THE EDUCATION OF GIRLS

Stephanie Williams was born in Canada, the daughter of an army officer. She grew up moving frequently across Canada, to Germany, England and the United States before studying history at Wellesley College, Massachusetts. In 1970, she moved to London. Since then she has travelled widely, working as a journalist, covering design, architecture and the environment. In 2005 she published a memoir of her Russian grandmother, *Olga's Story*. She lives in north London.

By the same author

Hongkong Bank
Docklands
Olga's Story
Running the Show

THE EDUCATION
OF GIRLS

*Coming of age in four years
that changed America
1966–1970*

Stephanie Williams

Highbury Books
30 Highbury Place, London N5 1QP

First published in 2025

Copyright © Stephanie Williams, 2025

The moral right of the author has been asserted

ISBN 978 1 0684931 0 2

Jacket design: Joe Ewart
Book design and typesetting: Iram Allam

Contents

'Was anyone ever so young?
I am here to tell you that someone was.'

JOAN DIDION, *SLOUCHING TOWARDS BETHLEHEM*

Four of us are gathered high in a box in the Boston Music Hall, a wonderfully baroque theatre in red and gold. We are here for Jefferson Airplane: musician gods, triumphant headliners of Woodstock the summer before. It's not a big place – a few hundred are packed in down below. We wait and then the lights come down. From somewhere a guitar sounds on a blacked-out stage, slow and easy, warming the room. Slowly, hallucinating lights emerge: green, red, acid yellow, purple. They begin to curve and swirl, catching a carved edge on the ceiling, playing on the faces below.

Chords from an electric guitar. Then, a second.

The beat picks up.

Grace Slick steps out of the darkness, slim, dark-haired. She floats above the stage, velvet coated in the shadows of some purple light. She pauses on her toes, swaying to the beat, swinging her black hair back and forth across her face. Pale hands lift the mic to her lips. She opens her mouth and her eyes meet mine.

We can be together.

Her song starts out sounding all peace and love. But I find out fast what it's really about is chaos. Anarchy, violence, lawlessness, and destruction.

The beat hardens. The pace speeds up. And we are on our feet. For, more than anything, what we need now is relief. Some kind of catharsis.

The music dies away. There is a pause. Then other songs, pale and watery, echoes of gospel blues. They soothe the crowd and we sit back, feel better. The guitar moves on gently, riffing the chords into *Good Shepherd,* mellow harmonies and visions of heaven.

But soon the sound picks up again. Strobe lights arc, blinding, shining on tired bits of golden detail on the ceiling, falling on the faces of the crowd.

'*Don't you want somebody to love?*'

Slick is back in front of the crowd, belting out the story of her own sad love affair. Of what happens when truth turns to lies. The death of joy, the loss of friends: a song that for four years now has echoed through our rooms, touching our souls.

She bows to us. Turns to face her players. The drummer nods.

She moves to the beat in her head. It steps up, the guitars again, the drummer follows, the beat is rough, tougher. Insistent.

Slick turns back to the crowd. Her voice is slow gravel, narcotic. Alice in a wonderland of drugs. *One pill makes you larger...* Tension rises with the beat. *And one pill makes you small...* Logic and proportion: where have they gone?

There is no pause now. Slick started with *We can be together.* We are finishing with *Volunteers.* She strides across the stage, hair streaming, face as hard as nails. She's belted, battle-hardened, ready for anything. She whips the mic to her mouth, and out come the words: 'Look what's happening in the street!'

Everyone is on their feet.

'Gotta revolution!' Over and over. 'Got the revolution!'

The exhortation of a battle post.

Revolution!

Fists raised high.

REVOLUTION!

Louder and LOUDER.

Slick swerves, the beat slows.

We can be together. Just you and me. Arms waving, everyone singing, ecstatic in unity.

'We are all outlaws in the eyes of America!'

There is something terrible in the power of this lyric. I think of the tanks, police in riot gear, chasing me and all the others I know down the street. And I realize – it's true! In the eyes of America: we *are* outlaws.

Rage fills my heart. I am *so fucking angry*. For the senselessness of the American government. For the non-stop violence on US streets. For the men I know, running from the draft. For Vicki, bloodied last night in a riot in Harvard Square. For the senselessness of the whole damn thing. Tears fall down my cheeks.

There is something very powerful in the moment you realize that you have gone beyond the law. That now it's too late. Even if what you are doing is trying to make the world a better place.

For yes, I really did believe it then: that we could make the world a better place. *A new continent of earth and fire.* Pristine, free of war and hypocrisy.

I am a student about to graduate from one of the finest universities in the world.

In the heat of the moment, I resolve that if I stay in America, I will go underground. Go to California and join the Weathermen or whatever other crazy anarchic group there might be.

1

First sight

It was 10 September 1966. I walked across the runway to the terminal at Logan Airport, my new fall coat hot on my arm. Inside a Customs and Immigration officer took my passport and turned the pages until he found my student visa. A rare and special status: permitting me to study and work in the United States for the next four years.

'Wellesley College, you say?'

I nodded.

'Speak up.'

I looked him in the eye. 'Yes.'

He looked me over carefully. Then he stamped my passport with a thud, closed it. As he handed me my papers, the officer relaxed and smiled.

'Welcome to the United States,' he said. 'You have a great time.'

Charlie – the boy who was responsible for me being there at all – and his mother were waiting for me. They loaded my luggage into their car and took me home to stay with them for the night in their big, comfortable house on a tree-lined street in

Brookline, on the edge of Boston. It was, I gathered over Sunday lunch the next day, a big thing – taking a girl to a college like Wellesley. Not just Charlie and his mother, but an actress who they'd invited to lunch decided to come in the car too. We drove along the banks of the Charles River, Charlie pointing out the landmarks: 'over there is MIT, that red brick tower in the distance is Harvard' – and then we were onto a freeway, moving fast for what to me seemed forever. At last, we swooped into a big clover leaf, and were off on Route 128. We made a turn. The traffic slowed. My stomach churned with tension. The road began to wind. Houses, trees, big lawns, gas stations, ice cream parlours. Finally, *finally* we reached the town of Wellesley.

The grounds were bordered by long stone walls and thick woodland. No gate, but a restrained bronze sign with the name of the college. As we swung into the grounds, we slowed. Like a wealthy country club. The sharp scent of fresh cut grass. Neat green signs with gold lettering showed up the names of buildings: rosy brick halls of residence built like battlements, Munger, Cazenove, Severance. Alumnae Hall. On we drove. Warm sun glistened on broad rolling lawns and wooded coppices. On a hill rose a nineteenth-century gothic unity I'd seen in the college brochure, a cluster of weathered stone buildings, roofed in the pale verdigris of copper, crowned with a high bell tower. Through trees, in the distance, I glimpsed the blue waters of a lake.

On, past a stone and timber chapel. A bank of tennis courts and a car park. At last, up a short steep drive, we arrived at the entrance of Davis Hall, a tall gothic-style entrance tower and a glass bowl of a dining hall: my home for the next four years.

I walked through the door into the cool of a white hall, hot in my pink wool suit. In front of me, a wide table with three girls behind it.

'Hi! So you are Stephanie Williams?' said one. I was struck by a kind of nasal-toned bureaucracy, one that I would come to know so well. I nodded.

'Hmm, let me look on the list. Oh, here you are.' She pointed to my name. The second girl crossed it through. The third reached into a box under the table.

'Welcome to Wellesley! Here is your Freshman Induction Pack. Over there,' (a wave to the right) 'is the mailroom. Your box is number 208. The same as your room. This key will open the box. Now Nancy here will show you upstairs to your room – no, leave your bags, someone will bring them up in a minute. You ordered Gordon Linen? Then you'll find sheets and towels in your room. Tea is at four o'clock in the living room. Then you'll be introduced to your Big Sister. See you later!'

Room 208 of Davis Hall was on the second floor, overlooking the front drive and a pocket of woodland – a narrow cell with

a concrete floor and cream walls. There was a narrow bed, a dark chest of drawers, an old desk, lamp and chair, and a walk-in closet with a full-length mirror. In the middle of the floor, a beacon of home, my father's old tin trunk from Korea, filled with most of my life's belongings.

I opened the casement window. Station wagons were pulled up, trunk-lids clunked open, voices rose as fathers and mothers helped their daughters unload their belongings.

I wondered at the luxury of having parents who would drive you all the way to college, even the whole way across the country. And what a lot of stuff they'd brought! Typewriters, tennis rackets, record players, blankets and pillows, lamps, boxes of books, hairdryers. Coffee pots. Radios. All loaded into the back of the car in a state of lavish disorder my father would have taken out and efficiently repacked.

I had no time to get my bearings. Voices echoed in the hall, and around the door poked a girl's face, pale with wide dark eyes, backed by a scarlet headband and a mass of shiny straight black hair.

'Hi! I'm Vicki.' Hearty mid-Western tones, the catch of a giggle. 'I'm just two doors down the hall. And this is Anne. She's right next door. We're all, like, going down to tea now. So why don't you come too?'

Together we descended the stairs and I followed them, uncertain, into the living room, large and comfortable, with sofas and armchairs overlooking a blue lake. By the windows was a table with a white cloth, ranks of cups and saucers, and plates of cookies. A line of hesitant girls had formed in front of it. With Vicki and Anne, I edged towards them, feeling as fragile as the china cup that was put into my hands. A silver urn stood on the table, and a junior poured pale, clear tea into our cups.

'Milk or lemon?'

'Ah... milk, please,' I said.

Everyone else seemed to have lemon. Worse, as I gazed at the glossy girls gathering in the room, I realized that the pink wool suit I had made over the summer vacation was a disaster. Vicki was wearing a dark skirt and a turtleneck sweater and Anne was in a simple, navy sheath dress. Around the room the older girls all seemed to be in peter pan collars or pastel cable knits, crisply ironed shorts or A-line skirts, and new brown loafers.

'Where are you all from?' A junior came up to us.

'Cincinnati, Ohio,' said Vicki.

'Champaign, Illinois,' said Anne.

The junior looked at me. 'Canada,' I said.

'Oh, whereabouts?'

On top of a hill high over the St Lawrence River. 'Kingston, Ontario.'

'Where's that?'

'I know.' Anne smiled at me. 'My cousins live in Detroit. I've been to Niagara Falls.' Just like I would, she sketched a map in the air. The junior's eyes glazed. She drifted away.

The noise level in the room rose. Thirty new freshmen, 102 people in the dorm. Waiting to meet our Big Sisters, everyone was making new friends. A rumour ran round the room that the real function of a Big Sister – they were all in junior year and lived in Davis too – was to kick-start your social life and fix you up with a date. All of a sudden, a group of about a dozen of them, tanned and lean from summers in the sun, and definitely in command, moved into the room and began to pick up their charges.

Ros was mine. Tall and lean, with thick dark hair and green eyes, Ros told me she was majoring in biology and was practically engaged to a man from MIT. She smiled and said she was sure I'd be fine, 'everyone loves Wellesley.' But if I had any problems, just come and see her. She told me where her room was. Then, not too sure of how much more to add to this basic information, she told me she would be in touch and said goodbye.

That evening there was a meeting with the housemother, a widowed southern belle with fading blonde hair, and Debby, our 'Vil Junior' – queen of her year in the dormitory, responsible for overseeing the care of the freshmen – who filled us in on the house rules. We were each responsible for keeping our rooms clean and tidy: there were inspections. Four evenings a week

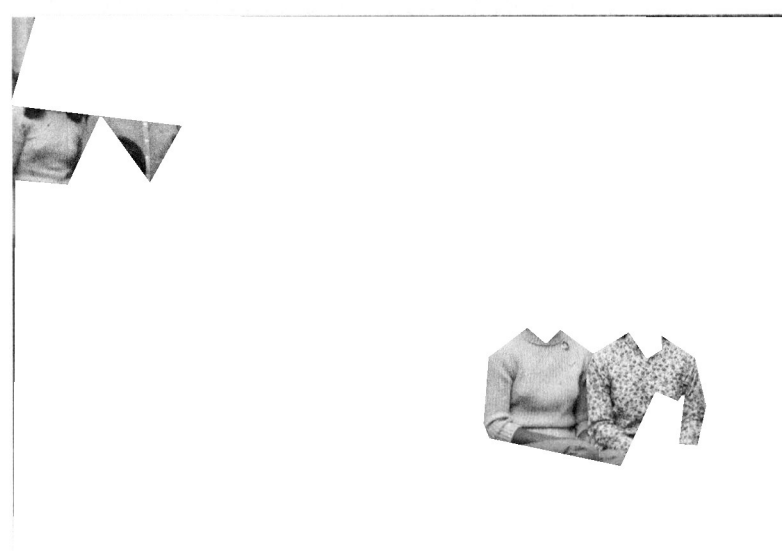

we were required to wear a skirt or dress for dinner and sit formally at table, laid with candles and silver and preceded by sung grace. Everyone had a task to make the dorm run smoothly, from waiting at the dinner table, to answering the telephone (no calls after 11pm) or greeting visitors at the bell desk. You had to sign in and out if you were going off campus overnight, with a contact name and address as to where you could be found. But first, your parents had to give the college permission for you to do such a thing. Curfew was at midnight. Men, including fathers, were never allowed upstairs in the dorm, except for Sunday afternoons, when you could have them in your room from two until five-thirty pm.

As I heard the rules expounded – curfews, clean your room, skirts for dinner, I felt faintly ridiculous, as if I was back in the Girl Guides, promising 'on my honour to do my duty to God and the Queen.'

Wellesley, we were told, operated on an honour system: based on integrity. No one checked up on you. You were expected to be responsible for yourself, trusted to obey the rules.

And if you didn't, there was always someone who would rat on you.

✱

I was seventeen years old. My life to date had been as the daughter of a colonel in the Canadian army – Jeffery Williams. I had a brother, Rod, and a sister, Sue, four and six years younger: as the eldest I was required to set a good example. I'd grown up attending church parades of soldiers, Sunday lunch at the officers' mess, making polite conversation while, instructed by my mother, Irina, handing round canapes at drinks parties. I knew how to ride a horse and fire a .22 at a target on a firing range. Dad had fought in Europe, and after the war decided to become a career soldier: he'd seen more action in Korea and, now that he was too old to go into combat, wanted nothing more than to work to keep the peace.

All my life, our family had been on the move, every eighteen months or so: Ottawa, Calgary, Fort Worth in Texas, Washington DC; Camp Borden, Ontario; Soest, West Germany. School for a while in England. Halifax, Nova Scotia. Back to Ottawa in time for the Cuban Missile Crisis in 1960. But while we were stationed in Germany in the mid-fifties, a fire in a warehouse back in Canada destroyed most of our possessions. We were wildly underinsured. I was always aware that money was in short supply, but now it was much worse: it took years for my parents to recoup the losses of having to furnish and equip a home for five, first in Halifax, and within less than a year, in Ottawa. Finally, in 1962, when I was thirteen, we settled into a standard military issue house high on a hill overlooking old Fort Henry, which commands the magnificent point where Lake Ontario flows into the St Lawrence River at Kingston, home to the Royal Canadian Military College – Canada's answer to West Point or Sandhurst. Because Kingston was just across the St Lawrence from the United States, the place had always had a military significance. My father was teaching at the Canadian Army Staff College. My mother was a part-time secretary at Queen's, the local university. They played tennis with friends on Saturday afternoons. It goes without saying that everyone in the neighbourhood knew everyone else.

I loved so much about our life: the travel, new people, the adventure of strange places. I considered myself adaptable, able to meet all kinds of people. But somehow, we could never acquire a piano, or take up skiing, or see the same doctor or dentist twice. I'd arrive in a new classroom and be made to sit at the back. Every time I made a really good friend, it seemed, I had to say good-bye. Mother tried to comfort me by saying we could always write. But of course, it wasn't the same. And she wasn't easy.

My mother had been educated at an English girl's school in Shanghai during the 1930s. There was always a 'right' way to do things in our house. How to set the table for dinner, how to greet a guest. Some were related to good manners, kindness and thoughtfulness to others. Others depended on keeping up appearances or were based on sheer snobbery. Mother found the unruly rowdiness of the large co-ed high school I attended hard to come to terms with. When, unknown to me, my friend Mary Ellen, the daughter of a general, went 'too far' on the school trip to Cedar Island early in the summer when we were still fourteen, my mother, who was already proving difficult about my scooter driving boyfriend from the 'wrong side of the tracks', had tea with a couple of officers' wives. Within weeks, in the autumn of 1964, three other girls and I were despatched to a convent 150 miles away, to be taught by nuns. It would be a sacrifice for them, my parents told me, but it was for my own good. Like so many other moves: however much I protested, I really had no choice.

✳

Convents have always held a popular fascination: women enclosed altogether, cut off from the world. Who are they? What do they think?

In my case, l'Académie St Michel was run by Les Sœurs du Sacré-Coeur de Jésus, an order founded in France at the beginning of the nineteenth century. It stood on the outskirts of a small pulp and paper town, half an hour west of the border with Quebec. When the wind blew from the mills a strong smell of sulphur, like rotting eggs, engulfed the school. Cornwall, Ontario, was strongly sectarian, split between 'privileged' English Canadians and 'down-trodden' French, a divide reflected in the convent and which made me, and my companions as English Protestants profoundly suspect. Outside the classroom, the language of the convent was French – or rather, Québécois – which bore little relation to the language I had so far learned at school. Like the nuns, most of the pupils were daughters of French-Canadian farmers. Coming from poor and isolated farms of the stony Canadian Shield, away from home for the first time, they were looked upon as potential recruits to the order. Four girls in my class were looking forward to becoming postulants. Most of the rest had their hearts set on leaving in another year, as soon as they turned sixteen. My dream was to go to university.

As Protestant heretics, the four of us from Kingston formed a mildly anarchic group. On Sunday mornings we were excused to go to the Anglican church, twenty minutes' walk away. Off we tripped to the centre of town in our high-heeled shoes, mascara and back-combed hair. It was the only day of the week I could wear my beloved winter coat, cut just like the one Jackie Kennedy used to wear, black and white tweed, lined with black satin. Out of sight of the convent, we skipped into the middle of the empty, echoing street singing *She loves you, yeah, yeah, yeah!* Then, while one of us went to church so that we could report back on the sermon, the other three repaired to the local diner, ordered big greasy plates of French fries and put on the juke box.

Before breakfast, while the rest of the convent went to daily Mass, I took drawing lessons from an ancient nun. Soeur François was over eighty. As I worked, I listened to her talk, her face creased, her gentle blue eyes, faded and benign.

She was born on a poor dairy farm. 'When I first came to the convent I could neither read nor write. I got up in the dark every morning in winter to milk the cows, and three times a week my father would take the wagon with the churns into town. My father—'

I looked up. Her old eyes were filled with tears. 'Who could call such a man by such a name, the one we call our Saviour, who lives in Heaven?' Her voice died away.

'He beat me. If the milk wasn't ready in the morning, he would bend me over and...' She gathered herself up. 'He made me do things I did not want to do. And when I refused, he hit me. I begged and begged my mother to save me from him. And, well, one day, she brought me here. To the convent.'

She was nine.

It was Soeur François who told me that the convent was where girls came when they had got themselves into trouble.

'Suppose a girl has sinned. So, she is going to have a baby. So long as she repents in her heart, God in his mercy will take care of her. A girl can come here and be safe. She can tell her parents and her friends that she is going to the convent. That she wants to see if maybe she has a vocation. After the baby is born, the nuns will see that it is taken by a good Catholic family. Then the girl can go home. No one need be any the wiser.'

I never heard a baby's cry or saw very young girls in the convent. But there was one long wing where the nuns lived, where we were forbidden.

Early one evening Soeur Monique, my pale and girlish home-room teacher, took me aside in the classroom. 'I have observed you have a habit of escaping. Of running away when there is something you don't want to face.' I felt the colour rise in my face. Moving so often, of course, I knew I could leave any situation I didn't like. But – how could she know this?

'You cannot go through life like this. You have to search your heart. Listen to it. And hear your conscience. Then you will find the right path.'

I wondered. My heart felt blank. So often I had no idea what I thought.

Sitting at the back of the room doing homework while the rest of the class had a lesson in religion, I would listen with half an ear as new forms of wickedness were laid before my class of half-formed Catholic girls. Lying, covetousness, disobedience (to parents, the Church, husbands, and fathers). Envy. Pray for guidance.

'It takes so little to fall. One taste of mortal sin, deliberately committed even though you know how wrong it is... And if you do, you will be condemned to hell for all eternity.'

I looked up from my books.

One girl spoke up. 'What kind of mortal sin must I be afraid of, for example, Sister?'

'Well,' Soeur Monique adjusted her glasses. 'You must be very careful whenever you are with a boy. A plain and simple kiss is one thing, but French kissing – well, that's a mortal sin, for example.'

*

Back home in Kingston the next summer, little had changed. But at the lake where we spent our vacations, there was a new family. American. From Boston. With four handsome sons. Two of them were at Yale. The younger of the two, the tall dark one, was Charlie.

Well, we had fun. We sailed and water-skied. There were big

family barbecues, and lots of swimming. Charlie especially was kind. Nineteen and into jazz. One rainy afternoon that August he put on records by Dave Brubeck and told me about the bars in Greenwich Village. There was dry Tom Lehrer playing 'The Vatican Rag' on the piano and Ella Fitzgerald singing the blues. Charlie displayed a laid-back sophistication I found completely beguiling. His parting shot as we said goodbye at the end of summer was to hand me the latest copy of *Newsweek*.

Inside was a long feature on the Seven Sister Colleges in New England – the famous women's colleges, like Bryn Mawr, Vassar, Radcliffe, and Smith which matched the all-male Ivy League. I had heard of them once, in a fashion shoot featuring a group of super-sophisticated girls in *Seventeen*. The last line of the *Newsweek* piece said they welcomed geographical diversity and offered scholarships to those who could not afford the fees.

'Why don't you go for it?' said Charlie.

As I left the lake that summer, I had a sudden vision of what my life might be like if I didn't escape the nuns soon. Maybe a place at Kingston's local university, Queens? Summer jobs working as a guide at the town's tourist attraction, Fort Henry, just across the street. Marriage to a boy like Frank Boxford, whose father owned the local sports store.

No travel, no adventure.

At this point in Canada, I had two more years of education before I could apply to university. For the Seven Sisters, I needed only one. Socially, my parents were very accomplished. They were well read and cultured, exceptionally travelled, and close to the heart of current affairs. But they knew little about education and nothing at all about what it meant to go to university.

I talked my mother into letting me stay home and go to the

local Catholic convent in Kingston. I argued I needed a proper English-speaking curriculum and more of an academic challenge than St Mike's could offer. My friends who talked of going to university were thinking of perhaps Laval in Quebec; you had to aim high for Toronto or McGill in Montreal. No one I knew considered studying in the US. Nor had I, until I spied the glimmer of a chance at the excellence of the Seven Sisters.

Mother wasn't in favour of my plans to go to America at all, even to an all-girls college – especially after she finished reading *The Group* by Mary McCarthy. But my father weighed in. His older brother, Jim, won a scholarship to Yale in 1939, but had not been able to take it up because he went away to war. It was something he always regretted. My dad believed in me. If this was what I wanted to do, I should be given the chance. But be warned: I was on my own. There was no money to cover the cost – not even of making the applications.

Four months after Charlie handed me his copy of *Newsweek,* my American SAT exam results came back. I'd only discovered I needed to take these exams six weeks before, just in time to meet the deadline to apply to take them.

Mine weren't top marks, but they weren't far off – and more than enough to get into one of the famous Seven Sisters. Six months later, in April 1966, four letters fell through the letter-box in the front door. A thin one held a rejection from Radcliffe, the sister college of Harvard. The three fat ones offered me full scholarships – to Wellesley, Smith and Vassar. My parents couldn't believe it – and neither could I. Nor could the convent. Even the local newspaper reported it. I opted for Wellesley, as it was just outside Boston. I knew I couldn't depend on Charlie and his family who lived there, but at least the fact that they were somewhere nearby gave me a kind of lodestone.

Now I needed clothes for college, and to find the money to pay for them. I got a job as a short-order cook, frying eggs and bacon and cooking hamburgers, on a boat taking tourists through the 'Thousand Islands' of the St Lawrence River, east of Kingston. Then I signed up for a Singer Sewing machine course in town, and in six weeks, made my ill-fated pink wool suit and two pleated skirts to take with me. My mother knitted me a heavy green V-necked sweater that I never wore, and bought me a dark cotton dress with long sleeves 'suitable for early fall' to wear. My things were packed into my father's old tin trunk and shipped off by the railway. Finally, I went to the doctor to have the full medical examination, the college prescribed, including a cervical smear test. (The doctor wrote 'N/A' and crossed it out.) As I left his office on that hot day in the summer of 1966, I walked past his open window.

'There goes another contribution to the brain drain,' he was saying to the nurse.

'How wrong you are!' I wanted to yell. 'I'm a Canadian! I'll be back!'

And I meant it.

I was more fortunate than I could have imagined. No sooner had I accepted my place at Wellesley, than my father was ordered to England to serve on the Canadian Defence Staff in London from 1 September. To go to university in Canada, I would have needed to take one more year of high school. To transfer into the English system, halfway through A-Levels, would have been almost impossible.

Days before my family were to fly to England, they saw me

off on the bus to Toronto, where I would stay with a friend until it was time to catch the plane to Boston. Everyone else was on board. I mounted the steps and turned to look at them one more time, a little group of four. My mother, trim, dark hair short and curly, her mouth set. She gave me a rueful wave.

'Don't forget to write.'

My father's hand was on my fourteen-year-old brother, Rod's shoulder. Next to him my little sister, Sue, twelve. Dad's eyes were soft and he was smiling, cheering me on.

'You're on your way,' he said.

The driver revved the engine. The sweet scent of gas rose. His hand was on the lever of the door, about to close. I blinked back tears and gave them one last wave. Then I set off into the heart of the bus and sank into a seat. We pulled away from the parking lot and headed out onto the highway, long and straight, flanked by a wall of dense forest. Three days later my family flew to England. I did not know when I would see them again.

2

Incipit vita nova

Incipit vita nova – 'Thus begins a new life' – the phrase from Dante used by Henry Durant, the founder, in an address to the college in its first year in 1875. At that time there were a total of 314 students, seven professors, and fourteen teachers, all but one of them female. 'The Higher Education of Women is one of the great world battle cries for freedom, for right against might,' Durant declared.

Wellesley would not only offer the same rigorous and demanding education as for the most able male scholars of the day, but prepare women for '…great conflicts, for vast reforms in social life, for noblest usefulness. Women can do the work. I give them the chance,' he said.*

The motto of the college is '*Non ministrari sed ministrare*' – 'not to be served, but to serve'.

The message was clear. We were being bred for action. We were to do great things, to lead the way. At the same time, we were expected to behave politely, as young ladies should.

---

* Glasscock, Jean. *Wellesley College 1875-1975: A Century of Women.* Wellesley College, 1975

No one seemed to realize as we acquired knowledge, and learned to research, analyse and conclude, these aims might prove contradictory.

In fact, Wellesley College in 1966 was one of the most cloistered and conservative of the Seven Sister colleges. More sophisticated than a boarding school, and a whole lot richer. In such an all-female institution, away from the distractions and competition of men, it was believed, women would thrive.

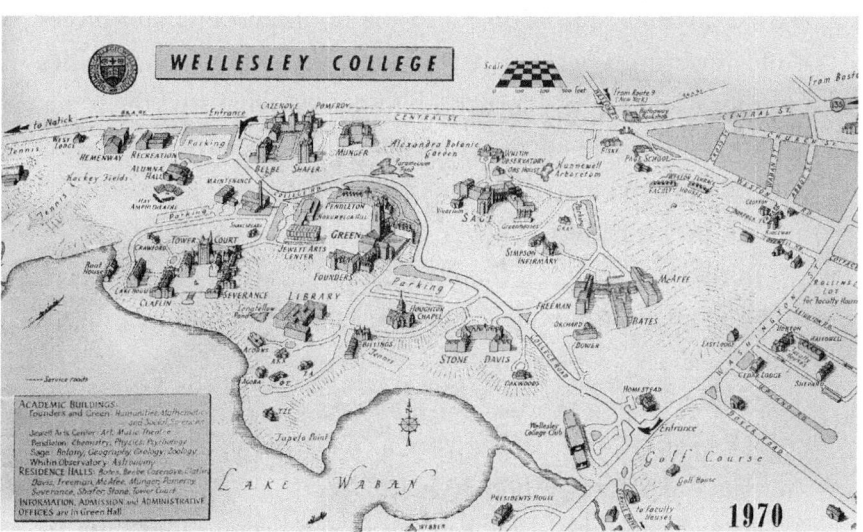

Campus map and a list of appointments in hand, I spent my first days at Wellesley in a rash of meetings, tours of the library, English tests, and assessments of my French, one of two languages I would be required to learn.

I kept getting lost, climbing the dark stairs under the arches beneath Green Hall looking for the way into Founders Hall for a professor's office on the top floor. I visited the scholarship office where I was told I had been awarded \$300* in spending money to last the year and that after the first term I would be working two evenings a week in the language laboratory, as small part payment towards my fees. Then I was taken next door to the Students' Aid Society.

The plump woman behind the desk did not look up from her writing. 'Please help yourself to anything you need.' She vaguely gestured towards piles littered about the room. Textbooks filled a bookcase and were stacked up in piles on the floor. Boxes full of used clothing spilled out onto the floor, and bits and pieces of old furniture – wastepaper baskets, table lamps and shades – were stacked up in a corner. I had nearly exhausted the funds my father had given me to get myself to college and I knew I was going to have to be careful to make ends meet. But I was shamed to think that I might need charity.

'I think I can manage, thank you.'

The woman looked up. 'Are you sure?' She sounded disappointed.

'Absolutely.'

'Like I said. Come back if you need anything,' she said. 'The Students Aid Society is here to help.'

'Uh, well. Thanks.' I backed out of the brown door with its frosted pane and closed it behind me.

That afternoon we were expected to attend the first meeting of the Class of 1970. I entered the lecture hall late – I'd been lost. I was amazed to see the huge room so packed. I started climbing the steps from the bottom looking for a seat. There were grey

---

* Around \$3,000 today.

stone walls to my left with high, west facing windows, sunshine streaming in. Here and there I saw a sari, half a dozen Chinese faces. Were there as many as ten Black students? As for the rest in my year: hundreds of clean-cut, shining, white-skinned all-American girls.

Until that moment I had no sense of the enterprise of Wellesley College. Sure, I knew about the one hundred years of history as pioneers of women's education, that it had scores of famous alumnae. But this was *reality*. At the top of the theatre, I found a seat on the edge of the back row and sat down to wait. The door at the bottom of the hall opened, and the president of the college, Ruth Adams – trim wool suit, large horn-rimmed glasses, cropped wavy hair – stepped up to the podium.

'Welcome,' she said.

She paused to look round the room, taking in the mass of ranked faces. 'You are the cream of your generation. Every one of you in this room today stood at the top of your classes in high school. Many of you were president of your class, or head of student government at your school. Many of you have already been to Europe. Most of you speak more than one language. Now you have all come to be at Wellesley together.

'You will quickly find out that you are learning beside girls who are all just as good, or even better than you are. You should not be surprised if at first your grades are not what you have been used to. You are going to have to work hard – sometimes very hard – to achieve here. But you will go on to achieve great things. There are women sitting in this room today who will be leaders, who will one day change the world.'

Later she reported to the college trustees that the new class of 479 girls had come from 43 states, Puerto Rico and 15 countries: among them Brazil, Colombia, the Congo, Egypt, Hong Kong... Libya, Pakistan, Saudi Arabia, Sweden and Thailand, and – Canada. Sixty per cent went to public schools. Nearly 20% had mothers or grandmothers who had gone to Wellesley. Of the graduates of the year before: half went into jobs. Forty per cent went on to further study. Most of those who had got married had chosen either to work or to continue their studies until they had a child.

But I was blind to the future. I had only just arrived. As we rose to leave the hall, filled with the strains of *America the Beautiful,* the girls broke into song. Someone whispered in my ear: 'That's by Katherine Lee Bates. You know she went here?'

I fumbled my way down the stairs. At the bottom I met my new friend Anne. She was incensed.

'Did you notice? There wasn't a man in the room.'

I was baffled. What did she expect, after all?

*

The gym and swimming pool were on the far side of campus, twenty minutes' walk beyond the green square of the academic quad, and on, up College Road. By now I had taken a speech test and had my hearing tested. It was time for a posture assessment. The girl before me was just leaving as I arrived at the end of a narrow corridor above the gymnasium. A pair of white-coated attendants were busy at a desk. One of them registered my name, my place and date of birth. I was told to step onto some scales. A rule came down on the top of my head, my height recorded. Then I was shown into a small blacked out room. A camera on a tripod stood in the centre. I was instructed to strip to my bra and panties.

Huh?

'Stand here.' The attendant indicated a measure on the wall behind me. 'Look at the camera.' I grimaced. A flash bulb popped. 'Turn around.' A second bulb. 'Now, face left.' Pop. 'Now, the right.' A fourth bulb flashed. I blinked.

'Thank you. You can get dressed now. That will be all.'

Back in Anne's room, we compared notes. *This was definitely weird.* Neither of us had any idea why it was required and what any of it meant. In the cafeteria that evening, we headed for a table with Deckie, a dark-haired, leggy sophomore, with a wide smile.

'I know.' She shuddered. 'Isn't it *awful*? But there's no getting out of it – everyone has to go through it. The posture photograph is a basic requirement for every new girl at Wellesley.'

We were stunned. We were so new. We had no idea of abuse in those days, and what, after all would you call it? Not long afterwards we learned our pictures had been stolen. We heard it took a lot of work to marry up the names and faces in our freshman directory to the appropriate silhouette. The raid had been carried out by group of Yalies, a typical 'boyish prank', and about to be published in a book.

It never appeared. The practice had been going on so long, since before the 1930s, the whole issue of posture photographs had become the source of legend. But it never occurred to us that the pictures might be filed and retained. And it wasn't just at Wellesley, where, since the 1920s concern about correct posture for women developed into a near obsession, but at numerous

[27]

Ivy League and other colleges. In 1992, a professor of art history at Yale, George Hersey, revealed in a letter to the *New York Times*, that the pictures had nothing to do with posture but were data for an archive being created by two psychologists, William Herbert Sheldon of Columbia and Earnest Albert Hooton, from Harvard, who planned an American archive that would match each freshman's body to their success or failure in life. Sheldon, who believed that measurement and analysis of people's bodies revealed much about their intellect, temperament, and probable future achievement, was inspired by the founder of social Darwinism, Francis Galton, who proposed such a photo archive for the British population, to support 'their theory on body types and social hierarchy'. The end game, like that of the Nazis was in selective breeding, eugenics.

As Deckie predicted, a few days later I was called back for analysis of my posture – hyper-extended knees – and assigned an absurd course of correction. ('Walk with your knees slightly bent.')

After that, we were eligible to go on to 'Fundamentals of Movement', a required course for every freshman. More lessons in posture and – what would prove invaluable, as pressure increased – 'conscious relaxation', adapted from yoga, as well as how to step out of a sports car in a short skirt, without showing more than a modest stretch of leg.

Oh, the glorious, honeyed days of those first weeks at Wellesley! Compared to the raw towns of Ontario, the pastoral green

of the college campus, with its lawns and burnished shrubberies, took my breath away. Nothing had prepared me for such
a sense of wealth and permanence, or the beauty of the place.

The town of Wellesley itself was straight out of a New England picture book: white clapboard houses with green shutters,
sweeping lawns fringed with maple trees, and great piles of rho-
dodendrons. In 1967 the town was reported to have the third
highest per capita income in the United States ('that means in the
world, practically,' I wrote home). There was Bailey's Ice Cream
Parlour and the Hathaway House Bookshop. Its windows were
hung with blue and white pennants emblazoned with 'Wellesley
College' and piled with books and college sweatshirts, tote bags
and special kinds of stationery all bearing the blue college crest.
Down the street was J C Penney, full of clothes for girl students:
brown penny loafers, neat A-line skirts and cable knit sweaters,
and further along, Filene's, where a single svelte black cocktail
dress was on display behind a plate glass window.

We were indeed *la crème de la crème*. Attractive, clever,
and, for those of us who were not well-off, sheltered finan-
cially in our places at the college. I could only bless my sudden,
extraordinary good fortune. I discovered, hidden behind grand
shrubberies, specialised greenhouses for botany, and an obser-
vatory for astronomy. Wellesley had a splendid contemporary
art gallery, light-filled and spacious, designed by the architect
Paul Rudolph, with paintings by Cezanne, and sculpture by
Degas. The Russian department had been founded by Vladimir Nabokov who wrote *Speak, Memory* there; the satirist Tom
Lehrer had just left the Economics department and was teaching
at MIT. During my first week, I sat in an auditorium listening
to Dean Acheson, the secretary of state who'd advised President

Kennedy during the crisis on the Bay of Pigs, address the student body. The teaching was a revelation.

Except for a handful of big lecture courses, classes were small, about twelve or perhaps fifteen, around tables, seminar-like. Every week you were handed a reading list for each class and were expected to be fully conversant with the contents when you arrived. So many of the girls – top of their high-school class, ex-presidents of their schools – did not hold back with questions and comments. To me they seemed scarily brilliant, full of new ideas and curiosity. The rate of progress expected took my breath away. Before long I was drowning in work.

Academically, in fact, there was little room for initiative. As a liberal arts college, no one was permitted to specialise, to follow a path deep into a subject. In the first two years – half my time at college – I would be required to complete a two-term course on selected portions of the Bible, four terms in the sciences, and more in English, languages and Greek Civilisation. At the end of four years, I was expected to have mastered one, if not two, foreign languages, have a good understanding of several of the humanities and one or two sciences.

I rapidly discovered that the Quebecois I had acquired at the convent was an embarrassment in my new French literature class. For the first time I discovered contemporary literature from France. Right away we were discussing Albert Camus and Jean Paul Sartre, moving on swiftly to Montherlant, Hugo and Giraudoux. In history, I was deep in the time of Louis XIV, taught by an enchantingly witty historian, Eugene Cox. I could not get enough of the details, the intricate etiquette of the court. He sent us to the library to analyse original sources and interpret contemporary diaries for ourselves: many by the important women of the time: Madame de Pompadour, Madame de Montespan, Madame de la Tour du Pin. How clever and powerful these women had been in their world of men.

Meanwhile, after a term of 'Fundamentals of Movement', formal 'physical education' was over and we had a breathtaking choice of sports: from synchronised swimming, to diving, rowing, field hockey, archery, lacrosse, tennis and skiing, golf and horse riding. Then there was the college newspaper to work on, plays to act in, madrigals to sing, life studios to draw in.

Things I noticed:

- How thick the teal blue carpets were in the Davis living room.
- Lots of girls had the *New York Times* delivered every morning.
- Everyone was raving about a subject that I'd never heard of called Art History.
- Peppermint fudge ice cream pie was the best dessert in the world.

Fresh from the convent, I was so caught up in my Wellesley dream I scarcely noticed the absence of men our own age in our lives. I was so happy going to classes where everyone kept coming up with sharp questions and amazing ideas, and there weren't any boys to laugh at you if you knew the answer, or shoot water pistols from the back of the room. But we were fifteen miles from the centres of life in Boston and Cambridge. Public transport was erratic. It rapidly became clear that if you didn't have a boyfriend, especially one with a car, you would be missing out on life. And the only way you could meet the boys from the surrounding men's colleges was through a blind date or a mixer.

The sophomores became our advisors. They moved easily through the dorm, in close fitting jeans and long sweeps of hair, swapping unpalatable tasks like waiting on table or serving in the canteen, for jobs on 'bells' on the front desk where they could see who was coming and going or getting the phone calls. In the cafeteria line that looped behind the glass dining room on the edge of the kitchen, they picked out salads and cinnamon coffee cake. They warned us to beware of the irresistible chicken fricassee and other demon dishes designed to tempt you into putting on the pounds.

One year ahead of us, they were much more friendly than the intimidating third-years, the juniors, to say nothing of the girls in senior year, who, at twenty-one or twenty-two, were four years older, nearly ready to graduate, and terrifyingly remote. We were more likely to find ourselves meeting sophomores in class, and as many were not yet settled into steady relationships with men, they might actually be seen in the dorm on a Saturday night. It was they who let us know that all the juniors and seniors who vanished from campus around noon on Fridays, startlingly smart and all made-up, had gone to spend the weekend with boyfriends at Yale and Harvard, Princeton or Brown. One or two girls were rumoured to be *practically living with* their fiancés.

'*Face it,*' I wrote home. '*I'm no longer in little old Kingston where pre-marital sex is so scandalous. Here what you do is entirely your own business – nothing fazes anybody. You've got nothing to lose in this day of contraceptives. It really makes you think.*'

Of course, it took no more than a single open house at an MIT frat house for us to begin to fill in the gaps for ourselves. A vast ivy-clad brick house, somewhere in Back Bay in Boston, rammed with people, crowding the stairs. Somewhere in a darkened hall, a band was playing so loud the music reverberated in your ears. Girls milled about the edges of the room trying for nonchalance until at last – *at last* – for this was the etiquette, some male came up and asked you to dance. Elsewhere girls stretched out with strange boys on sofas as the crowd surged around them, fending off hands feeling up their breasts. Others emerged blinking back tears from upstairs bedrooms, where ties looped on doorhandles indicated they were occupied. Meanwhile, on the front steps men were swilling beer and smoking cigarettes. They eyed up our legs as Anne and I slipped out.

Humiliated and miserable, we trailed back to Davis. Not one boy had even spoken to us. Deckie and other sophomores were all set to commiserate.

'If you thought that was bad, just wait until you get to Dartmouth!'

Dartmouth College lay two and a half hours north of Boston, in Hanover, New Hampshire. There, deprived of women for weeks on end, two long lines of baying males assaulted the buses of girls, coming to the first mixer of the year. I stepped down with Anne, to run the gauntlet to the hall where the dance was being held.

All the Ivy League colleges admitted only males. Each had their reputations. Brown was preppy. Princeton ditto and very far away. Yalies were fit and male, MIT was full of nerds, and Dartmouth men were animals. Boston University and Tufts men, with neither the brains nor the money of those from the

Ivy League were seen as slightly second rate, while the men at the various graduate schools of law or business were scarily mature. Everywhere one was warned to beware of 'jocks', a species of dumb sportsmen – *aka* football players on scholarships. They were often very nice to know but too stupid for long term investment.

And then there was Harvard. Founded in 1636, the oldest university in North America and among the most prestigious in the world, it was based around a handsome tree filled Yard, with a classical red brick church, and an enormous library. Here, fifteen miles from Wellesley, were the alpha-males, the *ubercool* of the dating fraternity – the most desirable men to be had.

In the first days of the term the weather held: warm days of sunshine and brilliant blue skies. But the nights were turning sharp and chill. Outside my casement window the leaves of the maples were beginning to turn. Around the lake, the trees were banked in oranges and rich yellows, scarlet and wine. One day my Big Sister Ros came up to me. She'd performed her main task. She had fixed me up, she said. He shared an apartment with her fiancé: his name was Ben.

Next Friday night.

3

Finding our feet

Five of us were slowly forming an alliance in this uncertain world: Anne and Vicki, a cohort from my first hour, then Linda. She was tall and slim and came from San Antonio, Texas. She had a mocking grin, a sugared drawl and a wide-armed gesture for every occasion. Diana by contrast, was tiny, rising just above Linda's shoulder. With a cloud of long, wavy auburn hair and a delicate complexion, she looked as if she had stepped out of the frame of a Botticelli. Small and exquisite, ethereal, somehow not quite real, she was a year older, and, having spent the last year in Florence, sophisticated. I found her fascinating.

Except for Linda, we lived in a row on the second floor of Davis. Green tiled washrooms with standard American metal toilet stalls, were at the far end of the corridor. We were in and out of each other's rooms, easy and friendly, asking directions, comparing notes, and in my case, borrowing Anne's typewriter to type up my papers.

Before long, by way of a raised eyebrow or stifled giggle we found ourselves joining forces to tactfully decline invitations to one rite after another. None of us could buy into Wellesley's saccharine traditions: wearing purple freshman beanies, taking up the class cheer, singing on the Chapel steps, or hoping our daughters would follow in our footsteps.

To me, Vicki seemed a natural leader. She had done tours of several East Coast colleges. An only child, her dad believed she could do anything, be a nuclear engineer. A friend of her mother's had gone to Wellesley. And that was sort of it. Her dark hair cropped in a long bob, she always seemed cheerful and open hearted, ready to welcome all, however difficult or compromised, into the warmth of her friendship. I had never met anyone so straightforward before, so down to earth, so gentle and who, much to my amazement at times would simply burst into song — a glorious mezzo soprano. With Vicki, what you saw was what you got, no sides, no hidden agendas. She smoothed the way, sorted out problems. It was only much later that I learned how homesick she was.

Diana's family came from Far Hills, New Jersey. To me, who knew no better, this sounded like it might not be far from the factories of the shoreline. No. Diana had attended the smart Concord Academy for girls, north of Boston. Her previous year had been spent in Florence following injuries in a bad car crash. Her skin was translucent, her hands, fragile and slight. In her clothes she favoured pastel flowered blouses and pale A-line skirts in fine herringbone. She wore a tasselled tawny suede jacket. On her feet: lace-up brown Oxfords, unexpectedly earthbound.

The word 'sensitive' was coined for Diana. She had a childlike way of fixing her eyes on you, that men often read for charm. Every conversation was one of great intensity, and in the end, exhausting. Her mother was unstable; her parents' marriage, which had ended in divorce, miserable. Her soon-to-be new

Vicki Van Steenberg
Cincinnati, Ohio

Anne M. Trebilcock
Champaign, Ill.

Linda Helland
San Antonio, Tex.

Diana C. Loomis
Far Hills, N. J.

stepfather was a world-famous Hungarian equestrian champion who owned acres of countryside. Her room was plastered with postcards she had collected in Florence: Botticelli's Venus, exquisite Fra Angelicos – her favourite painter. She was not only an artist, making thin-lined drawings that seemed perfect, but wrote poetry. Her plan was to major in Art History.

One evening after doing some homework, I sat on the floor in Linda's room down on the first floor. We didn't often gather there – Linda had a roommate. But the room, which had recently turned over from some public purpose to house extra freshmen as demand for places at Wellesley had increased, was huge.

Linda was from San Antonio, a city heavy with overlays from the former Spanish occupation, and home to countless thousands of Mexicans. From the ceiling she had suspended a Mexican piñata. Bright pink and shaped like some mythical bird, it struck a bizarre contrast to the Gothic decor of the room with its stained-glass windows. At the end of her bed sat her father's World War 2 footlocker.

The clothes her mother didn't make for her, Linda bought in the market. They were unlike anyone else's. In the summer, embroidered smocks in brilliant yellow, hot pink or lime. In the autumn and winter, short *serapes* in rose, magenta, or acid green. Linda was a connoisseur of Mexican food, full of exotic talk of strange foods like *tacos, tamales,* and *enchiladas,* and *tortillas* stuffed with chilli peppers.

Like Diana, she was artistic – bent on a major in Art History. But where Diana enjoyed neurosis, Linda was down-to-earth and practical. She had an eye for the ridiculous and for juicy bits of detail. Launching into a story, she'd laugh and spread her long arms wide. Or, in the heat of the moment, twist the gold bangle she wore on her wrist.

'Oh, I've just got to tell you! Daddy's just written to tell me about Fiesta Week. They're planning all the arrangements for next year's Coronation.'

'*Coronation?*' Like the kings and queens of England?

'Yeah, of the court. You've just *got* to hear this.' Linda was off. 'The dresses are AMAZING. *Really.*' She waved a newspaper cutting with pictures of women seated on thrones wearing crowns and holding sceptres. 'All those dresses covered in beads and rhinestones. They weigh a ton. It's completely ridiculous.'

Vicki glanced at me.

Anne's face was a mask.

'And the trains – they're getting longer and longer – it's all part of the hierarchy. They go from twelve feet for duchesses, to fifteen feet for queens.'

'STOP!' I said, 'What are you talking about?'

'So, at the top,' her fingers fluttered up, 'there is the Queen. She reigns over Fiesta.'

'Fiesta?'

'You know – every April. It was set up to celebrate the Battle of San Jacinto, Texas's final victory over Mexico. The actual Coronation is organised by the Order of the Alamo. Everyone in the Order has a vote.'

'For the Queen?'

'Yup. Her runner-up is Princess, and she's served by her Prince. The Queen gets a Prime Minister. Then there are duchesses and dukes and all sorts of pages. I was a page when I was eleven.'

'You *cannot* be serious.'

'Oh, I am. *I am,*' Linda laughed. 'You ain't seen the half of it!'

Anne was bunched over. 'This is a hoot.'

'You're telling *me?*' Linda spread her arms as if trying to gather her words. 'The whole thing's got nothing to do with beauty or talent. It's kind of like a debut. Family lineage and money are what counts.'

'A debut? Don't tell me they still have them?'

Diana rolled her eyes. 'In New York they do.'

'Every year the court has a theme. Like, in the first year, it was the Court of the Flowers, then came roses, fairies, and birds. Then they branched out.'

By now Linda was on a roll. 'The Queen is called Her Royal Majesty. The full title has her name, and the name of her family and the name of the court. So it goes like,' she pursed her fingers, 'Her Gracious Majesty, Dorothy of the House of Thomson, Queen of the Gods and of the Court of Olympus – that was in 1931.'

For a long moment there was silence.

'Are you going to have to do this?'

'Me?' Linda shrugged. 'Maybe.'

★

Lots of the girls at the college had mothers who had gone to Wellesley. Some, their grandmothers before them. Comfortable homes, good schools, summer camps, first-class colleges, suitable marriages. A tradition of wealth and stability, comfort and continuity which seemed to me extraordinary, not of this world and ultimately, stifling.

Every child takes their mothers' origins and eccentricities for granted. As I compared notes with my friends at Wellesley, for the first time I realized how far mine were from the usual thing. Mother was born in the city that is now Tianjin in north China. Her first name was Irina. *Not* Irene. Her mother, Olga, was Russian from the Siberian border with Mongolia, born into a well-to-do family in 1900, just in time to take a role in the revolution that engulfed the nation in 1917. Forced to flee her home in 1919, she took refuge studying law at the University of Vladivostok, until she was forced to flee again, over the border into China.

Mother's father was English from the East End of London. Frederick Edney had tried Calcutta first but soon travelled on to China – a better land of opportunity for a working-class boy. A job as a warehouse manager with British American Tobacco graduated to one buying fine papers for cigarettes.

Mother lived with her parents in the company compound of British American Tobacco with other English families. The women in particular despised my Russian grandmother. By the late 1920s Russian women were notorious on the China coast. Thousands of refugees like Olga, trafficked through the 'white slave trade', became the dancing girls in Shanghai nightclubs and the prostitutes in the shadier quarters of Beijing, Tianjin and Harbin.

'Go away, your mother's Russian,' the children hissed at Mother.

Olga survived in Tianjin because of her father's connections in the China tea-trade. With fluent French, she was able to get a job in a trading company. She, who had run guns during the Russian Revolution, despised the flirtatious manners of English women and the silly ways they deferred to men. She was at pains to always appear well-dressed, groomed and elegant: she and Irina had to be in every way above reproach.

Olga valued languages. Irina grew up speaking fluent Mandarin, as well as English and German. She was familiar with ballet and music and sea voyages around the world, to England on 'home leave'. When WW2 broke out, she and my grandmother became refugees on Vancouver Island, while her father was interned in a Japanese prisoner of war camp.

I found it difficult to imagine that my future could be laid down before I was born, defined by the expectations of generations long gone, governed by what your mother and grandmothers had done before. Surely if you were to live a free life, you had to make it your own?

I was seated at dinner one evening in our first few days of term: everyone very dressed up, silver settings and candles on the table, someone singing grace, a cocktail of ginger ale and cranberry juice to start. Fellow freshmen, neat and freshly turned out, who had been delegated for 'wait-on' that evening set down plates of lamb and roast potatoes before us. The conversation turned on what our fathers did for a living. I watched Anne shift in her seat. Her father was dead. Her mother brought her, and her older brother up, alone. But there was no escape. We had to go round. My Dad was in the Canadian Army, Linda's in insurance, Vicki's a mechanical engineer. Across the table sat Helen, one of two or three girls of colour in the room. She had a soft voice rich with the tones of the Deep South.

'He's a painter,' she said.

'A painter? What kind? Portraits or landscapes?'

'Houses,' she said.

Silence.

My heart went out to Helen at that moment. But it wasn't until much later that I began to grasp something of the vastness of the chasm between white and Black in America, the lives of someone like Helen's father, some understanding of the leap she made in attending such a bastion of white privilege only two years after the passage of the Civil Rights Act in 1964.

★

'You have a caller at the bell desk.' My name echoed over the tannoy in the hall outside my room, loud, for everyone to hear. This was a moment: the first time I'd been granted the coded signal indicating that an eligible male as opposed to a father figure or a woman, who were merely 'visitors', was waiting for me at the reception desk.

Ben was tall, with horn rimmed glasses and the brooding good looks of the classic NJB, as I was learning to describe a 'nice Jewish boy'. He came from Manhattan. Like my Big Sister Ros's boyfriend, Ben was a junior at MIT, but even though he planned to become a mathematician, he seemed the antithesis of the slide rule carrying nerds we had been warned against. He wore a scratchy tweed jacket and blue jeans, and he cracked a joke as he took my hand as we went downstairs from the bell desk. I was laughing when he held open the door of his car for me to get in. We swept out of the drive at Davis in a brand-new Ford Falcon.

I came back in a daze, just before midnight. The light was on beneath Vicki's door. Everyone was there – Anne, Linda, and Diana.

'*Honey!*' Linda flung her arms wide and gave me a hug. 'So – *how was it?*'

I told them how we'd gone to see *To Die in Madrid* at the Harvard Square cinema – a little sobering, I had to confess – and then out for coffee. Talking to Ben, I'd had a wonderful time. Every time he said anything, I told them, he made me laugh.

'Do you think you're going to see him again?'

'Well,' I said. 'He said he'd call me.'

'Steady there,' this from Linda. 'You've got to be careful with these NJBs. He could just be fooling around. They'll never bring a *shiksa* home to mother.'

'What's a *shiksa?*'

'You're a *shiksa*,' said Diana. 'You're not Jewish.'

By now the talk in the dorm was all about the Davis Hall mixer, when boys from Harvard and MIT, to say nothing of Brown and Yale, would come out to the campus for a dance on Saturday night. This mixer, Deckie promised, would be different. The rumour was that girls at Wellesley were so popular – not as fast as the ones from Vassar, or as immoral and studious as those from Radcliffe – that we would be outnumbered eight to one.

Anne and I had a nominal debate about whether we should go to it. Ghastly as the prospect was, there was no real issue. After all, this dance was on home ground. And how else, after all, were we to meet men? I'd had my first date with Ben, and I knew I really liked him, but after what Diana had said, who knew if he would call again?

★

I was finding it tough keeping my feet, floundering in English composition where the vogue was for writing stream of consciousness. An early paper came back with the remark that I had no imagination. Given some of the nonsense I had seen others produce, I was furious.

Things I noticed:

- Conversations at breakfast. Some girls seemed to have read *all* of Hemingway, John Steinbeck, J D Salinger, Tolstoy, Pasternak, Jean Paul Sartre (in French) and thousands of others, including one very 'great' German philosopher (Goethe?) in the original. It seemed you had to see all the going movies, i.e., *Who's afraid of Virginia Woolf* (with Richard Burton and Elizabeth Taylor. Did this really show the truth of their marriage?), all of Fellini, and anyone else who was avant-garde. Then there were all the old Garbo and Bogart films, as well as going to Symphony Hall to hear Leonard Bernstein conduct whenever he came to Boston – the tickets were $8.50 each, almost one quarter my monthly allowance.
- Dress code for a football game: suit, heels and white gloves. A simple wool dress (which I did not possess) or a decent, and different, skirt and sweater for everything else, including dinner four nights a week in the dorm.
- I couldn't keep borrowing Anne's typewriter for my papers. It was going to be $79 for the cheapest model new. No one seemed to know where you could get one second-hand.
- It took over an hour to get ready for a date. First take a bath or a shower, wash your hair and shave your legs.

Set your hair in rollers, tuck yourself under the dryer for the best part of 40 minutes, pluck your eyebrows. Select a dress or a nice skirt and sweater. Finally put on your makeup, using mascara you painted off a tiny palette with a wet brush.

- It wasn't just me who had started to put on weight – everyone except for one girl who seemed to eat mountains of food but was getting thinner by the day. Vicki told me that she'd heard her in the bathroom making herself throw up. (We would not hear of anorexia or bulimia for another 15 years.)

- Odd characters like the girl who kept taking showers, or the one who lived next door. She rarely came out of her room. She bought cans of Coca-Cola by the case, and drank it all the time. One day I knocked on her door to see if she wanted to come down to dinner and found she had started building a pyramid of empty coke cans in the corner of her room. 'Haven't you heard of Andy Warhol?' she said.

- Without fail, Anne's mother sent her a box of homemade cookies every week. Chocolate or butterscotch chip. And daily handwritten notes or newspaper clippings with 'thought you'd like to see this' or funny cartoons with a scribbled 'Can't you just see it?' on top.

These were a far cry from my mother's weekly screeds on airmail forms from far away across the Atlantic Ocean, telling me all the new things she and the family were doing, meeting new people and getting to grips with the practicalities of English life. In London they had found a flat. My brother and sister were starting new schools. 'I absolutely adore my bedroom (I should say ours because that is where you'll be sleeping),' wrote my sister, Sue. And I felt bleak, cut out of their new life, one I could not begin to imagine.

The Davis mixer arrived. It was held in the big round dining room with the glass walls, but you couldn't see much, as it was so dark. Anne and I didn't go down until the band got going, and there weren't so many lone girls and boys edging around the walls, trying to look as if they were just hanging around waiting for someone they had known all their lives. Vicki had confessed she didn't really know how to dance. Now she was giving it her all. Diana was dancing close with someone tall and dark. At the end of the song, he took her hand and they stepped out of a side door into the night.

Out of the darkness, a youth emerged. 'Wanna dance?' I had no idea who he was or what he was like but at least I had been rescued from the shame of being a wallflower. I set off onto the floor, moving to the music and looking around to see that Anne was all right. But things were okay. Both she and Linda were dancing too. Soon the boys finished picking the girls off from the crowd along the walls, and the floor was full.

Fortunately, I had my fallback position. Ben called.

His room, somewhere along a corridor in an apartment, was even smaller than mine. Dimly lit, beige and browns, a desk covered in books and papers, an armchair, and a single bed against the wall. He'd taken me to the movies – *Cat Ballou* – and we still had a couple of hours before I had to be back at Wellesley. Ben took my coat and hung it over the back of his desk chair, and indicated the bed.

'Sit down.' He took off his jacket, and loosened his tie. He came over to the bed and sat down beside me. He put his arm around me. 'Come on,' he pulled me towards him. 'Let's lie down.'

I lay down on the bed, next to the wall. In a way it felt good; the bed was soft and comfortable. I hadn't realized I was so tired. Ben stretched out beside me. He put his arm around me and for a while we lay there peacefully, looking up at the ceiling, and talking. After a while, he raised himself onto his elbow and lowered his lips to mine. Then I felt his hand reaching down my leg. 'Oh, dear,' I thought.

'What's the matter?'

All the siren warnings of my girlhood sounded. 'I'm sorry, Ben. I can't.'

'Can't what?'

'I just don't want to do this.' I struggled out of his arms, and sat up.

'What, don't you like me?'

'Oh, Ben, yes, I do like you. I like you a lot. It's just that,' my throat was tight. 'It's just that … well, this is a bit fast.'

'Stephanie, I really like you. I like you a lot. We've had a really good time together. I think we've really hit it off. I don't want to fool around anymore.

'Oh.'

'I mean, don't you think sex is a vital part of every relation-ship?'

'Well… not necessarily.'

'What do you mean?'

'Well, I think that you can go out with someone and have a really good time together, but you don't, well … you don't have to go all the way with someone to show that you really like them.'

Ben threw his legs off the bed and sat up. I stared at the rumpled shirt on his back.

'Look,' he turned to look at me, but somehow, the light had gone out of his eyes. 'Let's leave it for a while.' He got up and crossed the room. 'There's a song I want you to hear. Do you know Buffy St Marie?' He was slipping a record out of its sleeve. 'You ought to. She's a Canadian – Indian. Listen to this,' and he lowered the needle onto the record.

A rough and haunting voice filled the room. It seemed to go on forever. A slow, simmering love-song. A man and a woman making space in their lives for each other, until it was time for him to go.

Ben lifted the needle from the turntable. The words of the song hung in the air. I thought it was one of the most beautiful things I had ever heard.

But I didn't know what Ben meant by playing it, because when it ended he didn't tell me why he'd wanted me to hear it. Then he told me that pre-marital sex was really important to him (those were his words), and that he should have realized that I was just a freshman, and only seventeen, and really too young for him, as he would be twenty in two weeks' time. Then he helped me into my coat. We went downstairs and out into the freezing air, and he drove me back to the dorm in his car. I felt sick all the way. To give him credit, he honoured our date to go to see Wellesley's Junior Show the following Friday night, but even as Anne and Vicki and Linda gathered round for a post-mortem and said maybe there was hope, I knew it was all over.

4

Was anyone ever so young?

Up in Ontario, the snows had begun. At the college, dawn rose grey on trees that were bare. Lawns that had glistened in the sun of Indian summer were covered with hard frost, and mist floated above the lake. Huddled in my winter coat, I shivered on my way to 8.40 classes in the morning. Back in Davis, my room was snug: an old green wool rug on the floor, a red striped spread on the bed. I had found a baggy armchair abandoned in the attic of the dorm which I covered with a remnant of red corduroy from Filene's Basement and ran up some curtains to match. A standard lamp from a basement storeroom threw light from one corner. My parents sent me some posters of Inuit art to put up on the wall. Sitting in the pools of light created by another lamp beside my bed and one at my desk, I wrote to tell them I had created 'a fortress of Canadiana'. I had managed to get a part with a couple of lines in Aristophanes *Lysistrata*, the Drama Society's production for the autumn.

I had never heard of Aristophanes, of course, and wondered if performing a play by someone so ancient and dressing up in Greek robes was a bit old-fashioned and square. I reckoned without the seniors in charge. The play is about the power of women. Athens and Sparta have been at war for years. No amount of arguing and pleading by their wives can bring about a truce. Furious, Lysistrata persuades the women on both sides to unite. They will force their men to make peace by going on strike and denying them sex – the only thing, they realize, the men truly desire of them – until they agree to peace.

The production was raunchy and funny. And oh, how after all these centuries its themes still resonated with what we were going through!

This added a rehearsal most nights of the week and a drama workshop every Sunday evening, to my schedule. Meanwhile, mid-term papers were falling due, and my reading for history averaged 100 pages a day. To say nothing of my French course, which demanded reading a novel or two a week.

✳

It was sometime after ten. I had come to the end of writing notes on index cards stacked in order of the points I needed to write for an essay due the next afternoon. I wandered into the hall and knocked at Anne's room next door.

'Come in!'

The overhead light blazed. *Jumpin' Jack Flash* filled the room. Anne was cross- legged on her bed, head bopping to the beat, making notes on her knee from a book in her lap. In her left hand she held a mug of clear tea. Beside her was an open box of cookies.

She waved the mug. 'Have one.'

'Fatal,' I said and reached out to take one. You would never call Anne beautiful – her eyes were too small and her nose upturned – but she had a great figure and perfect legs. 'I can never understand how you can eat all these cookies and never put on a pound.'

She shrugged. I took another bite, savoured the sweet texture. 'Delicious. Your mother is a miracle worker.' I sat down on the floor.

'There's an ulterior motive, I'm sure.' Anne pointed to the box containing the cookies. 'See? Betty Crocker. My mom's saving the box tops.'

'What for?'

'She wants me to have a set of Twin Star stainless steel cutlery for my hope chest.'

Yours at special savings with Betty Crocker coupons!

'Your *hope chest?*'

'Yeah, like, for when you get married?' Anne flipped her palms up and snapped her fingers. 'You save up sheets and table linen so that when you set up house –' she spread he arms wide to expand the point – 'you've already got a lot of stuff.'

Marriage. Even though my mother talked of it, I always resisted her view that this was my destiny.

It was not what I wanted – not at least for a good long time – after I had travelled the world and established a life of my own.

But Anne was always surprising me.

For example: we functioned on entirely different clocks. I was always up early, eager to get on with the day, and asleep by half past ten at night. She could never get up before ten, and never go to bed before two. Her alarm clock was gigantic, like something out of *Mickey Mouse* – round and red with two big bells on top that rang like a fire alarm. She set it on top of the trunk at the end of her bed.

'Then I've no choice,' she said, 'I *have* to get up to turn it off.'

Just looking at that clock made me shudder.

Also, we worked differently. I moaned constantly about my workload, procrastinating to the ultimate hour before finally settling down to work. Then I complained about lack of inspiration. Somehow Anne never seemed bothered. She settled down at her desk at ten in the evening and worked through the night, to produce a paper required the next morning with no apparent effort at all.

But we could talk for hours. Unlike mine, her mother held down a full-time job as a lecturer, then a professor, in costume and textiles at the University of Illinois. A Mrs Weemer used to greet Anne when she got home from school. I sensed order and steady routines, Anne doing well at school, in her spare time working on the yearbook, writing for the school paper, taking holiday jobs. Her mother knitted her sweaters. She taught Anne how to make clothes. Once Anne got to Wellesley, she never let a day go by without sending notes of things Anne should know about. Little jokes, pushing ideas. Anne's grandfather had been an auto worker; her mother – not one of her brothers – was the first in her family to go to college.

Anne was six when her father died. 'Where would we have been,' her mother told her, 'if I hadn't got a master's degree?' No mistake about it: Anne was clear. A first degree at a liberal arts college was the nice-to-have. To do anything properly in life, she was going to need a second one to qualify for a decent job.

I listened to Anne outline a programme for her future that would include at least another seven years of education in a state of disbelief. My parents' attitude to what I did with my life had always been distinctly *laissez-faire*. Neither of them knew anything of higher education. I felt I had arrived at Wellesley more or less by accident. Merely getting the grades to stay there was enough for me at the moment.

Anne's father had been a newspaper reporter. He later taught journalism at the University of Illinois.

'You know, I used to sit on Hugh Hefner's knee at the age of four.'

'*Hugh Hefner!?*' I gasped. 'You mean, the man who founded *Playboy?*' While I was at the convent, one of the daygirls' fathers kept a stack of porno magazines hidden in the bottom drawer of his desk. While he was off playing golf on Saturday afternoons, we would pull *Playboy* out to explore: centre folds of wanton flesh and pumped-up breasts – we hardly dared look at the 'Playmate of the month'. How could *anyone* pose for such photographs?

But I didn't say that to Anne.

'Yeah. He was one of my father's favourite students. He used to come over for cocktails. We'd all be sitting around and I would sit on his lap.' She spread her hands wide and shrugged.

Another knock and Vicki poked her head round the door. 'Mind if I come in?'

'Join the party,' Anne said.

Vicki held a mug of black coffee in her hand. She settled her long frame beside me on the floor, curled her legs underneath her. She too came from the Midwest – Cincinnati, Ohio – and talked with a pronounced Midwestern twang. She dressed conservatively, in dark high-necked sweaters and neat skirts on the knee. Vicki's face was long and pale with large, round dark eyes, framed with thick black lashes, compelling, missing little. An only child, there was a sense about her of obedience, and of duty and care towards her parents, who I understood to be much older than mine: her father was 63 when she left home to come to college. She was protective, careful of what she told them: it was her uncle, the husband of her mother's sister, who had footed a substantial portion of her fees.

She kept a photograph of her father, strong jawed, thick grey hair smoothed back from a wide forehead, in a silver frame beside her bed. Vicki's father was an engineer. He wanted her to become a physicist. She preferred sociology.

Next to his picture, Vicki had a paperback copy of the latest novel by Joyce Carol Oates, John Updike or Saul Bellow. It amazed me that she had any time to read outside her courses. But Vicki, like Anne, could read and absorb at break-neck speed.

The girl who lived next door to us still wouldn't come down to dinner. 'I don't think I've seen her for three days,' said Vicki. 'Those coke tins are taking over the room. She tells me she's addicted.'

'I know,' said Anne. 'That pyramid takes up half of the room.'

'What can we do?' I said.

'If we tell anyone,' Vicki said, 'it's bound to get her into trouble.'

Meanwhile, the work kept piling up, keeping us hard at our desks. Then, every weekend there was another party or a mixer, or another invitation from a man you'd only just met to go away for a night or two to Brown or Princeton (5½ hours) or Yale, (or even Columbia, in New York City), to see a play, a football game, a concert (Harry Belafonte and Nana Mouskouri), or to a dance played by the Lovin' Spoonful.

Do you believe in magic, in a young girl's heart?

I couldn't resist it.

✶

By now I had taken my first glass of beer, sipped a light Dubonnet with lemon. All of us were all exhausted with 'fighting off the wolves' at the cattle shows, crowding into the 'powder room' to exchange notes, trying to keep clear heads among the pawing hands, while everyone's hormones raged rampant.

I was not the only one who was completely inhibited. None of us talked about the details. It wasn't that we couldn't conceive of being touched. It was the brutal presumption of it all. Nor did we give any thought to how the men we were meeting had been conditioned too.

All around us blazed macho adverts for cars and cigarettes. '*What sparks a champion, sparks you – and champions choose Wheaties!*' Tough, muscled bodybuilder Charles Atlas – a youth transformed from a 'bloodless, pitiful, skinny shrimp to this new muscular, red-blooded, head-to-toe He-Man', the quintessence of the popular ideal. There were rumours of unpleasant male initiation rites at fraternities. We had no idea what really went on in locker rooms.

But what it all added up to was the ideal of the super virile male, who would whisk away the woman of his dreams in the manner of *Me Tarzan. You Jane.* No need to speak, no need to seek some kind of rapport, much less respect.

And all the time we were trying to stay true to those upright values that had dominated our upbringing, that required us, above all, to remain virgins until the moment we arrived at the altar.

The facts were:

- We wanted it.
- We weren't really too sure exactly how you did it.
- Some said it hurt.
- That you would bleed the first time.
- You only had to do it once. Then you could get pregnant.

Just look what happened to my friend Mary-Ellen. She'd had to drop out of school. Her parents sent her away to have the baby. They told her to put it up for adoption. But in the end, she decided to keep it. The last time I saw her she was wheeling a pram in the distance. I was ready to say hello, but I was with a friend whose mother had told her she was to have nothing more to do with her. Drummed into us since our mothers first realized we might be turning into young women and needed an introduction to menstruation, there was a line you didn't cross.

In special classes at the beginning of high-school (boys into one room, girls into another) information about the facts of life were rudimentary, based on one or two simple line drawings: one lot for the girls, different ones for the boys.

I often wondered what the boys were told. As for the girls,

we learnt about ovulation and that bleeding for four or five days once a month was a normal part of life. A girl with her period just went on as she always does – playing sport, going swimming – even though she soon discovers she may often suffer headaches, nausea and outrageous cramps, fainting spells or terrible pain in her back or legs.

In the dorm our periods were either 'the curse' or, having ventured a little too far, 'the friend'. Everyone in the dorm was getting them at the same time. So striking was this information that Martha McLintock, a sophomore from along the hall, decided to make this coincidence into a biology project. Which started her on a path to her ground-breaking discovery of human pheromones, and a career today as a renowned biopsychologist.

Exactly how a sperm might enter the womb had been a puzzle for years. All we knew was that if you happened to get pregnant, you would miss your period and might have a bit of sickness in the morning. The key requirement was to preserve everything intact until you married.

And then?

'You might like it. Then you will want it more.'

We fussed over it. Obsessed about the right and wrong. Was it worth the contest to resist, in the face of a man you really liked? It hadn't taken us more than a couple of months to discover that pre-marital sex was common. 'It's entirely your own business,' the older girls counselled. You had nothing to lose in this day of contraceptives.

Except: how do you lay your hands on contraceptives when they are illegal to prescribe to single women in New England? It had taken a battle lasting years to bring a bill to the Massachusetts legislature in 1965 to legalise them for people who were married. It took another year to finally legalise contraceptive care – but only for married persons with a medical prescription.

No one uttered a word.

In fact, we knew next to nothing about how our bodies worked, and little of our sexuality. Like the good girls that we were, we wrote home for advice. Anne's mother: 'So I see you're really being exposed to the freshman rush ... take it easy kid and start dating freshmen rather than those seniors and PhD candidates who are so ready to take advantage of the innocent frosh ...' And from my dad: 'The gambit about 'naïve young freshman' is a standard ploy. Have you run into the one about being 'emancipated from the bonds of convention', 'let's see if we are really compatible', 'you aren't a whole woman unless...'

In November I turned eighteen, my first birthday away from home. The girls on the hall gave me a surprise party, complete with cake and punch. A couple of weeks later, Charlie and his family invited me to stay with them over Thanksgiving. Both acts of kindness, so unexpected, left me feeling curiously hollow – I wanted nothing more than to go home.

Early in December, a teacher was seriously assaulted by a man as she walked into the village at five o'clock in the afternoon. It was a friend of mine who heard all the screaming and ran to try and help. Warnings went up to take extra care when out alone after dark. The next evening, I opened my door to discover the Dean – who was never seen in the dorm – and the housemother in the corridor. They had come to take the freshman who was known to take interminable showers, to the infirmary. The next day we learned she was on suicide watch.

I'd noticed that no one talked about the marks they had

been getting on the papers we had to write two or three times a term. It was my turn to be summoned by the Dean. I was told I couldn't take the time to act in a play, go out on dates all weekend and still deliver the grades I needed to keep my scholarship. A decision on whether to renew my financial awards would be taken in the spring. My continuance at the college could not be guaranteed.

I was shocked. Clearly, I had to produce marks that were better than B-/ C+. I had to try and grip the situation. The next day I told the director of *A Taste of Honey* that I could not audition next term.

5

Pause for adjustment

I travelled to England to see my family for the Christmas holidays: a commercial flight from Boston to Montreal. Then a train to Ottawa. A taxi to a military airfield somewhere on the outskirts. All that day, as I travelled north, the weather had been getting worse. Low grey skies gave way to sleet, turned to flurries of snow. By the time I arrived at the hangar that night, a fierce gale was driving thick flakes of snow before it. In the floodlights I saw drifts taller than buildings being cleared away from the sides of the aircraft. Only two other passengers waited to board.

'Do you think we're going to take off?' I had no idea what I would do at this remote airbase alone so late at night if we did not. At that moment the pilot joined us.

'Don't worry.' It was just like in a war movie. 'The RCAF never flies if they don't think they can.'

Head down, he led us out into the blizzard. Snow flew into my face, and the wind rocked the steps as I climbed up into the plane.

A few minutes later we lumbered down the runway and shuddered up into the sky. Gusts of snow caught in the wing lights, and then we rose above the weather. Outside the porthole the night was black and moonless. A quiet dinner, some chat on the plane. I dozed in my seat until we touched down to refuel at Greenland. When we took off again, the stewards made me up a bed with sheets and blankets and told me to get some sleep. But the growl of the engines kept me awake.

What did I know of London? I had no picture in my mind at all. As we made our approach to land at Gatwick, I could see nothing. Minute after minute as we descended, I saw nothing but whiteness. Would we plough straight into the ground? All at once the sky cleared and the ground rose up to meet us. I saw a church spire, a strip of green lawn, and the runway, slick with sheeting rain.

Then: there were my parents, looking curiously diminished in the wide space of the terminal, my mother, slim and beautiful in an elegant tweed suit, my father in tweed jacket and tie.

My father had hired a Rolls Royce and chauffeur to drive me, on this, my first trip into London. My parents wanted to spoil me. But I felt overwhelmed by this extravagance, and faintly ridiculous sitting with them in the back of such a huge car, with its silver ashtrays, lacquered walnut veneer and beige leather seats – even resentful. After all, we were broke, and I was struggling, constantly, to keep within my meagre allowance. We were driven into London at a stately pace and all I remember was how alien England looked through the blurry drizzle on the windows of the car: the doll-like houses of the suburbs, with their neat green lawns and red pitched roofs, and the grey cloud of the skies, hanging so low overhead. The softness of the rain, the chill of the damp. On and on we drove, traffic whizzing about us, the cars – more than I had ever seen in my life – shiny and small and swift. Gradually the greenery disappeared, subsumed by grey brick and paving, shabby terraces of worn buildings. On. Roundabouts, Belisha beacons, traffic lights, zebra crossings, gas pumps in front of old white garages.

'Look, darling, Victoria Station! And just over there – the back of Buckingham Palace. Now: this is Belgravia!' Mother was my tour guide. We swept through a square of enormous buildings with cream pillared porticos – so vast, so cold. We emerged into the white stucco of what I was told was the Cromwell Road and, following a sweeping turn right, the bombastic rhythm of the white pillars lining Queen's Gate. In the distance I could see the gaunt outlines of trees, and massed shrubberies. 'Look,' pointed Mother. 'Kensington Gardens.' We turned again and entered a square and drew up before one of the high imposing houses. The chauffeur saluted. My bag was brought in. Before me a wide hall, scarlet carpet. To the side of the staircase, crouched an ancient iron lift, room for just four. My parents and I squeezed in, and we creaked up. At last we emerged at the top, the fifth floor. And then:

'Here is our flat,' said Mother. The door burst open and my brother and sister leapt upon me.

It was a grand reunion, hot milky coffee in an old-fashioned white painted kitchen, and much too much to say.

It did not take long before I had the feeling that my family were all set, living in this flat on top of a large house in Kensington. Once the servants' quarters, the rooms were low ceilinged, but spacious. The furnishings were old fashioned – striped walls and faded velvets. There were a few things – paintings and ornaments, which my parents had brought with them from Canada, but they were lost in the frills and furbelows of a pseudo-Victorian interior. My mother had told me she was in heaven in London, enjoying all the history and civility of the place. My father liked his new job. My sister was happy at a girl's preparatory school around the corner, where she wore a smart navy uniform and straw boater. My brother, who had been packed off to a boarding school ten days after arriving in the country, was miserable, 'but,' said my mother, 'he is sure to get over it'. Our dog was still quarantined in kennels.

'Here is your room, Steph.' My mother opened the door of a room at the end of a passage at the front of the house. It was papered a dull green with gold fleur de lys, long and narrow, with a gas fire below a tired marble mantel piece, and a lumpy bed under a wine-coloured candlewick bedspread in the corner. I looked out of the window.

Across the square was another identical terrace. Beyond, stretching away in every direction as far as I could see were the rooftops of London. Range upon range of pitches and flat sections, grey slates and lead guttering, dormer windows, attic rooms with window boxes, curving balustrades and chimney stacks, clay pots and iron ladders. To me it looked just like a backdrop for Peter Pan and Wendy – and I was one of the Lost Boys, aching for my newfound world in America.

I found London hard that Christmas. I missed the sharp, clear New England air; energy and colour and confidence. Anne's zany vitality, the warmth of Vicki's giggle. Linda's eager sketching out of a conversation in the air, Diana twirling before me in her new second-hand fur coat.

I didn't want grey pavements under my feet, I didn't want rain, and I didn't want the Victoria and Albert Museum and its

Raphael Cartoons, magnificent though they were. I wanted blue skies and sun shining on fresh snow, tall pine trees that gave off scent when you brushed by them and a frozen lake stretching out before me.

I hated the way it got dark so early, soon after three in the afternoon, when the day had barely started for me with my jet-lag and fatigue. I didn't like the Underground, which we took everywhere, grubby and blear, with men in grey overcoats and black bowler hats, and upholstered carriages smelling of damp wool and cigarettes. Its ill-lit passages, full of hurrying commuters, put me in mind of a world of troglodytes. The streets were lined with double-decker buses and black cabs that could turn on a sixpence and people who looked straight past you, as if you weren't *even there*, when you lined up to join a queue.

There were wide-eyed girls with pale lips and black-rimmed lashes, in skimpy mini-dresses that were at least nine inches shorter than the skirts we were wearing in the United States. They wore knee-high boots or vanilla tights from Mary Quant with neat black patent leather shoes. Technically, I had a good time. My parents poured me gin and tonics before dinner. I went to Harrods and Selfridges and bought my first dress from Biba. There were several family parties. The sons of my parents' friends took me to the theatre and trendy discotheques in smoky basement rooms in Soho.

And I felt strange, strange. Even the music of the Beatles didn't sound like it did on the other side of the Atlantic. And why did everyone talk about 'pop' not 'rock'?

6

Stirrings in the cloister

Life was much quieter when I got back to Wellesley. January was cold, with slush on the roads and patches of snow on the ground. Girls went about the campus bundled in big coats and thick boots, woolly hats and scarves. Everyone hunkered down for the long haul to spring.

The atmosphere at weekends for those who were left behind was one of solemn *ennui*. Introspection and depression festered. Darkness fell and silence descended on the dorm. There was little to do except study, study, study, or perhaps, go into Boston to the Museum of Fine Arts to see a Rembrandt exhibition. But that would cost money, and money was tight.

One morning I wandered into the dining room with my breakfast tray. Blinding sun reflected off snow piled deep outside the windows. Looking for a space to sit I saw three sophomores at the nearest table: a tight group of close friends, Hillary and her good friends, Jan and Betsy. I hesitated, unsure of a welcome. Then I took a place on the edge. Hillary was in full flow, leading the talk. She was wearing her dressing gown, glasses low on her nose, hair up in big curlers. Beside her Jan, small and dark, and Betsy, blonde, glamorous and immaculate. The three were talking about a new organisation, the National Organisation for Women.

'What do you think,' Hillary said to me, 'should Wellesley join?'

'What would it mean?' I asked, feeling my way.

Hillary told me NOW had been formed the previous October. Twenty-eight women who had attended the Third National Conference on the Commission on the Status of Women in Washington DC the previous June had been fed up with the way the federal government kept failing to enforce new anti-discrimination laws. They decided to set up their own organisation to campaign for women's rights – to push through, as they put it, a truly equal partnership with men and full participation in the mainstream of American society. The issue was whether Wellesley, as a college for women, wanted to affiliate.

'That would mean the college joining in, taking a stand for women's rights.'

'Women's rights?'

'I think the basic question is: are we feminists?'

I tried to connect a term I associated with militant Suffragettes fighting for the vote in Britain before the first World War to our situation in the comfort of the college. 'Feminists?'

'You *have* read Betty Friedan?' said Betsy. '*The Feminine Mystique?*'

I shook my head.

Hillary said: 'She's the founder of NOW – the first president.'

Feminism. It was the first time I heard the word – and from the girl who would go on to be Hillary Rodham Clinton.

Back then we were only girls, no knowledge yet of relationships, much less marriage, and of a working life. But it is no coincidence *The Feminine Mystique* was written by a woman who had gone to Smith College – like Wellesley, another female seminary.

You only have to look at pictures of Betty Friedan to see that she was not a conventional beauty. Brought up in the Midwestern city of Peoria, Illinois, Friedan was the brainy Jewish daughter of a Russian immigrant father and a gifted mother, who had given up her job as women's editor of the local newspaper to marry and have children. Outspoken and argumentative, Bettye Goldstein as she was known then, was ostracised by the smart sororities at her high school. But at Smith, where she arrived in 1938, she could be who she was. Friedan flourished. She graduated *summa cum laude* in 1942 and went on to do graduate work in in psychology at the University of California, Berkeley.

Smith was like Wellesley: enclosed, focussed on learning and intellectual achievement. No dangerous distractions from male companions and no men to put you down. Both breed an unusual kind of feminine intensity, and an awareness and curiosity about how other women live and think. Women quickly learnt they have kindred spirits, and how to tap into them. Women who do not compete, who they can trust, and with whom secrets can be shared.

The clues that set Friedan on the road to writing *The Feminine Mystique* emerged from a survey she conducted in 1957 for the 15th reunion of her graduating class at Smith. How were her educated classmates adapting to their roles of wife and mother? Time and again came back complex and troubling responses – 'nameless, aching dissatisfaction', 'the problem that has no name.'

Friedan reinforced her findings by sending the same questionnaire to graduates of Radcliffe and other colleges. The seeds of an investigation that would become *The Feminine Mystique* were sown. The women who were most unhappy were those who tried hardest to live up to the pervasive image of 'the happy American housewife.' What Friedan uncovered 'was a strange discrepancy between the reality of our lives as women, and the image to which we were trying to conform.' Always being a mommy, always being a wife and 'homemaker', a woman could never be herself. Friedan called the image of the manufactured housewife 'the feminine mystique.'

Her solution?

Social and economic equality for women, the right to control their own bodies and the sharing of childcare.

✱

Of course, Anne knew who Friedan was.

'You remember that piece by Gloria Steinem? When she went underground as a *Playboy* bunny and wrote it up in *Show*? That came out about the same time. And you know they both went to Smith?' She sighed. We had a grudging feeling that Smith might be a bit ahead of Wellesley in a number of areas.

'Look,' I said, 'the question is: are we feminists?'

An awkward silence.

Linda: 'Aw, me, no. Can you even see it?'

'I'm not so good at being labelled,' said Vicki. 'It doesn't matter what it is. Maybe I just see too much. Things are never really black or white.'

We batted the word around a bit. It sounded so daunting. As if we were joining an army.

Women who are feminists don't like men.

Maybe it's a byword for lesbianism?

Or standing up to be counted for women's equal rights in the workforce? Getting a bit shrill and shouty?

Isn't that a bit butch?

We were still so young, so close to our sheltered upbringings, our down-home comfortable, middle-class lives. Our favourite childhood TV programmes like *Father knows Best, I love Lucy* and comic strips like *Blondie*. Nothing there.

We considered such role models as we knew. Elizabeth Taylor. Sophia Loren? Hollywood movie stars, outside our purview. Jackie Kennedy and Eleanor Roosevelt? Exceptions, married to the President: Jackie no more than a glamorous hostess, really, and Eleanor – well – at that time little was known to us of her life. Golda Meier, Prime Minister of Israel? But just look at her...

If I only have one life let me live it as a blonde.

We fell back on reality.

I thought of my mother playing *La traviata* full blast while furiously vacuuming our house on an army base far from civilisation. Taking an hour every afternoon after lunch to read. Proud of having trained to be a ballerina in Shanghai under the same teacher as Margot Fonteyn, frustrated that her mother wouldn't let her join the Canadian air force during World War II. That university was an option she could never afford.

As for marriage, there had never been a moment of doubt: my father was the love of her life. Eight months after they met, she settled down to be a 50s-style helpmate: washing and ironing his shirts, cleaning their apartment, cooking, packing and unpacking, organising the family. We never lived anywhere long enough for her to have a job – but whenever she could she grabbed an opportunity: setting up a nursery and kindergarten for Canadian children on the base where we lived in Germany, book reviewing for the CBC while we lived in Ottawa, working as a secretary at Queen's, the university in Kingston.

As for the mothers of my friends, there were few fields in which women were able to get jobs in the Illinois of the early 1950s. Fortunately Anne's mother, Lorraine, had two degrees She taught in the business school of Washington University in St Louis during World War II. When she married and she and her husband moved to the University of Illinois in Champaign-Urbana, nepotism rules barred her from working at the same institution as her husband. When he died, she got a job in a new division in textiles at the university. All her life she battled men promoted over her to carve out a role. It took her fifteen years to become a full professor.

Linda's mother, Ruth, had never had to work. But she had been to the University of Texas and on to Vassar which had opened her eyes to a world beyond Texas: this was what she wanted for Linda.

Once she took us out to dinner at the Wellesley Inn. Ruth had impressed me as well-dressed and worldly, with a confidence born of a life of comfort and stability. She was pragmatic and down to earth. 'Get over yourself,' she would say when things got difficult. 'You do what you have to do.'

'I don't know if she's read Friedan or not,' said Linda. 'I've got the feeling she would be irritated by her — she'd say those women should have come to terms with their situations and dealt with it.'

As for Vicki: her mother, Doris, would have liked to go to college when she graduated from high school in 1922, but had no choice but to get a job. Any job. Doris didn't marry until she was 41.

'My Mom always gave me two pieces of advice. The first was: don't marry unless you are sure. The second: always have your own career.' She thought it very important for women to be independent, to have a career and be able to support themselves – without a man.

These other mothers seemed so much more grounded than mine. Pragmatic. Capable. Sure of themselves and their daughters' potential. Mother feared my coming to college in America, of leaving the life she knew behind. She had no idea what going to college could lead to, or of a career for me. When I talked of my own ideas, she often remained silent. Her own early life had been one in flight from the Japanese in China, and during WW2, watching her own mother struggle to make ends meet working in a naval shipyard in British Columbia while her father was a prisoner of war in Shanghai. Later, she held a basic job as a secretary. Mother wanted nothing more for me than what had been her own solution: a secure marriage, following my husband.

It never occurred to us to think very much about the fact that we'd already achieved far more than most of the boys at our schools. We knew we were every bit as good as any man.

But we also wanted them in our lives.

And more than anything, right now, we wanted love.

*

The first weekend of February was Winter Weekend: Wellesley's social event of the year. Centred on a huge dance on Saturday night, this was the moment when, if he were going to ask you, he would pop the question. As you blushingly whispered yes, he would pull a velvet covered box from his tuxedo pocket, open it, and place a huge diamond ring on your finger. And you would have realized the pinnacle of social success, the dream of your dreams. *You would be engaged.* After that, the photographs and the announcement in the society pages of the *New York Times,* and a June wedding, straight after graduation. The atmosphere in the dorm in the run-up before Winter Weekend was electric.

But none of us was going.

'It's more for juniors and seniors,' Deckie comforted us. Vicki, Anne and I prepared to go on the offensive, design-ing amusements in Boston for the weekend. On the Thursday evening before festivities started, I was washing a sweater in the sink in the little kitchen on our floor when a friend put her head round the door.

'How'd you like to go down to Yale for the weekend?'

'Tell me more.'

'It's Jonathan Edwards' College's big weekend of the year: you know, lots going on, big dance – full formal – on Saturday night. The thing is, the girl who was going with my date's room-mate has just called in. She's sick. I wondered if you'd like to come. Quite a few of us are going. We're driving down tomor-row afternoon.'

My date for the weekend was Bill. He was short, with a friendly smile, a mop of dark hair and glasses. He took my bag and steered me along a path carved out between banks of snow across a wide quadrangle. The light was fading, and the bare limbs of the trees stood black against the sky. Around the quad, the stone buildings loomed large and grey.

'You're staying with the Coffins,' said Bill. 'He's the chaplain and a really good guy.' Bill had met Reverend Coffin through music: he sang in the freshman glee club and played the violin. He told me Coffin had a fine voice – in fact, the whole Coffin family was musical. Mrs Coffin was the daughter of the famous pianist, Arthur Rubenstein, and had been an actress in the movies.

Eva Coffin was tiny and graceful, with long dark hair which she wore swept up, and round glasses. A corduroy dirndl, nipped into her waist, served to emphasise how small she was. She wel-comed us into the kitchen, and we stood about as she made us cups of tea. In the midst of light chat, Reverend Coffin poked his head round the door. Horn-rimmed glasses, dark receding hair, bold red check shirt: he didn't look like any churchman I had come across before.

'Hi there,' he said. To me: 'You Bill's date for the weekend? Well, welcome to Yale. Have a great time tonight. See you later.' He was out of the door.

In the evening Bill took me to the theatre. Yale Drama School were performing Ben Johnson's *Volpone*. It was a magical evening. Snow was falling, catching in the glow of the campus lights, and throngs of couples were making their way towards the theatre. Bill and I crowded into the foyer and found our seats. The performance was set to rock and roll, with props and costumes from 1610 to 1967. We huddled together, rocking with laughter. We emerged from the theatre flushed with good humour. Bill walked me home to the Coffins to get some sleep before for the next day when he would be singing, and a dinner and dance in the evening.

I came in about midnight. I didn't feel like going to bed, and went into the kitchen to make tea. Through the door, I saw a light shining in the living room. Coffin was sprawled in an armchair beneath the lamp, smoking a pipe. Two other men were ranged on the couches along the walls on either side of him. Philip Roth – not famous then – with piercing eyes, black receding hair and heavy brows, then writer-in-residence at Princeton had started working closely with Coffin. He would go on to draft some of the fiercest polemics against the war in Vietnam for a newsletter called 'Resist'.

'Come on in here,' Coffin beckoned. 'Sit down and join us.' He indicated an ottoman in front of him. 'We're just having a little discussion.'

During the evening Bill and his friends had talked a lot about Coffin. Not the kind of man you'd think of as a priest. For one thing, he didn't wear a dog collar, for another he was fit and athletic, and rode a motor scooter. He delivered sermons worth hearing. Coffin believed that a minister's job was to be both priest and prophet, to warn his flock where they might be going wrong, challenging you to stand up for what you thought. Courage, he was fond of saying, is the first virtue. 'It makes all other virtues possible.'

Bill told me that five years before, in May 1961, Coffin was one of a group of seven Freedom Riders who travelled from Atlanta, Georgia to Montgomery, Alabama where they joined three local leaders to request service at the bus station lunch counter that had been desegregated the day before. All were arrested. On his return to Yale, Coffin declared he was only setting a moral example. Two years later, while protesting segregation in Baltimore he was arrested again; and again in Saint Augustine, Florida at another lunch counter that he and others were trying to integrate.

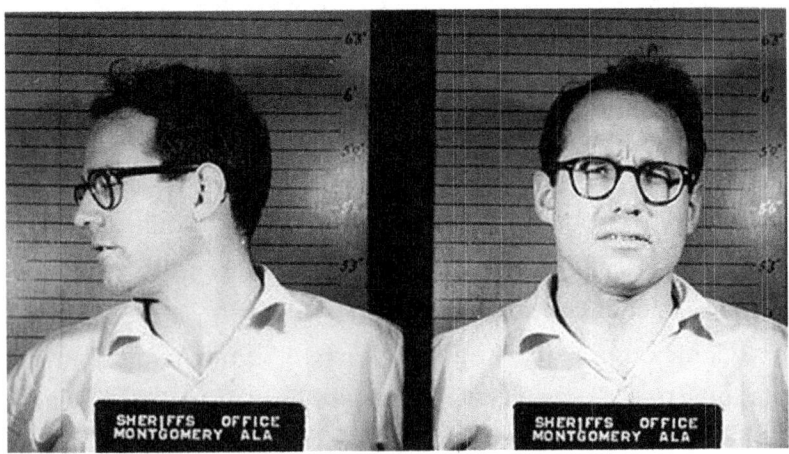

Over the talk I recalled the cold pit of fear that used to open in my stomach back home in Canada whenever the television used to cover the Ku Klux Klan going about its nightly raids, murdering Black people in southern states. Or my baffled horror watching white crowds attack Black children bussed into schools in Alabama. I had often seen news of the Freedom Fighters' arrests. But I never imagined I would meet anyone who had been on the marches or gone to jail. Or who was a friend of Martin Luther King.

Lounging back in his chair that night, Coffin was young (he was 42), funny and just a bit scary. I clutched my mug and sat down.

'Let's see, you're from Canada, you say? Ever have any Black kids in your class?'

Not an orthodox question. But an issue. The seventeen Black students at Wellesley had just announced the formation of a 'Negro study group' called Ethos to discuss their role at the college and in the country. They called it a place for 'personal self-discovery of one's racial heritage through group interaction... only Negroes would find membership meaningful.' I wanted to go. I wanted to know who these girls were and what they thought. But I also felt if I were them, feeling as strange as I often did at Wellesley, I would like my own space, with my own people – in privacy.

As for Coffin's question, the answer seemed to be no. Then, I remembered. I told him that when we lived for six months on the outskirts of Halifax, Nova Scotia and I was about eleven, there were fair number of Black kids in my school and three or four in my class. They came from a shanty town even further out of town than the newly built subdivision where we lived. Years later, I would discover that these kids could have been descendants of slaves who had fled north at the time of the American Revolution.

'Well, I can bet you there aren't many boys here at Yale who ever had any Black people in their class.'

I sat down to listen. About how many Black boys were being drafted to go to Vietnam. How the National Selective Service Act was written in such a way to defer to the rich and better educated. I had known nothing of this. It did not seem right. For me, for years, the issue of Vietnam lay in the background. Despite America's pleas for troops, Lester Pearson, the Canadian prime minister, had never permitted Canada to become involved in what was essentially a civil war: between the communists of North Vietnam, and the corrupt remnants of a French colonial regime in the south. Vietnam was not my problem. But now, how could I avoid it?

In the early summer of 1963, not long before President John Kennedy was assassinated, a Buddhist monk burned himself alive at a busy intersection in Saigon – a breath-taking protest against the persecution of Buddhists by the South Vietnamese government, backed by the United States. The scene was filmed live and broadcast round the world. You can be traumatised at long distance at fourteen. The composure of the monk as his body in its saffron robes became engulfed in flames remains scarred on my memory.

Now almost half a million American troops were fighting there. Every day more were going. Each month the American government was drafting almost 40,000 boys. I knew that all males over the age of 18 had to register with the Selective Service System for military conscription at their local draft board. From what I'd heard, no one seemed to know exactly what the terms of eligibility were; it often appeared you were at the random mercy of your local draft board. For the moment, anyone at college was entitled to defer the draft until they had finished their degree.

Coffin was softly spoken. The talk that night was electric. About conscience – so familiar to me from uncomfortable discussions with the nuns – now combined with the issue of civil disobedience.

Was it right that boys who were drafted, should have to fight in a war they did not believe in? What did the issues in Vietnam have to do with their lives in America? Both Congress and the Johnson Administration were seriously divided on the rights and wrongs of the war. There had been protests – a handful of draft cards burnt, scores of citizens refusing to pay their income tax. College presidents and thousands of professors, clergy and journalists had seriously questioned the aims and conduct of the war. How far should you be prepared to let something go before you stand up to be counted?

As far as Coffin was concerned, the war was not only unjustifiable, but illegal. Now he was mulling the text of a big speech he was to deliver in Washington in two weeks' time.

'Ultimately you have to do what you think is right,' he said, 'and accept the risk of consequences. You can only be effective, by doing what's right.'

I wondered, did I – could I – have his courage?

Coffin thought it would be a good thing if students got organized. He'd love to see thousands of those opposed to the war gather on some specified date in cities around the country. And then with a moving, simple statement, surrender their draft cards at designated federal buildings.

It was dawn before I went to bed.

Two weeks later I joined Wellesley's first demonstration in the history of the college. It was a grey February day, not too cold, and I milled about with the others, three hundred and fifty students and faculty gathered in Founders Hall parking lot. The issue, on which I felt strongly, was the straitjacket of the college's liberal arts curriculum. I resented the fact that half my time at the college would be spent studying biblical history, sciences and maths in order to fulfil arbitrary 'liberal arts' requirements. No one was permitted much freedom to explore the many wonderful courses Wellesley offered, or to specialise as I wanted, to dive deep into history, philosophy and the history of art.

Various speakers offered different points of view. Hillary was campaigning for a seat on the Student Education Committee. 'Anyone who isn't here right now is probably in the library studying for one of their required courses,' she quipped, and everybody laughed.

'Not a stand-in, teach-in nor demonstration: rather a conscientiously conducted rally,' the *Wellesley News* piously described it. Perhaps because so pious, the approach worked. Small steps. The President appeared to be listening. I had a sense that change could be coming.

Another weekend, another Saturday night in the dorm. Vicki and Linda and I were left to fend for ourselves, cleaning out our cupboards as stated by college rules (there would be a room inspection the following week) – washing and – Linda and I – ironing our clothes.

'How many commercials can you remember?' Vicki started to sing. There was Ajax, and Colgate's toothpaste and—

'Oh, Mr Clean gets rid of dirt and grease and grime in just a minute!

Mr Clean will clean your whole house and everything that's in it!

Mr Clean...

Mr Clean...

Mr Clean....'

'I can't be bothered anymore.' Vicki thrust her sweaters into a drawer. 'I'd much rather cook instead.' The three of us congratulated ourselves on our fine housekeeping, brewed a cup of lap-sang souchong and went to find Anne.

She was looking over her clothes: two long-sleeved blouses, one in bright yellow and another, equally vibrant, in orange, reserved for 'good' occasions. And a baby-doll type dress, brown with white polka dots. She'd worn it to a mixer at Harvard – where she was the only girl in the room who was not asked to dance.

'A literal wallflower,' she said. 'Imagine the humiliation. I've had enough of mixers. ' And announced she was taking up computer dating. The service was called 'Contact'.

Bizarre.

I'd heard vaguely of computer dating – *Glamour* ran a piece. 'Operation Match' was conceived by a couple of 'mixer-weary' Harvard graduates to find the kind of people they enjoyed dating at Radcliffe. 'If you're the modern adventurous type, you'll probably want to take part in one of the most interesting social experiments ever,' was the story.*

But *really*? Engineering encounters with perfect strangers? Produced by a machine? Anne could take her chances, but I hung back. Her argument: how was this any different from being set up for a blind date?

So she went ahead and sent off $3.00 for the kit by mail. In due course a questionnaire arrived. She filled in the answers by pencilling in circles on manila-coloured cards to coincide with the desired qualities in a date. Within days of posting off the cards, Anne received three 'ideal matches'.

The first was a witty guy from Harvard with whom she exchanged post-cards before they met. Tall and blond, on the first date he unfortunately made some reference to belonging to the 'master race' and Anne came home claiming to have met a Nazi. The second was a football player from Columbia, who by way of enticement, wrote to tell her 'my thighs are thick as is my chest and arms'. He invited her to New York, but at the last minute she bailed. The third was a guy from MIT called Hal, with whom she went out for a while. Very nice, smart, but no sparks.

She was well out of it.

More things I noticed:

- The quiet girls were the ones who were getting the boyfriends.
- Sunday mornings in the dorm sitting room were spent poring over the engagement columns of the *New York Times*. To say nothing of the weddings.

---

* https://archive.computerhistory.org/resources/access/text/2020/12/102797880-05-01-acc.pdf

- Skirts were getting shorter by the month. Soon they'd be at least an inch above the knee.

March came with 70-degree heat, with two feet of snow still on the ground. Vicki had stopped coming down to dinner and was living on Rice Krispies in a bid to lose weight. Anne was playing Aretha Franklin non-stop at high volume.

I was enjoying my courses, one in contemporary French drama, taught by a M. Galand, a bubbling Frenchman. I was reading Apollinaire and Euripides, discovering the Russian poet Yevgeny Yevtushenko, and, wherever I could, trying to read more about China's Cultural Revolution, to fathom Mao Tse Tung's quotations and his *Little Red Book*. Twice a week I worked in the evenings in the library to top up my scholarship, and in the mornings got fit by rowing for crew.

In Cambridge that spring, the maples sprang into leaf, shading the red brick-paved side-walks around Harvard Yard. The Coop was stacked with the latest Beatles albums, and full of books on Aubrey Beardsley and Alphonse Mucha. Art nouveau was everywhere. Beardsley's exquisite pen and ink drawings, with their androgynous figures, luxuriant hair, and extravagant voluminous dress, so often sensationally explicit, were exquisite. They epitomised the fin de siècle decadence of the 1890s, when many feared that civilisation had reached its pinnacle, that the future was doomed, though I'm not sure we thought of that then. Everywhere posters, record sleeves, and underground magazines echoed his vision.

I lay in the sun reading *Notes from Underground*. From someone's window sounded the latest Beatles, weirdly wonderful:

Picture yourself in a boat on a river...

Everyone was talking about romance, the inspiration of Wellesley's spring rites: walk three times round the lake with a boy, and you'd be sure to get engaged. Seniors raced hoops to Tupelo Point on the lake below Davis: the winner would be the first to be married. It was awfully dull when there was no one you knew who you could care for.

In her room, Diana and I talked about love. She sat cross-legged on her bed among heaps of clothes and cushions, her blue eyes fringed with pale lashes, fingers twirling the ends of her auburn hair. The bed was covered with a blue Indian paisley spread. Her desk was deep in scarves and books and papers. They spilled onto the floor, covering the carpet. Among her post-cards of Renaissance paintings pinned to her wall, was a sixteenth-century poem Desiderata: *'go placidly among the noise and haste and remember what peace there may be in silence...'* I was impressed. It looked lovely. She'd copied it in exotic lettering. What none of us knew was that it was a fake, written by a Max Ehrmann from Indiana in the early 1920s.

To me, everything about Diana seemed beautiful and assured. In fact, she interspersed periods of effortless brilliance with crippling anxiety. Here she was, this beautiful girl, who was getting straight As without appearing to do any work at all. Her drawings were delicate, acutely rendered. She could paint, compose music and write poetry. This term, in addition to her work for class, she was drawing up the outline of a book she planned to write over the summer. But every moment of her spare time and every night of the week was devoted to one or other of her boyfriends.

'But how do you *know?*' she kept asking me. 'How do you *know* you're in love?' Whenever she asked me a question, she would look at me intently as if trying to read the answer behind my eyes.

How could I tell her? I didn't know myself. She was so absorbed in her own world of emotions she never asked about mine. And in the end she could tell me so little specifically about whichever of her men she was obsessing over, I was at a loss. Certainly, what she'd seen of her mother's marriage and love affairs had not set a reassuring example. As a child she had seen little of her mother and father. Packed off to summer camps and boarding schools as soon as she was old enough, she was kept safely away while her mother, seeing one man after another in New York, abandoned home for weeks at a time. When they were together, she watched her parents' marriage dissolve into vicious fights, an angry separation, and when she was fifteen, divorce.

'I think I might be... oh, Stephanie, what do you think?'

*

I sat in College Hall taking notes for Dad as I listened to Arthur Schlesinger, former Special Assistant to President Kennedy, deliver his analysis of the 'Dilemma of Vietnam'. This was a test case of aggression, he told us, of wills between the US and China: a carefully premeditated and co-ordinated plan of the Chinese. A suspension of American bombing would only encourage Beijing to think the US was weakening. The only way to negotiation was by escalation. But if the US did so, it could increase the risk of Chinese entry.

The problem, he said, was that bombing had never been decisive against what was basically guerrilla warfare in a rural economy. Just as the US hadn't been able to control Korea from the air, bombing in Vietnam had failed in its objective – it couldn't stop infiltration from the North. Instead, bombing had increased it and hadn't stopped supplies. His analysis coincided with what I had often heard from my father, who regarded the American intervention as doomed to disaster.

More and more, I was becoming convinced that the war was unwinnable.

Our first year of college was drawing to a close. My grades were still bumping along near the bottom. And I had yet to hear whether my scholarship would be renewed the next year.

7

London

I spent the summer of 1967 working in the Canadian High Commission in London, on Grosvenor Square, opposite the US Embassy. In the square there was a statue of Franklin Delano Roosevelt and a garden where I could sit on the grass and eat sandwiches at lunchtime – correction: yoghurt and an apple. London was still strange, a city of red double-deckers and black, chunky taxis, screeching to a halt whenever I looked the wrong way and stepped out into the street. I heard the milkman's white electric cart come round the square at 6.30 in the morning. On top of the bus on my way to work, I watched well turned-out riders trot along a sandy track in Hyde Park. The few people of my own age I knew were the sons and daughters of friends of my parents. In between going to the theatre, promenade concerts at the Albert Hall – and, for the first time, the opera! – work was stultifying.

I get up every morning, go to my office, smell the heat and stale of the military halls, I wrote to Anne. *I make a cup of coffee – type a few lines – pick up the mail – more coffee, etc. In between I encounter one or other of the 'girls'.*

They were tough, seasoned typists and stenographers who had left school at sixteen. Varnished nails and mini-skirts, hair teased and lacquered into a beehive hair do. Their talk was continuous – about food, their flats, money – but especially, they talked about their men: husbands, boyfriends, even sons. '*Always*, the main talk is about the opposite sex,' I told Anne. 'Just like us. This provides firm evidence in favour of the hypothesis that women live for their menfolk, while the latter don't give a damn about their women.'

Still, in London in those days there were always the clothes. Wonderful kooky-looks, so cheap by comparison to American prices. All the girls were wearing fine white stockings from Mary Quant which laddered like lightning. I had an orange hat and a pair of huge oval horn-rimmed sunglasses, which made me look like an owl – but 'dreadfully sexy at the same time'. I had my eye on a miniskirt and a pair of hot-pink shoes, and had had my hair cut for free on a 'come and be a model' night at Vidal Sassoon, a long evening filled with humiliation while trainee hair-dressers *oohed* and *aahed* over my younger sister's long blonde tresses. Reluctantly, they turned to me, scarcely disguising their distaste. They knew my wavy hair would never stay sleek in a bob.

At home I lounged around the flat wearing bell bottom trousers and listening to the Stones. The few people of my age who I knew gradually left London to go on holiday in Italy and Greece. Others said they would get in touch and forgot. Wellesley 'friends' popped in and out for a free bed and meals – with rarely a word of thanks and Mother didn't like that. *Whiter Shade of Pale* kept playing on the radio.

'Oh, the long *ennui* of the sweltering summer.' I knew my real life was elsewhere. Diana was somewhere in Europe. From my friends in America came word that the dating scene was non-existent. The fear went up. What would happen next semester if we still didn't find a boyfriend? If we never got one? And if/when we ever did – would they be suitable marital material?

Linda was running errands in the advertising department of the fanciest San Antonio department store, saving up to buy a reel-to-reel tape deck for her room. Others were working in Howard Johnson's, getting driving licences and sewing dresses. In Cincinnati, Vicki was a soda-jerk, getting tennis elbow scooping ice cream and bruises all over from lifting milk crates. She was meeting some 'real characters'. One of them gave her a lesson in self-defence. The Pepsi man made a pass at her. One night she got home at 11pm to find her father had had a heart attack. 'The world temporarily came crashing down.' She and her mother ordered a hospital bed to set up in the living room, and after a couple of weeks he came home from hospital. She kept on working, while running errands, shopping and cooking, and helping her mother until, by the end of the summer, he was able to walk around the block by himself. It shook her.

A hot pink envelope decorated with elaborate swirls and curlicues landed on the mat in London. 'FLOWERS ARE HAPPY — ARE YOU?'

God, is Illinois ever FLAT, Anne wrote. I was so glad to hear from her. She was at home in Champaign, taking a course in zoology at the University of Illinois, so that she could get ahead with her required science credits for her degree. Not much was going on. Her friends either had conflicting work schedules, or boyfriends they were with day and night. And she'd got a job at the post-office.

Getting her job in the post-office had been a coup. She wanted it because it paid $2.44 an hour as opposed to the minimum wage of around $1.15. As it was a federal office, she'd had to take some tests and have an interview. As Anne faced the man in charge, he told her the post office didn't hire women.

'What about the Civil Rights Act?' It was a bluff. She didn't know that at the time the Act didn't apply to federal government offices.

Neither did he.

'You realize you're gonna have to lift 80-pound mailbags.'

'No problem,' said Anne, and crossed her fingers.

It turned out two other girls were also working through the summer vacation. The girls weren't assigned to deliver mail, because that would have exposed them to 'all kinds of dangers. They didn't just mean from dogs.'

All the same, work in the sorting office was hellish: the air-conditioning was broken, there were no windows. 'It's like 1000 degrees.' And exhausting. The punishment for gossiping was to stuff nineteen empty canvas mail bags into a twentieth. Impossible. The permanent staff resented the students: *Miss ANNE*, one Afro-Caribbean man kept mocking her. The other students she met were working their way through school, some of them completely self-supporting. 'Makes me feel like an absolute sloth.'

Early Sunday morning on 23 July, police raided an after-hours bar in Detroit, arresting 82 people. An angry crowd gathered outside to watch. Within minutes the street erupted; violence turned into a vicious battle with the police and federal troops. For five days Detroit boiled over. Street fighting, killing, burning and looting: in all over 1200 buildings were destroyed, 43 people killed, nearly 350 injured. Terrifying scenes captured on camera were broadcast on the BBC in London.

Anne was devastated. She wrote, *It's my parents' hometown, my aunt and uncle used to live in my grandparents' house, which was probably burnt in the riot. They moved out just over a year ago. The head of the SNCC was quoted as saying the black people are just asking their rightful due – that America is a thief, having stolen Negroes from Africa and land from the Indians (all true) and that America was just being paid back. Well, the irony is that the people who were hurt most by all this looting and burning were non-insured, hard-working, respectable, law-abiding fellow blacks.*

Cincinnati was in trouble too, and Newark, New Jersey.

I watched as fears of Black insurrection haunted the British airwaves. In London, press and politicians speculated that such riots could easily blow up in Britain too, stoking the flames. Stokely Carmichael, the charismatic Black civil rights activist, was barred from entering the country again.

Despite first impressions of my London office, I had succeeded in making a couple of friends. One of them, Clare, invited me to stay at her parents' home for the weekend. 'An old, old cottage like you never see in North America – all rose and creeper covered,' I told Anne. Her family had lived there for years – Clare knew everyone around. So when one of her friends called early Friday evening to ask us out for a drink, it seemed the most natural thing in the world to go off pub-crawling.

Clare was showing me new ways of going out, in groups with friends for a drink. Or at the last minute with some friendly bloke. It was so much more relaxed. At Wellesley, if someone didn't call you by Wednesday at the latest, you figured you would have no date for the coming weekend. In England, friends rang at 6.30 to ask you out at nine.

'Men don't seem to need women as 'dates' the way they do in America,' I told Anne.

But before long shades of mixers, hourly exams, lectures, note-taking and talks with the Dean returned. I ran through last minute preparations before leaving for the airport: pick up a US dollar bank draft, go to the dentist, get my hair cut, pick up new glasses, bras, slips, three pairs of Mary Quant tights.

And a fabulous shocking pink coat and matching wide-brimmed hat from Biba.

8

Do you believe in magic?

Underneath the surface gloss, there was a harder edge to Wellesley that fall. The posters up on people's walls were trippier, the music more hallucinatory. The harsh, magnetic tones of Bob Dylan ran as counterpoint through the corridors of the dorm.

The summer's riots in Detroit had left a bitter aftertaste. My eye was caught by an introduction to Black Power offered in the *Wellesley News*. Fran Rusan was a leading Black voice at the college. She was slight and pretty, sharp as a blade. Civil rights had been okay as far as it went, she said, but white students who tried teaching for, say, a summer in Mississippi, and tried to secure rapport with African-Americans simply couldn't. They could always choose to leave and go back home. What would she think of Bill Coffin? Was he a hypocrite?

I don't think most whites realize what real black people feel towards each other. Black people understand whites. After all, we've swept your floors, cooked your food, and raised your children, smiling all the while and listening and learning... There is a whole tradition of persecution which binds all blacks in a way whites usually misunderstand.

I knew nothing of Black history in America. All at once I began to see how far the popular truth had been distorted on television and in movies. Think of *Gone with the Wind*, where a smiling 'mammie' looks after a Southern belle, as benign and faithful Africans toil in the cotton fields.

As Fran went on, I could feel the swell of an underground movement rise.

'*The civil rights movement is dead. The Black Power move-ment is taking its place. We don't need white support anymore. As a college educated elite, we have an obligation to go back to the ghetto.*' They were the only ones '*who could push the door open for others, educate their children properly, start black the-atres, read black poets, and teach American history that includes the history of the negro.*'

'*Many people worry about our movement and our power ... they don't need to worry. The objective of Afro groups is to pull together to lift the foot off every black neck. We don't want to tear down, just to build up. We just want what is ours, not what is theirs.*' She made the point that the American tradition is a violent one, that no one should see Black nationalist activity as deviant from the norm. '*We don't like to use violence, and I hope we don't have to. But we are not afraid to use violence to obtain our rights.*'[*]

Fran's vehemence and anger shook me. Her words about vio-lence scared me. The distance between her history and mine was so vast. However much I sympathised and tried to understand, I knew I could never be part of her world. I also knew everything she had to say was true.

My new room for sophomore year was just along the corridor from my old one in Davis, a door or two away from Vicki and

---

[*] *Wellesley News*, 16 November 1967

Diana. Linda had moved near too. Anne, though, had elected to live on the French Corridor at Tower Court, an intimidating brick and stone Gothic monster of a residence, like an upscale New York apartment block, on top of a hill about twenty minutes' walk away. She would eat, sleep, and live in French. I missed her already. But I knew Anne was set to achieve – and she wanted to be fluent.

A new cohort of freshmen arrived, filling the living room overlooking the lake, drinking their first cups of tea. We looked at them with sympathy, treated them kindly and found many new friends. Hillary had been elected Davis's new Vil Junior. Besides counselling freshmen, her job was to call the house to order and take our views to college government.

The choice was inevitable. No one else could touch her. Ever since I first met her I was struck by Hillary's aura, her natural authority. But she didn't always have my sympathy. I favoured the Democratic party; she was a Republican. She was not afraid to dominate. But she was dynamic and organized and seemed to know her way around in a way I never felt I could. People wanted to know what she had to say, gain her stamp of approval. She and her roommate had a huge two-room suite on the top floor – the best rooms in the dorm.

There was a tang of autumn in the air, the scent of turning leaves. Indian summer days, and the campus was beautiful. I'd signed up for Art History and enrolled in English History with a visiting professor from London University, John Scarisbrick, a specialist in Henry VIII and the Reformation. Scarisbrick was tall and lean, with a dry style of lecturing, talking for 80 minutes straight without notes.

For Classical Civilisation: Emily Vermeule had just returned from Greece where she had been part of a team which had unearthed a Minoan city, buried for 3500 years by a volcanic eruption on the island of Thera, now Santorini. Over the summer her find made headlines around the world. Now, here she was – *this world-famous archaeologist!* – down in the front of the amphitheatre, taking us through the elements of early Greek sculpture.

My nightmare was the science requirement I had been assigned: physics.

Incomprehensible.

Meanwhile Diana, dear fey Diana, had opted to enrol in computer programming. It was the first time the subject had been taught at the college. She came back from her first class, bearing cream oblong cards punched with holes like some kind of curiosity. She handed them round to those of us gathered in her room and we looked them over: just like the cards I used to take my SAT exams, where I filled in multiple choice answers on oval blobs in pencil.

We had hardly been back a week when a huge bouquet of red roses arrived on the corridor.

For Diana.

A couple of weeks later Davis held its annual mixer in the glass globed dining room. It was the last Saturday in September and it started grimly. The usual scene of girls frozen demurely to the curving brick walls of the dining room, waiting to be asked to dance (for that in 1967 was still the etiquette) as posses of males swaggered past, sizing up the meat on offer.

Taking a break from the soul-destroying parade, Linda and I climbed the stairs and walked past the waiting-room beside the bell desk. Two lone males were sitting on the sofa: one dark, one blond; tweed jackets, wool ties, khaki trousers and polished loafers. Why I thought we could just walk in and start talking to them, I will never know. Linda took a chair. I sat on the table. But glory of glories, as Linda would later record, the pair didn't seem too frightened of a couple of apparently intelligent girls.

After talking for a while, they suggested we go downstairs and dance. I crossed my fingers. Who would they choose? Sigh of relief: the dark one, David, nodded to Linda. Mike, the blond, whose broad grin and good looks had already captivated me, took my hand.

Hey, Mr Tambourine Man, play a song for me
Oh, to dance.

How we danced!

Mike came from California and was a year ahead of me, in his third year at Harvard. He shared rooms in Winthrop House with David. His older brother Jim was in his senior year. Mike was a head taller than me, broad-shouldered and slim. He was a wonderful dancer, light on his feet, moving to the beat, guiding me effortlessly round the floor, wrapping me close during the slow songs. He was not only attractive, he couldn't seem to keep the smile out of his eyes when he looked at me. We took time out and talked until midnight. He was the first American boy I'd met who I liked right off the bat.

Before we went to bed that night, Linda and I regrouped in her room, slightly pinching ourselves at our good fortune: both of us meeting people we liked and having such a good time. Vicki poked her head round the door and settled down on the floor. Did Diana come in too?

'You say his name is Roosevelt?'

'And so?'

'You don't know?'

'Know what?'

'You must realize, Stephanie, that Roosevelt is not the most everyday name in the telephone directory.

'What do you mean?

'What do you *mean*? That guy is the grand-son of FDR.'

'Don't be silly – he comes from Pasadena.'

'So? He's a Roosevelt. It's rumoured he will inherit millions when he's 21.'

How did they know so much?

'You've got be kidding,' Anne said the next day. She'd seen me dancing from across the floor and recognised Mike from a Young Democrat's conference in Boston the previous year. Later that day I pulled a stamp out of my desk. On it, the face of the famous war-time president in profile. There was no escaping it. He looked just like Mike.

It was one of the things he liked about me, Mike always said, that I never asked about his family.

The evening after I met Mike, Walter Cronkite aired a Vietnam special. With everyone else in the dorm, I piled onto a sofa in the living room to watch him front the CBS News. It was Sunday, October 1st.

For the past year, US troops had been holed up on a muddy hilltop called Con Thien overlooking the Demilitarised Zone between North and South Vietnam, keeping an eye on movements over the flat plain that stretches twelve miles to the South

China Sea. The story of trying to hold Con Thien was one of slow, steady attrition and increasing demoralisation. Now the outpost had been under heavy fire for a month. Under cover of darkness, North Vietnamese units crept up to the barbed wire to plant explosives at night. As soon as the Marines fired back, big guns north of the DMZ opened up. Rifles jammed in the mud. None of the US armaments had the reach they needed. Without reinforcements, without the aid of B52 bombers, they knew they couldn't take out the enemy's big mortars across the DMZ. There was nothing to do except keep their heads low in the trenches and wait for the next attack.

'We're just like bull's eyes, waiting to be hit.'

The faces of the men on the screen looked just like the boys I knew. Some had only been in Vietnam a few weeks. My friend Elizabeth's brother was in the field. She fled the room. Other girls were crying. I felt sick.

The war was getting bloodier by the day. Every morning there was some new horror on the front page. Every night on the TV, grainy scenes of wounded men on stretchers being run to hovering helicopters. The US stepped up the bombing. Bridges, railroad yards, petroleum dumps – only ten miles south of the border with China. Infantrymen slogged through rice paddies and fought on beaches in the Mekong Delta. Vietcong guerrillas emerged from the jungle to pick them off a few at a time. Their forces were supplied on bicycles. American casualties now exceeded 100,000.

*

The next day another bouquet of red roses arrived for Diana.

Then Mike called. The autumn was underway.

It was the traditional Ivy dream: beautiful autumn weather, sharp chill in the morning, hot sun in the afternoon. The scarlets of the sugar maples, others gold, bronze and yellow, glistened in the sun. Work was demanding, but (except for physics) going well. The Saturday after we first met, Mike invited me to a concert with an Indian musician called Ravi Shankar. We sat at his feet, listening to this strange music, intoxicated by the measures of the sitar, transfixed by his quiet dignity and charisma. A few days later he brought me books I needed for a history project from the rare books library at Harvard. I took him to hear Julian Bream play the lute. And so it went on. Linda and I took him and David cookies we had baked in the dorm. One Saturday we tried to study in his room but had to give up – the weather was just too beautiful.

We drove out to Wellesley and walked around the lake hand in hand, kicking leaves, inhaling the scent of decay, watching the sparkle on the waves. Linda was seeing David, and over the weekends we would cross at parties and dinners.

Diana's conquest was someone called Harry. She was out every evening. The debrief and analysis when she returned would go on for hours, and only Vicki seemed to have the stamina to stick with the drama to the end. Then our friend Ginny announced her engagement. She'd been dating Ken since she met him in the first weeks of freshman year. The next Sunday morning there it was: official, her picture over a couple of columns in the *New York Times*. 'Miss Thorndike is a sophomore at Wellesley College. *Her father is...* The bride-to-be is *a granddaughter of...*' (a whole genealogical string).

The first girl in our year was getting married. (And sadly, it didn't last, but that's another story.)

Two weeks after Cronkite, the gossip in the dorm was all about the news that Bill Coffin had fronted an anti-war rally of over 4000 on Boston Common. I'd heard something was going on – just as he had talked about. A new organisation called Resistance, with slogans and texts by Philip Roth, had emerged, backing protests breaking out in city after city across the country: New York, Chicago, San Francisco. In Oakland police hurled tear gas, and a flying wedge of officers swept through the centre, injuring more than twenty people. One hundred and twenty-five were arrested, including Joan Baez. People had finally come together and were standing up to be counted.

By Coffin's side in Boston was Dr Benjamin Spock – whose handbook on child rearing had sat by Mother's bedside for all the years we were growing up – and three others. The action was brave and thrilling and amazing. After gathering on the Common, the protest headed to the Arlington Street Church. Coffin addressed packed crowds from the pulpit.

'Let us be blunt. To us the war in Vietnam is a crime. And if we are correct, if the war is a crime, is it criminal to refuse to have anything to do with it? Is it we who are demoralising our boys in Vietnam, or the Administration which is asking them to do an immoral thing?

'The issue IS one of conscience.'

Then sixty-seven young men, neat in jackets and ties, rose in silence to set their draft cards alight in a bowl in front of the pulpit. Another two hundred handed Coffin their draft cards. He packed them into his briefcase to deliver to the government in Washington.

I devoured the stories in the papers. I could not believe his audacity. Maybe it wasn't exactly illegal to burn your draft card. But the law said you had to carry it at all times. The word went round: Coffin was at serious risk of jail for five years.

Two days later, crack units of the 82nd Airborne Division flew into Washington to contain a huge anti-war protest planned for the following Saturday. Dozens of people I knew were going. I hung back. In the face of all-out war, I wasn't sure what a march could achieve – and this one was a good day's drive away. More fundamentally – as a Canadian, was this my fight? What right did I have to a say in US politics?

Around me, the conversation was getting heated. Emotions were running very high. Davis was divided. Hillary and her friends were known Republicans. Were they Hawks ('we must honour our commitment/ counter the threat of Communist expansion/ safeguard our national security')? Or Doves?

Coming along behind were peace militants from all sorts of quasi-organisations preaching nothing less than all-out revolution.

A rising crescendo.

Vietnam...

Vietnam...

VIETNAM!

*

The football season was upon us.

I shortened my skirts once more. Harvard had already played Columbia and Cornell. It was time for the big games of the season: Dartmouth, Princeton and Yale. Edgy with excitement, crowds piled into the stadium. Brass bands from opposing teams competed to make the most noise across the bowl. Scarlet pom-poms waving, Harvard's cheerleaders leapt and yelled and cheered. I chose that day to break out my knee-high boots with my hot pink coat and big brimmed hat from Biba. Mike was in his father's enormous 1930s overcoat. We were spotted by friends across the stadium as he took my hand to stride across a corner of the field.

Harvard always lost, but just by a whisker. At the parties afterwards, beer and whisky flowed and the lights were low. Everyone danced as the music rolled, waving cigarettes like sparklers. The Supremes and the Four Tops, the Bee Gees, the Beach Boys and other clean-cut outfits intercut with the raunchier tones of the Stones and fey Sergeant Pepper. The scent of marijuana – I hadn't smoked it yet, and thought it was burning carpet – wafted through the rooms. Then a group of us headed off to dinner in a small French restaurant in Beacon Hill or a place like Durgin Park. The next day, Sunday, Mike came out to the college for Sunday lunch, and study in my room – but it was such a gorgeous day, the autumn colours so magnificent, we just had to get outside and kick the leaves and stroll around the lake.

With his blue eyes and horn-rimmed glasses, short curly blond hair and tweed jackets he was so clean cut and 'all American' that I just couldn't quite believe I liked him quite so much. He was conservative, with beautiful manners, he guided me with confidence everywhere we went. He was open and funny and thoughtful and we couldn't stop talking.

I was having a lot of fun, but I didn't consider myself Mike's 'girl'. Everybody else did. By Thanksgiving, the noise around me of dating a Roosevelt was getting louder. Mothers of friends were the worst, speculating about my future and regaling me with gossip about the family.

I liked Mike because he never talked about money, and despised people who showered it around. Mike rarely talked about his family. Whatever there was to say, I'd much rather hear it from him.

But over Thanksgiving weekend in New York, I saw something of the power for myself. On Saturday, Mike picked me up and took me window-shopping on Fifth Avenue. Lights twinkled and the glamour built as we strolled past Saks and Tiffany's to a restaurant beside an ice-rink full of skaters in Rockefeller Centre. Twilight was falling as we walked north to the Plaza

and climbed into a horse and carriage to ride through Central Park. Later we took a yellow-cab down to Greenwich Village. We peered into the windows of antique shops and walked over to Washington Square where he showed me the house where his grandmother, Eleanor, used to live.

By now it was raining and it was cold, but it was my first time in New York, with someone who knew it well. The next day, Mike took me to the Harvard–Yale game in New Haven on the way back to Boston. Then he drove me back to Wellesley along darkened parkways. In the *lingua franca* of the time, it was a complete snow job.

✱

It was all so easy when you were going out with someone you really liked and they seemed to like you too. I couldn't stop smiling. Plus: a small reform in the social order of things at the college. Hillary, our Vil Junior and now with a seat on the College Senate, where the changes had been drawn up, was in charge of the Davis meeting. Glasses on her nose, clipboard on her lap, she sat in an armchair in the living room, the House Mother beside her. The meeting was all-house, with roll call. Girls squashed up on sofas or sat cross-legged on the floor. Hillary was energetic and clear. The issue for discussion: a revolutionary extension of the hours (from 2–5.30pm) on Sundays when men could be in our rooms to *every day* from noon to 10pm and *until 1am* on Friday and Saturday nights.

For days there had been argument. Girls were worried. How would you cope with a man in your room if you had a roommate? Suppose you ran into one in the bathroom as you came out of the shower? But the heart of the issue was: could we, as women, be trusted to be in charge of our own lives? Ninety-five per cent of the dormitory had to vote; and 75% must approve for the rules to change.

The meeting lasted 35 minutes. Three days later, the ballot was counted. Support was overwhelming: men in our rooms most of the day *every* day. *Amazing*: at a stroke, our rules had become more liberal even than Harvard's.

Which was great in theory.

But what was a good girl to do? We'd long known we were in trouble, living out the conflict between being the nice girl who says 'no' and the bad girl who rocks the boat. Between the boy you fancied rotten, his hand up your skirt and begging for more, and our own lustful desires. The last thing you wanted was a pregnancy.

Of course, we knew about the pill. You took it every day. It could take away menstrual pain, regulate your cycle, and was thought to be around 93% effective in preventing pregnancy – so still, not 100% reliable. We also knew the formulas for it were crude, sometimes brutal on the system. For some, periods vanished completely. For others it brought on depression. Blood clots, hormone changes.

The big question for me remained: how did I get my hands on it?

It was around this time we first debated putting an end to a foetus. Abortion was illegal and dangerous – getting one, terrifying. Whispers of an apartment in New York from where you would be escorted by someone unknown to somewhere in New Jersey, or perhaps a motel in Pennsylvania. The prices in hundreds of dollars. Were a few cells a living being or not? Did it have a right to life? We didn't think in terms of rights. Just: was it wrong to kill it?

Few of us talked about it; we never considered joint action. The taboos around anything to do with sex, much less sexuality, were too strong. And it wasn't just girls who were hung up. So many of the boys we knew had been brought up the same way. Mike was keen to do the right thing; besides, he was a Roman Catholic. Sex before marriage was a mortal sin.

*

The fall semester was coming to an end. Exams loomed. I was teetering on the verge of love: losing things, forgetting things; emotionally conflicted, unable to sleep. On the day I had to submit the application for my scholarship for the following year, I got the news I had failed my mid-term paper in physics – badly.

I dropped in to see Diana, hoping for tea and sympathy: computer science hadn't been up her street either. She was in a state. Tales of her father, this time, behaving like a character out of a horror film – 'he's positively malignant' – or that is what I noted at the time. She lay on her bed among clothes and papers, chain smoking cigarettes. Her hair hung limp. Her right leg was encased in bandages.

'What's wrong with your leg?'

'Thrombosis,' she said. 'I've got a blood-clot in my leg.'

'What do you do for it?'

'The doctor's put me on blood thinner. I've got to come off the pill until it settles down.'

Diana on the pill? I kept my tone light. 'Where did you get it?'

A vague gesture in the direction of the window.

'Diana?'

'Oh, I've been on it for ages. Some doctor in Newton. Look, what I was saying, about my father—'

It was Mike's twenty-first birthday. I joined his friends at Winthrop House for surprise champagne and cake in his room. Then I buried myself in preparation for my exams and writing the final history paper.

But I was exhausted, overwrought, paying the price for a term of good times and procrastination. I checked myself into the infirmary to get a couple of night's drugged sleep. In the morning Mike sent me a telegram. 'Good luck on the exams. Remember: the grade on an exam is inversely proportional to the amount of time spent worrying about it.' The next day I randomly ticked off the multiple-choice boxes for my physics exam in the morning and spent the rest of the day cramming for Biblical History eighteen hours later.

The following morning Mike picked me up at ten and we drove into Cambridge for a Harvard-y day. I went with him to a modern drama class, where I was amazed at how the men carried on, coarsely interrupting and yelling over each other, punching and fighting. We browsed around the Co-op and the Design Centre shop with its Marimekko dresses and went to Cronin's for lunch. Afterwards we drove out to Concord. We picked out idyllic New England houses to live in, and he told me about growing up in California. I kept thinking how amazing it was that the two of us came from such different environments and yet thought so much alike. Then he took me to the airport where I flew to London for three weeks over Christmas. Another life.

✳

It was good to get home and sit in the frowsty English sitting room in the family flat high above Queen's Gate Gardens. The traffic roared along the Cromwell Road at the back of the flat, and I could walk to the V&A in minutes. I saw a few friends that I had made last summer, went to Christmas parties and the theatre. My mother and I went for walks in Kensington Gardens. In the evening my father poured me gin and tonics before dinner. I was full of tales of Mike. He was in California, seeing a lot of family, having a wonderful time, but alarmed to discover so many old friends did not have the facts on the war, and even more alarming, planned to vote to re-elect President Johnson the following year. I wanted their take on the Roosevelts ('Careful,' said Dad) – and Vietnam.

It was good to hear Dad on the war, and a relief to know his views chimed with mine. He had spent two years fighting in Korea. He was now working with British intelligence and the Ministry of Defence. He didn't dispute that the Chinese Communists needed to be stopped. But the way the Americans were fighting the war, bombing from the air, was all wrong. 'You have to win over hearts and minds, work slowly, piecemeal, in small units, in villages in the jungle, showing people that your way of life – democracy, freedom and justice – is the better one.'

In his view, America's approach would only lead into a quagmire, and disaster. The war could not go on like this. There would have to be a peace move soon.

9

Take a little piece of my heart

I'd gone about London draped in Mike's long red and white Harvard scarf, conscious how much it was a vivid statement of America. I returned to Wellesley at the dawn of that fateful year of 1968 eager to see him and keen to find out the results of my exams. A blizzard was blowing as I came into land in Boston.

The snow kept up. Wellesley seemed marooned. At last, the weather cleared enough for Mike and me to meet. We went to see *Bonnie and Clyde* in Cambridge. We were somewhere on the road back to Wellesley, both of us staring ahead at the headlights glimmering on the snow-packed road, when, out of the blue, he told me that he loved me.

I think my heart stopped. I couldn't think of anything to say. And then I thought – I like him. I *really* like him. In fact, I liked him so much the words just tumbled out.

'I think maybe I love you too.'

I don't know what he said next – but what I do know is that then I said:

'*Phew.*'

'What?'

'What a *commitment.*'

'Commitment?'

'Yes, of course. Commitment.'

'I don't get it.'

'When you really love someone, you never want to let them down. It's a real responsibility.'

'Yeah,' said Mike. He paused. 'I see what you mean.'

We became inseparable. On the weekends we went out to dinner or the movies (*The Graduate, You're a Good Man Charlie Brown, Gone with the Wind*) or double-dated with his older brother Jim, and his fiancée Ann. Other times we studied together in the library, fell asleep in his room or talked late at night on the phone. It was like playing a backdrop to a Simon and Garfunkel album. Ali McGraw in *Love Story*. I was blithe to the world and everyone else. I went to my classes and worked my evenings in the language lab. Mike had a dream for us: of how we'd get married at some point after my graduation and set up house on a Christmas tree farm in the mountains outside San Francisco. Mike would be an unpretentiously brilliant lawyer who would give quiet and sound advice to the President (who might or might not – lots of laughter – be his brother Jim). But I couldn't conceive of getting married yet, not to Mike, not to anyone. My own dreams were nebulous. Being a girl, I couldn't follow my father into the army, but what about diplomacy in the department of External Affairs? Or maybe the CBC? Whatever my future held, I knew I had to have lots of travel.

And so I thought: *maybe*.

We talked a lot of politics. I suppose it was in his blood. He was standing to be Winthrop House's representative on the Harvard undergraduate council. Mike knew all the history of the coming of the Vietnam war: it was a civil conflict. He was convinced America's involvement was immoral. He knew that he was going to have to take a stand. Not long after Christmas, the US rejected a North Vietnamese overture to talk peace. Every day the war was getting worse.

On 21 January the North Vietnamese surrounded the Khe Sanh Combat Base and began a siege of the 6,000 US marines stationed there that would last for seventy-seven days.

A week later Vietcong and North Vietnamese troops launched the Tet offensive: a major assault against almost every urban centre in South Vietnam. The US forces were caught by surprise. The push-back was almost unbelievable.

Two days later the North Vietnamese reached the grounds of the US embassy in Saigon. Live in front of our eyes on TV, Marines were fighting for their lives, falling dead on staircases in the heart of their own embassy.

The dorm was a fevered hothouse. Rumours spawned and multiplied. The front pages carried pictures of live executions. Sobbing fathers carried broken bodies of their children. Women fled in terror from flaming villages. Thousands of civilians were slaughtered in the crossfire. Refugee numbers were over 350,000. Walter Cronkite on the TV in the living room every night. Shots of Marines lying dead in the mud. These were scenes our fathers had never talked about when they came home from the war – and after Vietnam, were no longer permitted to be shown by news crews.

I couldn't bear to look.

On 29 January, Bill Coffin and Benjamin Spock were arraigned in a Federal District Court in Boston, charged with conspiring to help young men evade the draft laws. They were released on bail for fifty days. The trial was scheduled for the spring. Later that day they held a packed teach-in at Arlington Street Church. Two days later, on 1 February, Richard Nixon entered the Presidential race for the Republican nomination.

But in the moment, all that mattered to me was that it was Friday night. The Four Tops played Harvard, swinging in sync back and forth on the stage, and Mike and I danced.

Ooh, sugar pie, honey bunch
You know that I love you
I can't help myself —
I love you and nobody else

I had to keep up with my work. For history I was researching a paper on the early non-violent militancy of the Suffragettes in

Britain. In 1906 women, led by Sylvia Pankhurst, were arrested for demonstrating. When the case came to trial, they refused to acknowledge the authority of the Courts. Pankhurst's argument: if women are not allowed to have the vote, they cannot make the laws. How then, could they be subject to them?

Coffin.

Pankhurst.

State wrongs.

What I was getting was a message. As Coffin kept saying: no one has the right to break the law. Everyone, on occasion, has the duty to do so.

There were roses for me on Valentine's Day. Linda, Vicki and I baked cookies and fudge to take to our men at Harvard. Gordon Lightfoot, for years my Canadian folksong hero, was playing in Cambridge on Saturday night. Mike and I grabbed a quick bite before the concert. The Winthrop dining hall was packed. A golden light shone down on the room, people milled around the tables. A sudden swirl of news skittered across the floor: the National Security Council had just announced that there would no more draft deferments for graduate students except in medicine or dentistry.

No more safe haven from the war, for the boys I knew.

Did anyone that night give a moment's thought to the inequities of the system then in place: letting people who had the opportunity and means to go to graduate school, escape from military service? It was five years in prison if you didn't want to go. Conscientious objections were difficult to get: religious reasons were one way out, but most people I knew didn't object to war *per se* – it was Vietnam that was unjust. Everyone was talking about Bill Coffin's offer of sanctuary in the Yale chapel for war resisters. What about the other alternatives?

People crowded up to our table, heads leaning forward.

'What's Canada like?'

I was surrounded.

'A lot of fir trees and pines, a lot of snow…' As I told them of the cities, where they might go to university, or canoe in northern Ontario, all I could think was: if you run away and dodge the draft you will never be able to be that civil rights lawyer you want to be. Never be that NASA scientist. Cross the border back into the States and you'll be arrested in an instant. Five years minimum. You can *NEVER* come home again.

But to end up being one of those bloody bodies on a stretcher in the middle of a foetid paddy field?

To be sent away to fight a war that you think is wrong? That night Gordon Lightfoot captured the mood.

In the early morning rain
With a dollar in my hand

Maybe Mike could somehow get a desk job.

Or get sent to Germany?

The navy didn't look too promising.

Out on runway number 9
Big 707 set to go

Mike said he was going to try for the Coast Guard first.

★

Eugene McCarthy was a senator from Minnesota, and a published poet. Greying, clear-eyed, he had a reputation for a high-minded approach to politics and known to be sceptical about the war. He was 51. The previous October, McCarthy had been persuaded to take his political life in his hands and stand against President Johnson for the Democratic nomin-

ation for the upcoming election in November. No one before had ever defeated an incumbent president for the nomination. Early in January, Gallup showed 12% support for McCarthy. But the national mood was shifting dramatically. To students like us, raised to believe in the promise of America, McCarthy's integrity held instant appeal. The New Hampshire primary, the first stage of the presidential election, was less than six weeks away. Mike's brother, Jim, head of the Harvard Democrats, was already in touch with his campaign, marshalling students to canvass on his behalf. It was time for me to get involved.

Mike and I spent a day on a low-cost housing project in South Boston, collecting signatures for a petition to put McCarthy into the Presidential primary – a dispiriting effort: of 102 people who were registered as Democratic or Independent voters we got just fifteen signatures. We consoled ourselves it was a holiday. Many weren't at home. Others wouldn't open the door but just shouted from the inside. Of those that signed to endorse McCarthy, five had sons in Vietnam.

At seven on Saturday morning on 9th March, Mike and I drove up to New Hampshire to join an army of students canvassing on the ground. Gallup was registering 28% support for McCarthy. Through mushy snow, we knocked on doors and handed out leaflets, scrawling names on clipboards. People were smiling. The race was hotting up.

The primary was the following Tuesday. On the returns that day, McCarthy secured 42.4% of the vote to Johnson's 49.5%. We were jubilant. The primary should have been a shoe-in for Johnson.

Back at Harvard in Jim's rooms, it was very late. We were still on a high about McCarthy's performance. Bright lights overhead, Jim smiled and poured Scotch into our glasses, a pile of us heaped on the sofa. Everyone speculated about what might happen next as McCarthy continued to pick up steam. In the midst of it all the phone on his desk rang.

Jim picked it up. Nodded to Mike: their mother from California. He turned away, bending his head to shield the call, talking for what seemed like a long time. When he hung up, he turned to Mike. Her pitch was that the two of them should try to get on Bobby Kennedy's slate of California delegates to the Democratic Convention the next summer. McCarthy's delegates had already been chosen. If Mike and Jim wanted to go to the Convention and not be associated with Johnson by going with their father – James Roosevelt was already a Johnson delegate – Kennedy was their best chance.

For a long moment there was silence. All I remember was a chill. Desert the candidate we were convinced was honourable, for *Bobby Kennedy*? A smooth, self-seeking opportunist who none of us liked. Jack, his older brother, had had a magic charm, a golden appeal. But underneath the surface of the Kennedy family swirled dark forces. Jim's dream – he made no bones about it – was to go into politics. Bobby Kennedy was already hitting out about the war. So, what's the difference?

For a while, Mike was with me. How could he and Jim abandon McCarthy? After all our hard work and our belief that we were doing right? How could we just throw over the delegate who first stood up to get the US out of the war?

I hear what you say, said Jim, but let's be realistic. McCarthy hasn't hit the West Coast yet. Nobody out there knows much about him.

It didn't take long before Arthur Schlesinger, Kennedy's advisor, was on the phone. He told Jim if he could deliver the Harvard Democrats for Bobby, he and Mike could be delegates for California to the convention. Jim was nodding.

It was a done deal.

Four days later, Bobby Kennedy, closely calculating the odds, went back on his earlier statement that he would not run for the presidency and announced his candidacy for the Democratic nomination.

Fascinating – seeing power politics up close. Men who can turn on a dime.

A few days later Mike and twenty-five buddies left for spring break in the Bahamas in the back of a truck.

*

At Wellesley I prepared for my end-of-semester exams. Everyone in Davis was hunkered down, finishing papers. Someone offered that as Mike and I had been so lucky to fall in love in the way we had, there could never be anything to worry about.

I could only laugh.

My life was in an emotional churn. Things hadn't been going so well with Mike since the news came in about no further exemptions from the draft, spreading doubts over his future, and his plans to go to law school. He was fit and well. It was impossible to get out of the draft. I was filled with dread that he might actually be required to serve on the front line. I wanted to help him, but what he wanted now was for us to slow down. I was the only part of the mess, he said, that he could do anything about.

Hot on this news, my parents wrote to tell me my dad was going to retire in the spring of 1970. They assumed by that time I would be married. They planned to live part of the year in Malta and the rest in England. And not go back to Canada at all.

My home, such as it was, was disintegrating.

I couldn't see what the future held. The world was closing in. Fifteen minutes after getting into bed at night, a phone would ring in the hall. Doors would slam, voices call. I was feeling claustrophobic, stuck with the same group of friends at the college day after day, fighting an assumption that we would all do everything together. Diana, her blue eyes anguished, kept trying and failing to give up smoking. Vicki – so kind, so good – had been elected to succeed Hillary as Vil Junior the next year. This carried with it an assumption that she, Linda, Diana and I would all stay together, living in Davis Hall again. Girls I didn't know so well were in and out of my room, helping themselves to change or loose stamps, borrowing my clothes.

I sought refuge with Anne in her room in Tower Court. She sat on the floor of her room in a tired navy skirt and what she called her 'frumpy' blouse – pale pink with pintucks stained from leaky BIC pens. LPs were stacked up ready to fall into place on her turntable. She was scribbling notes, her head bobbing to Aretha Franklin. The pitch was at full volume.

'Don't talk to me.'

'Yeh?' I sat down.

'I am SO MAD.' She put down her pen. ' I am completely sick of the petty affairs of this college. All the giggly little girl bit. No chance of realistic relationships with boys. No intellectual challenge. Political science like rote learning. I'm making a list of schools. I'm definitely going to transfer in the fall.'

I stared at her. As far as intellectual challenge was concerned, I didn't understand what she was talking about: I was loving Tudor history and my required science course in geology; even my required course in Biblical History was proving fascinating. I stifled envy that Anne could afford the option of a change. Sorrow – and worse – that she might actually leave. All I needed now was for my best friend to cut and run.

'You're really going to do it?'

'I feel like a trapped animal.'

I decided to take a rain-check on Vicki's invitation to go home with her to Cincinnati for Spring break and take refuge with my father's sister, my beloved aunt Margaret, in Montreal instead.

Exams were due to start on Tuesday. On Sunday evening we put down our books and went down to the living room to take our places in front of the television. President Johnson was due to address the nation at 9pm. There was an air of grim anticipation. More bad news about the war.

The President looked so exhausted as he came on air, blood-hound eyes lifted wearily to the camera, that I almost felt sorry for him. Then, with no introduction he made three simple, astounding statements.

- He would not 'seek or accept' the presidential nomination that year.
- He would now begin to de-escalate the war by calling a halt to the bombing of North Vietnam.
- He had invited Hanoi to join him in a series of moves towards peace.

The President signed off and everyone looked at each other, for a moment overwhelmed. Was the war – could it be – over? All of a sudden there were cheers and tears. We hugged each other, tears spilling down our cheeks.

The next day Johnson announced he was meeting Bobby Kennedy in a bid to work together towards national unity. On the Wednesday, Johnson announced the North Vietnamese were ready to talk peace. He was flying to Honolulu to meet representatives from South Vietnam to pave the way towards talks.

Early Thursday evening I was in my room, tidying up the mess after studying for my three-hour Biblical History exam when I heard feet pounding down the hall. There was a ghastly shriek. I opened my door. Girls were stampeding down the corridor, wailing and crying.

'Martin Luther King's been shot!'

Someone had their arms around Helen. I ran towards her and joined everyone heading to find out more in front of the television in the living room.

King had been standing on a balcony of the 2nd floor of a motel in Memphis when a bullet exploded in his face. Authorities said he had been shot by a well-dressed white man. King was 39.

Johnson came on air to express his shock and call for peace. He cancelled his flight to Hawaii. Hanoi cancelled plans for the talks. Across the country, riots broke out in the streets.

*

The next evening, Friday, I flew to Montreal. National Guardsmen armed with automatic weapons roamed Logan airport. Riots weren't just happening in Memphis. Cities were up in flames all over the country. Washington, Baltimore, New York, Boston. Seven were dead in fires as looting spread across Chicago. Tens of thousands of demonstrators protesting King's slaying marched down Broadway.

I landed in another world. That day Pierre Trudeau – young, dynamic and heading for the top – had been elected leader of the Canadian Liberal Party. People in Montreal were overjoyed. Everyone seemed relaxed. Canada was peaceful – and superior: aloof from the war in Vietnam, repulsed and horrified by the race rioting going on south of the border.

I sank into the sofa at my aunt's, her kind warm face like balm, and opened my heart.

*

I got back from Montreal to uncharacteristic silence from Mike. The call when I got it was bad – and oh, so rational. He repeated what he'd said to me before. He was feeling pressured from all angles – the draft, four more years of school, what kind of career he might have – things he couldn't control. But I was the one thing he could put a hold on. We needed to wind down, he said. We were way too young to be so committed. I don't think he could bring himself to say good-bye.

I was stunned.

A week or so later it was Linda, dating his roommate David, who told me the truth. Mike had a new girl, acquired on Spring Break. Linda could not look me in the eye.

I wandered about in a daze, trying to figure out where it had all gone wrong. The words he'd said, the promises he'd made, kept running through my mind. He was the one who had talked about marriage. Had I been too demanding, wanting to see him all the time? What else should I have done? I couldn't turn my attention to anything. I stopped by Diana's room. She was curled up in a chair covered with a blue flowered Indian bedspread. She didn't want to hear me out, just handed me a cigarette.

I'd spent a lot of time telling Mike off for smoking. I'll pay him back I thought, and reached out to take it.

∗

Six weeks left to the year. The usual: classes, papers, mid-terms, exams. A geology trip to Cape Cod. Lovely spring weather, a few painful meetings with Mike. Joni Mitchell on the record player, day after day.

It was all I could do to hold myself together.

Three weeks after the death of Martin Luther King Jr, I was dimly aware that rage was still rising on the streets. A genteel one-day strike took place at Wellesley: against the war, the draft, and racism. Students and prominent faculty fronted workshops on racial awareness, repression and civil disobedience. Ethos, the Black organisation on campus, took centre stage: 'We want you and Wellesley College to get off your haunches where you perch, spouting the platitudes of liberalism...And act.'

Back then, we never thought for a moment what it cost the women in Ethos to stand up to the white complacency of the college. They first came together as a group of seventeen a little more than a year before. As they compared notes, they uncovered the reason each had been given a Black roommate or assigned a single room: no white girls had volunteered to share with them. Investigating further, they uncovered a *de facto* segregationist rooming policy at the college, of rooming Jews with Jews, Blacks with Blacks and Chinese with Chinese.

Ethos decided to write to the National Scholarship Service and Fund for Negro Students, which funded their places. Hearts beating fast, terrified at their own audacity, they could only summon the courage to post the letter with all of them holding onto the envelope together to push it through the letterbox. Upon its receipt, Allene Talmey Plaut (class of '24), the wife of the president of the foundation and associate editor of *Vogue,* declared herself 'utterly appalled by this pre-Civil War psychology.' How the college decided to move would determine the Foundation's future contributions to Wellesley.*

Now Ethos swiftly organised a petition that went round every dorm. It demanded a big increase in Black admissions, the number of Blacks employed on campus, and the establishment of a new major in Afro-American studies, to be headed by a Black professor. They wanted a Black psychiatrist on campus

---

* Wellesley College Archives, Ruth Adams papers, 1DB9 Ethos General (2 0f 8) 1967-71

and an annual lecture in honour of Martin Luther King. Then they called a press conference. If the college would not support their demands, they would declare a hunger strike. Before they missed a meal, the president of the college had agreed to meet them. A committee was set up to see their demands through. It would report early in October.

But it was from Columbia in New York that news and pictures exploded over front pages. A thousand students invaded five campus buildings, including one that housed the president's office. 'Up against the wall, Motherfucker!' They threw him out and took over the main campus switchboard.

They were led by a few radicals from 'Students for a Democratic Society' (SDS). SDS grew out of a student peace group set up at Harvard in 1960. In March 1965, its founders organised a sit-in at the Chase Manhattan Bank in Wall Street to protest loans to South Africa, and a month later, in April, the first major demonstration against the war in Vietnam in Washington, in front of the White House. With the growth of opposition to the war, by 1968 its membership had expanded beyond students to embrace a huge number of activists from a range of political persuasions from across the country – hippies, loonies, and militants – all keen to take action into their own hands.

At Columbia, student anger had been simmering before Martin Luther King's assassination, over the draft and the discovery of the university's involvement in weapons research. Black students added fury about the university's plans to build a new gymnasium with separate entrances, one at high level for students and another, lower down the hill, for Harlem residents on Morningside Park, owned by the city. Not only did the designs smack of 'Jim Crow', but they represented another step on the University's encroachment on Harlem.

Now police set up on the boundary of the campus. The students held fast to the buildings. A constant stream of people – some from the neighbourhood, others, important, like Stokely Carmichael – even, a telegram from Chairman Mao – arrived to show solidarity. Friends brought food and supplies. *Life* featured a picture of a student lounging in the president's office, smoking one of his White Owl cigars.

The scale of the disobedience was stunning. The authorities refused to yield. I thought – how *could* these campus administrators, who claimed to be so in touch with their students, be so deaf and blind?

[127]

One week later, a thousand police in riot gear moved into Columbia's campus at 2.30 in the morning. The students walked out of the buildings escorted by police, holding their heads high. No sooner did the paddy wagons set off for the station, when police on the edge of the campus charged, clubbing everyone in sight, including the university rabbi, a professor and hundreds of students. By the end of the day, seven hundred and twenty students had been arrested.

Then, from far away at vast distance, came news from France. The Sorbonne had closed. Students had taken to the streets, burning cars, looting buildings. Hundreds were arrested. Countless injured. The Latin Quarter was overrun with fighting students and police, streets clouded with tear-gas. Lots of fractious leftist groups, Communists, Socialists, anarchists and Marxists had joined forces. Soon ten million workers were said to be on strike in France, and ten thousand battled with police in Paris. The issues in France were different – France was not fighting a war. It was not drafting its young men to fight in the military.

Or killing its Black people.

And almost as a footnote, in Boston the trial of Dr Benjamin Spock, Bill Coffin and three others opened. They were accused of conspiracy: to counsel, aid and abet men eligible for the draft to avoid military service.

A big, nasty charge, with overtones of treason.[*]

★

Vicki and I got a job that spring doing 'heavy outdoor work' on the Hunnewell Estate on the other side of the lake from the college. Six hours a week, at $1.70 an hour – the plan was to earn $60.00. The job was to grub out heavy-duty weeds that had taken over the base of a never-ending yew hedge that surrounded the house and garden. Neither of us had any idea what we were doing. We didn't even have gloves. The weather was glorious and the sun on our backs was hot. Hopeless, simply hopeless! Our eyes on our watches, as soon as our three-hour stint was over, we raced to the lake, stripped off and plunged in.

Vicki, though, wasn't really with me. Phil was tall, blond,

---

[*] In mid-July Coffin, Spock and all but one of the 'Boston Five' were convicted of conspiracy to counsel and aid men to avoid military service. They were sentenced to Federal prison. Previously, Coffin's actions as a Freedom Fighter ended with the Supreme Court throwing out the law segregating bus passengers in Mississippi. This should have been a landmark case – one that decided the legality of the war and the constitutionality of the Selective Service Act. Instead, after four weeks in a packed courtroom and acres of news coverage, people called the trial a national disgrace. Not only had the judge appeared biased, but the indictment was so loosely construed it might as well have included the scores of distinguished people from senators and congressmen who testified in their defence. In the end, it only seemed to strengthen the legitimacy of the draft resistance movement.

with the carved features of an Adonis. He shared a room at Harvard with a friend of Linda's from San Antonio. A day or two after Linda returned to college from spring break, she and Vicki took him some fresh *tamales* she had brought from home.

Phil appeared in the room, bearing a daisy he had found on a walk. Vicki thought this was pretty interesting and unusual for a guy. And that was it.

Phil. Kind of quiet and shy. A typical reserved New England guy. A bit like her father. Vicki tried to talk to me of other things, but he was all I ever heard about. Except for when she absolutely had to be there, she simply disappeared from the campus.

10

Summer of '68

I was blind to the way things were adding up. A little disbelieving, really, that so many twists to life and outside horrors could be happening all together. After all, I was not yet twenty years old. I discounted each event one at a time – living through shock, picking myself up, adjusting my expectations. Slowly they added up. Disbelief here, deep hurt there, slowly forcing a change in my direction.

I was in London in the summer when Bobby Kennedy was assassinated in June. He was in the bowels of the Ambassador Hotel in LA, having just accepted the California Democrats' nomination as their candidate for President at the upcoming Democratic Convention in Chicago at the end of August. He was so handsome, Jack's younger brother, only 42, another golden Kennedy, although not to me. Unlike Mike, I had clung to the integrity of Eugene McCarthy. I thought Bobby was just too smooth, too opportunistic and underhanded.

But his murder was awful. In England, new firearms legislation had just come into force: shot guns had to be kept under lock and key and you had to have a good reason to own one. Nobody I encountered could understand how America could put up with so many shootings – say a dozen in a weekend in Houston – let alone allow just anyone to buy guns. Bobby's murder took place exactly two months and one day after Martin Luther King was shot.

Another signpost, it seemed to me, on the road to America's disintegration.

I was still in the throes of heartbreak. My friends wrote: nothing lasts forever. Better sooner than later. Get a life, they said. I tried. All around me was London.

I got a job in a team setting up polling for Canadians abroad to vote in the upcoming federal election, then counting the ballots as they came in from Kashmir and Saigon, South Africa and West Germany. It was exciting to be counting the votes that led Pierre Trudeau to win. Miserable to eat lunch outside in Grosvenor Square on the grass at the feet of FDR, who Mike so resembled. Next, I got a job on the shop floor at Harrods, as famous then as it is now – but not so much a stop for the well-heeled tourist as a bastion of supplies for people living around the corner. Clocking in and out through the grubby staff entrance, I was selling 'turnery' – anything turned on a lathe – from brooms and brushes and coat hangers, to pepper mills, vast wicker picnic and laundry baskets and the most exquisite wooden bowls and boxes. It was punishing being on my feet all day, tedious when there were no customers.

I danced in Soho discotheques, took in the theatre, shopped on the King's Road. At home, I noted my mother curled on the sofa deep in Simone de Beauvoir's *The Second Sex*. She said how wonderful it was, that I should really read it, but I was in a rebellious state of mind, closed to what she might offer. I felt it was another way she might try and control me. In my state of mind, it looked like too much hard work for me.

My friends wrote. Linda was in San Antonio, seeing old friends from school, coping with a rash of house guests in town for the 1968 World's Fair. She'd stopped at Yale on the way home to visit a friend of Vicki's from her home in Cincinnati: an archaeology student called Bob. They had a good time, but his packing methods so offended her sense of order that she seized his clothes and, like the good girl she was, folded everything up neatly and finished the job for him. Now she was taking a course in geology to earn college credits. 'Summer school is, well, summer school.'

Diana was somewhere in Europe.

For Anne and Vicki, the deal for the start of the summer was a mild experiment in communal living. Vicki's new boyfriend Phil and his friend Elliott had taken a lease on a house for the summer on Norris Street, in a tired but leafy neighbourhood a couple of miles north of Harvard Yard – an arrangement for three or four guys. Until, in a moment of inspiration, they decided maybe it would be fun to have a few girls around too. Elliott, a slight balding fellow, was entangled with a girl called Lou, fair-haired and voluptuous. Vicki had a month before she had to be in Cincinnati to take up a job in a department store. Anne had got a job in Boston until she planned to go to the Democratic Convention in Chicago in August. Maybe she could come too? A stocky red-haired guy called Nigel from MIT, working in a lab somewhere, helped split the rent.

A big front porch and roses round the door. A living and a dining room and a wide kitchen spread across the back of the house. Upstairs the bathroom and two or three bedrooms.

Nigel, who kept a hamster which he fretted over, took over the attic at the top.

Vicki moved into a room in the basement with Phil. The hours she had spent consoling Diana late into the night paid off. This was the way it worked. You went to the doctor at the college infirmary and told them you had been having trouble with your periods for two or three months – irregular and very painful. They would tut, advise you see a gynaecologist, and refer you to a nice man in a local clinic. Legit, Harvard Med school etc. He (doctors in those days were invariably male) would put you on your back with your legs up in stirrups and proceed to give you a full internal examination – a humiliating experience for which no one prepared you. And during the chat you would confide that you were engaged and getting married next summer. And he would ask if you would like the pill or the cap. And in view of the trouble you were having with your periods, he quietly wrote out a prescription for the pill.

Vicki had finished cleaning the house by the time Anne arrived. Within hours she had made chilli, coffee cakes, brownies and a lemon pie. Vicki didn't have a job, so – partly guilt trip, partly because she was pretty happy covering domestic chores, but also because no one else would do it – she cleaned and shopped and cooked for everyone else, balancing brown paper grocery bags on the handlebars of her bike, or coming back from Stop and Shop on the bus so overloaded it took her three trips back and forth from the pavement to lug everything into the house. In search of cheap ideas for food she'd go down to the Co-op and jot down recipes from cookbooks. Took care of dividing up the communal phone bill, and charges for the food.

Back in the spring, Anne had applied to the US civil service for a summer job in Boston. Her letter of appointment came from the Defence Supply Agency at Boston's Army base. The idea of Anne anywhere near a military operation was like asking a cat to take a bath. Still, not knowing exactly what was in store, she researched the commute and took a series of buses out to the base. Bright and efficient, she reported for work at 7.45am the first morning. The buildings were grey, factory-like. Men in green fatigues marched briskly past.

'Take a seat here.'

Anne sat down with other summer hires and looked at the walls. Heavy bootsteps echoed along the corridors. She signed papers declaring she was not a Communist. Took the oath of allegiance (hand up, facing the flag). Three hours of 'processing' crawled by. She listened to the clump of boots and could not stop thinking about the war. Any war. '&', she told me 'I was getting all sort of convoluted inside.'

Around 11.30 the personnel manager came in to talk to the new recruits.

'We here at the Defence Supply Agency are here to supply all branches of the armed services with whatever they need, wherever they are. From basket balls to bombs – that's what we do. And we do it well.

'Now, some of you will be aware that occasionally problems crop up with college students who are opposed to the war in Vietnam. If you are one of those, I have only two things to say. One is that you can work here all day, like anyone else, and then go to your peace meetings at night. Or you can quit now.'

Anne was home by lunch time. She ran across the street to where Linda's boyfriend, Mike's roommate David – with big fuzzy dark hair and his legs in blue jeans, now popularly known by his surname as 'the Ach' – and a bunch of his friends were living. Together they went down to the employment office. She came back with two gigs: one for an operation supplying psychedelic sound and lighting for concerts out of an upstairs apartment on Monday, Wednesday and Fridays. The other, typing for Samuel Bullock, the pastor at the Baptist church in Roxbury, in the centre of Boston's Black community.

She worked at his dining room table, pounding out the same letter day after day, asking for funds to support him and his church's 30th anniversary. During her breaks she watched children from the neighbourhood play with his grown-up daughter, who ran a day-care centre from the back of the house.

The guy who ran the sound and lighting outfit, was a weird and savvy Harvard Law grad. While he was away on his day job, Anne ran errands, washed the floors and typed. One day he came home early.

'Aw, Anne,' he said, placing his hand on her hip and moving her towards the bedroom. 'I'm so worn out, won't you rub my back?'

'I don't think this is a good idea.' Anne grabbed her purse and left.

Back at Norris Street, everyone was running around on varied schedules. The Ach and his friends dropped by all the time. Next door lived another group, windows thrown wide and porch doors hanging open, better to let the beat of the stereo play out into the street. In the evenings on the front porch. they hung out testing all kinds of drugs, new, interesting and experimental. Lou imported her sister and her fiancé. Then there was Elliott's cousin, a handsome Jewish guy called Lenny. The house for four became home to ten. A single bathroom in the house. The etiquette was never to lock the door while taking a shower so someone could come in for a pee if they needed one. I didn't envy Anne.

Elliott had a taste for hard rock. Cream, Iron Butterfly, Jimi Hendrix. He played it loud. Wasn't bothered about when he turned it off. He sat on the sofa, Lou draped over him, turning on with a bit of dope. Then they chased each other round the house, in pursuit of constant sex.

Lenny took refuge in the kitchen with Vicki. She stood at the stove, hair tied low on her neck, her feet bare, tasting bolognaise. Lenny had graduated from Yale a year ago. He was a runner, tall and lean with curly dark hair and a bemused smile. He was in Cambridge that summer to finish a thesis for his MA. He'd also been labelled 1-A by his draft board, and unless he could produce something pretty exceptional for his thesis he was going to have to go into the army in a year. He hunched over the kitchen table, trying to write, trying and failing to get on with his work. He talked. One existential crisis after another. Intense, anguished monologues on the war, politics, his latest girlfriend, his parents' disappointment in him. Vicki buttoned her lip. Just listened.

And listened.

Five people lined up in the morning waiting for the shower. Tension was rising in the house. About the mess and squalor and the cat, who Vicki picked up at Mr Do-Nut across the street. The frenzied rushing-in and out, the music blaring all the time. By early July, as many as fifteen people were staying in the house. Then who should drop by but –

The landlord.

'Cute, *really* cute,' said Anne.

He didn't wait for an answer to the doorbell, but marched straight into the living room with two health inspectors. They were violating three codes. No one could live on the third floor because there was no fire escape; no one could live in the basement because it was not two-thirds above ground.

'I have no idea how many people are really living in this house,' the landlord said, 'and from the chaos I've seen, I doubt that you do either. According to regulations, this house can sleep four. We will be back tomorrow morning to see you are complying with the law.'

A crisis meeting was held. From that point onwards, it would be as if there were no girls living in the house. Nothing beat getting up in the morning, having to tear up beds to make rooms look uninhabited. Every day Anne, Vicki and Lou packed all their belongings into the back of a closet. Phil and Elliott slung their jackets over a chair and littered the floor with their workboots.

*

On 20 August my family and I set off for our summer vacation via the ferry across the Channel to Boulogne and the long drive down the N7 to the south of France. We woke up on our first morning in Normandy to news that Russia had invaded Czechoslovakia. Nothing in Europe since the war had been as scary as this: Russian tanks barrelling down the narrow streets of Prague, where only a few short weeks ago, the politics of hope had brought forth a few months of freedom. My father rang

London. Did he need to return to the office? The answer was 'not yet'. For a long time that day he drove south in silence.

★

Five days later in America, the Democratic National Convention opened.

Chicago in late August. The weather still hot during the day, turning cooler at night. The sunshine sparkled on the waves of Lake Michigan. Handsome buildings, green trees and mown parkland, wide streets, and big cars – a beautiful city with a nasty reputation. Chicago's mayor, Richard J Daley, was one of the last of America's big city bosses. Daley was large, florid and self-satisfied. A big supporter of JFK, he was a man with the ear of the President. Chair of the Cook County Democratic Party central committee, Daley was the *de facto* leader of the Chicago Democratic party. Hours after Martin Luther King's death, riots broke out in over 100 cities across the country. In Chicago, they were the worst: at least nine people were killed and 1200 injured, over 200 buildings were destroyed. At the end of the riots Daley beefed up what he saw as his faint-hearted police force, with orders to shoot-to-kill in cases of arson 'or anyone with a Molotov cocktail in his hand. Maim or cripple anyone looting.'*

In Daley's book anti-war demonstrators were revolutionaries, bent on the destruction of America. He was ready for trouble.

All demonstrations had been banned. The International Amphitheatre, where the convention was to be held, was ringed with barbed wire. Security check-points inside and out.

---

* https://chicagoreader.com/news-politics/shoot-to-kill-shoot-to-maim/

Six thousand armed National Guard troops were camped out with armoured cars. Another eleven thousand police. Tense and febrile, the authorities waited for the mob to arrive.

Anne drove west with Nigel. She found him infuriating. Pudding-like, Anne wrote to me, he sat on the fence over the war and refused to commit to McCarthy. Her mother, worried about her safety, had found them a place to stay, in an apartment not far from Chicago university. They would be meeting up with Lenny, who, Anne said, had done a lot of work the previous summer for Allard Lowenstein, a lawyer and the charismatic organiser of the 'Dump Johnson' movement. 'A political whirling dervish' (as one of his obits put it when he was shot dead by one of his disappointed followers in 1980, at the age of 51), Lowenstein had failed to persuade either Robert Kennedy or George McGovern to challenge President Johnson for the Democratic nomination. Nobody in history had successfully challenged an incumbent president for the nomination. Except – Eugene McCarthy. Lowenstein had led the campaign that had brought him into the race. He had a reputation for gentle intensity – a bit like Lenny himself. He gave Lenny a pass for the night before the final vote at the Convention. Anne said she and Nigel planned to ride in on his coat tails.

They landed in town with tens of thousands of others. Lenny followed on a plane from Texas. The media was arriving in droves: the Convention was meant to be 'open' to all comers. Even though McCarthy's campaign was faltering, it was crucial that delegates to the Convention be convinced of the strength of opposition to the war in Vietnam for themselves. Thousands cheered him as he drove from the airport to the Conrad Hilton. The time had finally come to stand up and be counted.

The Boston Movement Centre, home-from-home to a coalition of political and anti-war organisations from the Boston area, was in the basement of an old Methodist Church in a dicey neighbourhood. On Sunday, the day before the convention opened, Anne and Nigel turned up, fresh-faced and keen, Anne, in neat A-line skirt and pressed blouse.

'Hi,' she said to the few she knew. No one seemed too glad to see her. Not much seemed to be going on. She and Nigel were given some leaflets. A map of Chicago, a list of delegates. Everyone seemed to assume everyone knew what to do; no one cared to explain it. Activity for the day was to picket three hotels where delegates were staying, then meet again in the evening for an update.

'Be clear,' she was told, 'these pigs are mean. Here's how you get legal aid.' In case of tear gas, she was to cover her face with a wet cloth. Coat her face with vaseline to protect against Mace. A doctor would be on hand from 1–2 am each night to treat minor wounds. She watched two women she knew from Wellesley put on white jackets with red crosses on the arms – first aiders to the crowd. They set off in various cars for the picket. They arrived: no picket signs. A few people milled about in black arm-bands. A wash-out.

Anne's next days were spent trying to prise more passes for the convention out of uninterested delegates, crashing drunken campaign parties, watching TV in McCarthy hotel rooms, but mainly trying to keep track of Lenny and Nigel – with no mobile phones, scant knowledge of Chicago, and only a hit-and-miss strategy of trying to stay together while joining in as much of the action as they could.

All the main players were there: Students for Democratic Society (SDS) under one banner; the National Mobilization Committee to End the War in Vietnam (MOBE) another. The Yippies, led by Abbie Hoffman and Jerry Rubin, wild and unpredictable, were taking the piss.

Waiting around – there was a lot of waiting around – the three of them went to the Lincoln Park Zoo to pass the time. Helmeted National Guardsmen drilled on the fringes of the park; a group drank beer in a circle on the lawn. They ogled Anne: 'Hey, honey, whatcha' doing tonight?'

Seas of people strolled or cycled south towards the convention centre. Lots of different folk: white-shirted college students, the odd stoned hippy, salsa bands, a handful of Hell's Angels. An older man draped in mourning carrying a poster of Bobby Kennedy. People set up a Free Store trading in left-over clothes under a tree. A 'Good Humour' ice cream van tinkled past. Peace flags waved and hands were raised in peace salutes. Tim Hayden sang folksongs. The occasional couple danced. Blue shirted policemen, with helmets and billy clubs, waited for trouble.

Everyone cautioned against winding up the police. They'd already arrested and gassed people in the park the night before. Respect the curfew of 11 pm.

A heady moment that Tuesday night, 27th August, walking into the Convention Centre. Lenny'd got a gold medallion with a red, white and blue forked ribbon hanging from it – and a pass. There was no name on it, so they could pass it back and forth through the barriers. Anne was tricked out in her McCarthy badges and a campaign blue and white scarf. Past the tanks forming blockades to the north, and the cordon of helmeted blue-shirted police. Inside, the halls were crowded. Security still tight. Balloons, people handing out leaflets, lining up to make calls at banks of telephones. Well-fed white men in crisp shirts and ties, smoking cigars, cradling pipes. *Hey, how y'a doing?* Caucus meetings in the Boulevard Room. Here and there a woman in a hat. Paul Newman. Phalanxes of cameras, more police. The excitement and the glamour – Anne could feel it – all that money and *power*.

They found their seats, high in the bleachers above the scarlet carpet on the main floor.

NBC anchor-men Huntley and Brinkley were suspended in the box in the opposite corner. The band churned out *Chicago*. The states each in neat boxes: Illinois near the front. High podium for the speakers. In front of the microphones, flags from all the States.

And when the saints go marching in…

In all the noise and razzmatazz, she tried to hear the speeches from the podium. Watched the deal-making on the floor. In the press boxes journalists hammered out copy, TV cameras rolled. The delegates were deeply divided. The Southern and the Northern Democrats seemed like species from different planets: one was convinced of the rightness of the war, the other pleaded for peace. The booth harbouring honoured guests bore the slogan 'Promises made. Promises kept.' It was pure fiction that McCarthy had admitted defeat. Lobbying was going on in every corner. Security was so tight delegates couldn't move across the floor without jostling one another. It wound up the tension. A CBS correspondent was grabbed by security guards while trying to find out why a Georgia delegate was hauled out of the hall. Walter Cronkite was livid.

Five miles north, in Lincoln Park, the police charged. Tom Hayden of SDS was arrested. The poet, Allen Ginsburg closed proceedings chanting *Om* in time for curfew.

Wednesday, 28th August, the final day of the convention. An anti-war demo – the only one for which a permit had been issued for the week – was planned that afternoon. Anne and Nigel joined huge numbers gathered in Grant Park, opposite the Conrad Hilton hotel where the cream of the delegates were staying. In one speech after another, Dick Gregory, the comedian, McCarthy, the candidate, Tom Hayden from SDS, called for an end to the bombing in Vietnam. More Ginsburg. Jerry Rubin and Bobby Seal from the Black Panthers. Peter Paul and Mary strummed *We shall overcome* and the crowd sang along. Young men offered up draft cards like communion chalices before the crowd. Then ceremoniously burnt them. The crowd chanted.

'*Hell no, we won't go.*'

Rumours issued from inside the convention hall of the ongoing battle for the nomination. Kennedy's assassination had left nearly four hundred delegates to the convention uncommitted. Senator George McGovern, with his appeal to Kennedy's supporters, was coming up fast. Johnson's favourite, Hubert Humphrey, was trying to pave the middle way, saying he would call for a bombing pause.

At some point someone lowered the American flag in the park. Police broke into the crowd. Hayden grabbed a megaphone and yelled for people to separate and move into the street. 'The pigs are coming!' People picked up their things and ran.

By nightfall, it was cold. Inside the convention hall, Humphrey was in the middle of a passionate three-hour debate. Everyone knew the Convention had slipped away from McCarthy. Even McGovern seemed doomed. The war would go on. Things would roll on in Washington. Nothing would change.

Outside in Grant Park, Anne was exhausted. There were SO MANY PEOPLE. Floodlights glanced off police helmets. *Peace – Now!* All of a sudden – no one knew why – the army's huge armoured cars were on the move. Barrelled down the street. The National Guard fired tear gas. Twenty short-sleeved, white-shirted police with clubs and helmets moved in a line. Took off in a run, swinging clubs. The crowd moved faster. Canisters popped. Smoke rose. The air was burning. Sirens wailed. Anne's eyes teared up. She couldn't breathe. Bull-horns sounded, clamoured for order. Police charged the crowd, flailing billy clubs and gun barrels left, right and centre. Protestors seized trash cans. Hurled them back at the pigs. Anne covered her mouth and nose with her McCarthy scarf and ran. She heard a shriek as a baton came down hard on someone's head. Saw a girl dragged by her hair and tossed into a paddy wagons. People were screaming. Anne kept running.

All of it, seventeen minutes, was broadcast live on television, around the world. And when Anne got back to her apartment, she wrote everything down.

In the rain, in the pretty main square of Hyères, I read the head-lines in the newspaper. I wanted to weep with despair. I had no idea what had happened to Anne, only knew that she was there. My family climbed back into our car. 'Tune in to Radio Caroline,' I said to Dad.

Hey Jude, don't make it bad.
The Beatles.
Just released.

11

No more dancing

In September I landed from London and went straight to Norris Street, to see for myself how everyone had been living. Vicki had just arrived back from Cincinnati: she had washed the floors and cleaned the house. She and Linda stood gossiping in the kitchen. Sunshine streamed in and the sky was very blue. It was early afternoon.

'Honey!' Linda cried as I walked through the door. She threw her arms wide and gave me a hug. Vicki turned from the stove, and gave me her big, wonky smile.

'Hey, how' ya doin?' I thought she looked too thin. Her dark hair, grown long, was pulled back in a loose pony-tail. She wrapped her arms around me and squeezed me hard.

'Come here y'all – I'm just telling Vicki about this wedding...' Linda's Southern twang twitched into a giggle. Her fingers raised, pursed for detail, and I just had to chuckle in anticipation. I was so glad to see them.

'Okay. So: she's the daughter of a San Antonio oilman. Her sister is my age. *Seven* bridesmaids, all decked out in matching finery. And a ring-bearer – the bride's three-year-old brother. Place is packed. Standing room only. We then went on to what must have been one of the largest receptions in country club history. Neiman-Marcus did all the decorations. They must have flown them in from Dallas.'

Her face crinkled. 'Ugh – it was *not* fun.'

'Aw come on, Linda,' I had to laugh. After a summer of swimming laps at the country club pool, she was fit in shorts and a sleeveless blouse in orange linen. She went on to tell me how her parents had driven her in her new car, a second-hand Opel her dad had bought for her, north from San Antonio to Vicki's home in Cincinnati. There she'd been able to see Vicki's friend Bob from Yale for a couple of days before they headed for Massachusetts and 'Achland', as she had christened David's stomping ground at Harvard.

'It was just great. Phil was there too.' Phil came with them for the drive across country to Cambridge. 'Which pleased the parents mightily,' Linda said. 'You know – the magic of a male in command?'

We laughed. Vicki's feet were bare on the wood boards. She wore a shirt of Phil's and wide-legged sailor's pants slung low, buttoned on the hips. I noticed a new aura about her. She was relaxed, at home in this place. I looked at her pants.

'Where'd you get those?'

'Picked 'em up second-hand from the Army and Navy surplus store.'

It was warm in the kitchen, heaped with bowls of vegetables, piles of this and that. No place to sit down. I'd come straight from the plane in my new London look – pale lips and deep-shadowed eyes, cute bob, and a tiny gauzy dress from Mary Quant, with cream tights and black patent leather loafers. It wouldn't do. Whatever passed in Britain was here too racy and smart, my skirts too short. I went into the room where Linda was staying, opened my case and put on my old corduroy bell-bottoms and a pair of sandals. I never wore the gauzy dress again.

This year, the five of us, Vicki, Linda, Anne, Diana and I were to live side by side in rooms on the ground floor of Davis. My new room had a view of the lake on one side and green lawns on the other. But shrubs blocked some of the windows, and it was dark. The plaster was peeling and my mattress felt like it was stuffed with straw. At night the radiator clanged.

I set about acquiring light bulbs and laid my green rug over the concrete. My clothes reeked of moth balls packed in my trunk over the summer. I had come back to the college a few days early, to sell second-hand furniture which I'd picked up cheaply in the spring from departing seniors, to incoming freshmen. It was a frenetic three days, organising, cleaning and pricing furniture, and riding 28 bicycles left behind by students, across campus. I sold them for an outrageous profit.

Anne came back as late as she could, driving in from her home in Illinois in her new car, 'Volksie', her mother's old red Volkswagen bug. I couldn't wait to see her. Aretha was belting out *I say a little prayer* when I knocked on her door. But she was racing out for a meeting for *News* and couldn't stop. It wasn't for a few days that we had time to talk through all that had happened to her in Chicago.

We sat side by side on her bed, our backs to the wall, a box of her mother's cookies between us. She drew her knees up to her chest, hugging them tight She talked fast, taking me through her story, starting with the moments at the beginning of the convention when she was trying, sensibly, to learn about the political processes; and how quickly her curiosity turned to disgust with the self-satisfied Democratic party hacks in the committee rooms. The drunken delegates' parties. All the time, the false promises and the lies. And afterwards, the tear gas and the pigs. She just could not get over the viciousness of the police.

'I could see blood pouring out of open wounds. Kids were beaten as they lay on the street. Girls forced into paddy wagons.' I recalled the shocking pictures I had seen in the papers and watched as she twisted her fingers.

'All I could see was just this vast mob pitted against lines of cops, gas masks in hand. The National Guard rolling up behind. Everyone was singing *America the Beautiful* – and *never* had it meant it so much before. All of a sudden from somewhere someone shouted UP AGAINST THE WALL, MOTHER-FUCKERS — you know, the chant from Columbia last spring?

'The police started pushing the crowd back. Someone jumped on the back of a police car and bashed in the window with his boot. And suddenly here was this irrational – animal-like – vicious thing coming at us, pushing kids against the buildings, hitting anyone on the way – *and there was nothing we could do.* I looked one of them in the face and just screamed, '*PIG!*' Then I just ran.' Afterwards, she told me, she couldn't stop shaking.

She shivered.

'They didn't listen to us when we asked for peace, and *THIS had to be the result?*' Her voice shook. She was so angry. Then she paused.

'I don't think things will ever change.' Her voice was low. Tears of despair filled her eyes. 'It has never been so clear to me before that now there are two Americas. We are sitting on one side of a fence, battling to be heard. On the other – there's this vast machine of power, ingrained with self-interest and complacency. Deaf to anything anyone else has to say.'

From that moment, and for some years to come, Anne never used the word police. They were always the pigs. Now, with the Presidential elections in November imminent, with Hubert Humphrey as the Democratic candidate and Richard Nixon running against him, she could see no hope of ending the war. She was miserable, talking of throwing up her plans of going to law school after graduation. Why bother if the law couldn't be a force for social change? She'd tried to transfer from Wellesley last spring. She hadn't succeeded. Now she was going to double down on the work she needed to do to get the credits for her degree as soon as she could. She would keep on working for the *Wellesley News* so she could go out and report on everything, on and off campus, and plunged into work.

In the dormitory we had moved up a notch: Hillary, now in her final year, was president of student government. As the most important senior in the place, she occupied a suite on the top floor, with lofty rooms, views of the lake and built-in bookcases under the eaves. Vicki had been elected to take over her old role as Vil Junior in Davis, dealing with tricky issues that arose in the house.

I saw little of her. Before term started, she'd been away for a couple of days on Cape Cod, getting trained for the role: what to do with homesick freshmen, girls who had never lived away from home, or who found themselves overwhelmed by the work. Closeted in her room, she held little meetings of new girls, comforted sobbing freshmen, then went off to choir to sing madrigals, and, as soon as she could, jumped in Linda's car to Cambridge and Phil.

Linda wrote home:

19 Sept 1968

Now then, to the other prime aspect of life: the social. Bob is fine. I'm going to Yale the 28th or so. The Ach is fine. I like them both. I shall have schizophrenia by the end of the year, or whenever the end comes.

As time was to go by that autumn, I wondered how Linda really felt about these two men in her life. She settled into her new room along the hall from me: lots of Mexican colour, and a reel-to-reel tape recorder playing her homemade tapes of Brandenburg concertos or Vivaldi's *Four Seasons*.

By now Diana had returned from Europe, as ethereal and dreamy as ever. No one had heard from her all summer.

'You were so *dear* to write,' she hugged me tight. 'If only you knew. The letter you sent came just after such a time of tribulation with my mother about whether or not she *would* phone her friends, and whether or not we *would* mix everyone up at the big lunch for her birthday.' And so she went on talking non-stop, funny understatement intercut with huge exaggeration, about the wonders she had seen at the Uffizi and her trials with her mother.

I'd only met Emily in passing. She was fair, like Diana, with a pale, languid beauty. From Diana's tales I couldn't help imagining her as a more neurotic Bolter from *The Pursuit of Love*. In 1965, the year before Diana started Wellesley, Emily had married Bertalan de Nemethy, a former Hungarian cavalry officer, who had been the coach to the American Olympic show-jumping team for the past ten years. De Nemethy, the son of a pre-war Hungarian state governor, was a high-priest of the international show jumping world, fastidious, upright and elegant.

'And they're riding at Madison Square Gardens in November and I *really* want you *all* to come.' And I wondered if she really meant it. Or whether I'd be able to afford it.

Soon her new room was furnished in her trademark paisleys, cushions and heaps of clothes. But underneath the piles on her desk the pencils were sharpened, the typewriter aligned, the drawers impeccable. The previous term Diana had used her charm to wage a single-handed campaign on a stuffy professor of fine art. Her object: to persuade him – and in turn the powers that be – that if drawing, painting and sculpture were to be properly taught on campus, there ought to be a store for students to purchase art supplies closer than downtown Boston. Her wish was granted: with Linda to help, she was now in charge of a cubby-hole in the art centre. Four hundred pounds of clay, two hundred sketch books, rulers, knives, pencils and watercolours were unpacked, sorted and inventoried, sold, and the account books (no calculators!) kept. If it all worked well, Diana would be allowed to stock oils and turpentines the next term. And the two of them could make money.

It was harder coming back than I had thought. My heart was still bruised. I hadn't heard from Mike all summer. Now Linda was back with his roommate, the Ach. Vicki entwined with Phil. Our rooms were too close. Too easy to pop in and out of. It was a hard job shielding me from gossip. Whenever we went into Harvard together, they took care to steer me away from any possible encounter with Mike, and all the time I was conscious of how I missed talking to him. I put on Leonard Cohen and a lot of Joni Mitchell, in the search for some kind of wisdom. Finally clear of the required courses for my degree, I loaded myself with history: heavy courses in the history of the Renaissance, a seminar on domestic problems in Victorian England, and the novel in nineteenth-century France. This required me to read a doorstopper of a book – Balzac, Flaubert, Stendhal – in French each week. At night I worked in the library, putting books that had been returned back in their places on the shelves. I went to the Army and Navy surplus store in Boston and purchased a pair of thick serge sailor trousers to wear, and put away my London patent leather loafers.

Meanwhile, no question, there was a new vibe on campus. Girls were going about fresh-faced, their hair loose and growing long, in cut-off jeans and bare feet. A few of the African Americans had adopted Afros – emulating Angela Davis, California's shining light of Black Power. People talked of the relief of not wearing bras. There was a lot of talk of co-education coming to the Ivy League: Princeton, Vassar, maybe, Yale. In a new departure, Wellesley had come to an agreement with MIT to share courses.

And then there was the issue of civil rights.

Early in October, I went to an All-College meeting in the chapel to find out what was happening on Ethos's demands of the previous spring to increase Black student admissions and introduce a new major in African American studies.

Darkness had fallen and it was chilly walking to the chapel for the meeting that night. The scent of autumn was in the air, leaves drifting to the ground. Inside, there was hardly a seat to be found. It was reported that an embryonic major in African American studies had been introduced and a part-time lecturer had been recruited. Okay. Then the director of admissions delivered her report: there were still only 29 Black girls at the college, including a mere seven new freshmen. She went on to explain how much competition there was among top colleges for Black applicants who had 'the ability to adjust' to places like Wellesley. There were issues of 'overcoming differences of life-style.' Said one professor: 'It is difficult to recruit when many 'coloured students' come from homes where the only literature is comic books.' It was when the Dean stood up and promised to bring students with 'deficient backgrounds' up to Wellesley standards, that half the Black girls rose to their feet and walked out.

A week later the following letter appeared in *News*.

14 October 1968

On BLACK Pride

*To the editors of **News**:*

*The terms 'colored' and 'negro' have unpleasant and degrading connotations for Black people today. We realize that the majority of the faculty and students has long associated itself with Afro-Americans exclusively in a master/servant relationship and may find it difficult to adjust to a more equitable arrangement. However, we ask them, when speaking to us, to refer to us as Blacks or Afro Americans, and **NEVER** as 'colored girls,' which alludes to latter-day Prissys and not proud Black women.'*

*Ethos**

*

---

* *Wellesley News*, 14 October, 1968

Over the summer a woman in Cambridge called Roxanne Dunbar advertised for women to set up a 'female liberation front'.

'Stop using the word 'women',' she declared. Replace it with 'female'. Why? Because it covers all the bases from babyhood to old age. She and others in 'Cell 16' were now working full time for a female revolution – a 'thorough social revolution' not just in America, but across the world. They quoted lots of Mao, whose handy pocket sized *Little Red Book* of political quotations was stacked up high in the Co-op: *A revolution is not the same as inviting people to dinner, or writing an essay, or painting a picture, or doing fancy needlework; it cannot be anything so restrained and magnanimous. A revolution is an uprising, an act of violence whereby one class overthrows another.*

The women confessed they had no real idea of what they were doing. They met in intimate groups, and connected with similar ones around New England, bent on raising consciousness, to make women aware of the degree to which they were currently enslaved.

The talk arrived at our dinner tables. We discussed it over breakfast, as we stood in line for coffee, as we came out of the showers. Before long, I realised, to my amazement, that everything that I read, saw or heard had taken on a new dimension. It was unsettling to discover how every bit of life seemed to turn on the world of men and their view of the world. All of us began to see how control by men began in childhood with divisions of activities thought appropriate for boys rather than girls – playing with cars or kicking a ball, versus dolls and playing house. Stories, TV shows, films and plays: everywhere we looked, the underlying assumption was that men were in charge. Men did the thinking; they were in charge of operations; they controlled sexual game-playing (women however, we noted, were responsible for birth control). We were seen as passive, inadequate, unable to negotiate the world by ourselves. And hired only for the menial jobs.

Women had been taught since girlhood to wait on men, smile coyly and soothe, play up to make them feel clever and important. We learnt that the family model, in which the male ruled over his wife and children, was derived from the Latin *familia* – a household of slaves. Marx had taken up this idea, remarking that the nucleus of oppression lay in the family, where wife and children were slaves of the husband. The male is noble and dominant; the female a possession, required to be charming and beautiful – and to reproduce the next workforce.

Cell 16 advocated self-defence, karate and kick-boxing, to develop strength and agility to enable women to meet an attacker with aggression. They liked the trickiness of judo, where a woman could use the strength of a man's momentum to flip him to the ground. The single woman, they felt, should either cultivate a proud and honourable celibacy, or – if you must have a child – live in a commune 'set up on the right basis (female liberation)' as the only humane arrangement.

Cell 16 told us there was a lot to do. To be a free woman, you had to be prepared to sacrifice everything. Abandon cosmetics and uncomfortable clothes. Stop following fashion. Despise consumption. Start reading (the lists were not extensive, falling back on De Beauvoir's *The Second Sex* and Virginia Woolf's *A Room of One's Own*). And start thinking for yourself.

Most sinister of all, they opened our eyes to the ways in which we had been programmed, rather than coerced, to accept our lot, to consider the 'psychological castration of the female' – not just by men, but by other women. They showed us that the programming of traditional man-woman-child roles was designed to fit the need of the system. That we were slaves in a male world. There was much talk of the family as the most basic unit of female oppression. Some were convinced that ultimately, all women might need to live lives separate from men and male institutions, if only to be free.

The talk was tough and heady. Celibacy? Lesbian separation? The message: you cannot rely on men to fight our battles for us.

This was the moment when male chauvinism entered the language.

Over the weeks of that term, the scales fell from our eyes. Anne and I spent many hours digesting the arguments. We could easily see how far the world had been designed to favour men. How far they trampled over us, designed and controlled almost everything around us. We talked of the way men had always run whatever jobs we'd taken. We knew we wanted control of our own lives.

At the same time, we didn't *feel* enslaved. We shrank from the idea that we might be seen as aggressive and angry. Or unable to appreciate the good qualities in our friends who were men. We weren't sure we wanted to throw away the whole idea of the private home. Or change our patriarchal names to break any connection with our fathers. We didn't want to get involved in revolutions.

We started to call out the men we knew. A lot of the time

they laughed, but then, realising we were serious, they paused. Agreed that we might have a point, and thought better.

Anne and I couldn't decide how far we were prepared to go. We resolved that we'd be free and independent women. Liberated! But we were too fond of having a good time. In spite of the contradiction, we could not resist the appeal of being someone's cool girlfriend if we got the chance.

*

Social life, as usual, was focussed on the weekends. I still had not got over the pain in my heart, the sense of bitter betrayal. I summoned the courage to face the first mixer of the year with Anne. Across a crowded floor we were surprised to spot Diana. She was in the arms of someone new. He was fine featured and tall with glasses and thick dark hair. As we would, much later, discover he was called Douglas.

Now that we were one step away from senior year and graduation, most of the men we met, seniors and post-grad men, admitted shamelessly they were scouting the field for a wife. A Wellesley one – such an asset for the future – would more than do. I wrote my mother:

Larry is now in his third and final year of law at Boston College. He is a typically clean-cut American boy, good looking and quite nice. He is also a quite unimaginative and a blatant and disgusting capitalist. This time next year he will be earning $60,000 p.a. on the staff of the Supreme Court of New Jersey.

Marriage? Why did everyone seem to keep pushing us in this direction?

That was the autumn I gave up dancing.

*

I joined the Yearbook and was assigned to photography. I was given a good camera and a roll of 35 mm film a week. Every time I went to the darkroom it was out of one chemical or another. And my contact sheets always seemed to disappear. All my friends were away every weekend. They set me up with blind dates, some nice, even interesting, but no one could extinguish my longing for Mike and the easy chats we used to have. I did my laundry, cleaned my room, went to the bookshop, wrote letters and listened to the BBC on Vicki's AM–FM radio.

I took to seeing Steve, a friend of Anne's from home in Illinois, and a graduate student at MIT. He had a second-floor apartment in Cambridge at 882 Main Street. Steve was tall and thin, with long hair, a relentless case of acne and a stringy beard. We got on well; there was no question of romance. He rode a motorcycle which both excited and terrified me, clad in a giant parka like a sleeping bag, as the temperatures at night sank below freezing and we sped along the Mass Turnpike to Wellesley in time for my curfew at midnight. We went to the movies. We hung out with Anne and a boy from Harvard with leftish views she had met over the summer.

Charlie was shambling and rotund, hardly taller than Anne herself. He had fuzzy hair and the most beautiful golden-brown eyes. He couldn't stop clowning, found anything funny, even his well-documented woes.

After supper in Steve's apartment we sat around on the floor as winter darkness fell outside the windows. Steve rolled a joint and passed the toke around, exhaling the smoke. Charlie lolled on the floor, chuckling softly to himself. I watched it go slowly round the room. Someone, maybe Lenny, as tightly-wound as ever, would take a long heavy drag, the smoke curling out through his nostrils.

'Where *did* you get this grass?' Charlie said and Steve chuckled. Lenny giggled. It got to me and I took the paper weed. My first ever drag. Sweet, rich and far too hot in my lungs. I felt my head go light and could not help thinking, *if tobacco does as much damage to your lungs as they say it does, what does this stuff do?*

✳

We were two years into college. Two more years to go. The glamour was wearing thin. There would be a life after June 1970. What were we going to do? Anne was talking of some kind of grad school, probably history. Vicki some kind of further education ditto, 'I guess.' For Linda and Diana, it all seemed a haze. Long ago I had decided that I wanted some aspect of my father's career – a life at the heart of foreign affairs, of travel to

interesting places. Now there seemed so many other possibilities, I wasn't so sure.

We began to look around at women we admired, wondering how they went about their lives. Eugenia Janus, stylish in black tights, high heels and big owl-shaped glasses, delivered intoxicating lectures on the History of

Art. We knew nothing of her private life, but her career looked worth emulating.

Then there was Eleanor McLaughlin, thin and rangy, frizzy hair scraped into a tight knot on the back of her head, unfazed by motherhood. She was a stylish dresser — an elegant grey patterned knit sheath set off her figure. Round glasses, fine frames, completed the look. She was a medieval historian, keen on heresies, witchcraft and the role of dissident women in religious movements. She wore her lack of makeup like a badge of honour. She invited me and other students to supper with her husband – dark, and handsome – around a big wooden table in a rambling kitchen.  She turned from stirring a pot on the stove to debate ethics or fume about the war. I admired her clear sightedness, and her commitment. Strikes were a public demonstration of horror, she would say. But – 'It was not enough to stand up and be counted and have a conscience and be a good guy,' she would say. 'We've got to change things.'

The grandmother of one of my friends lived in Centre Sandwich, New Hampshire, a picture-postcard New England village, population 700, with a church, a general store/post office, and an antique shop (open by appointment). Mrs March had to be over 70 but looked no more than 55. She lived alone in a 1760 farmhouse, tiny from the outside, all white-washed and pine-floored inside, with fireplaces in several rooms, and one in the kitchen which she kept going all the time. Warm and kind, she lived a full life: books, music, the people she knew in the town. Her style was simple and elegant. I tried to imagine the day-to-day rhythms of her life as a woman on her own, in the peace and tranquillity of this beautiful place.

How did these women do it? I wondered. Keeping such a sense of themselves, running their lives as they wanted to?

∗

Anne told me she had met someone called Chi from Princeton, who she really liked. He was Jewish and his family was serious about that. She asked me: was there even any point to this?

∗

I was working hard, typically, trying to get through six-hundred pages of *The Charterhouse of Parma* by Stendhal in French in a day. Anne was drowning in back copies of *Good Housekeeping* and *The Saturday Evening Post,* for a paper she was writing on the popular image of American women in the ten years after they got the vote in 1919. She was also driving hours to see Chi in Princeton at weekends, and once a week she went to Somerville, a faded town northwest of Boston, to oversee production for *News* at the printers. Misty's inhabited hot, cramped quarters in an old brick house. While Anne proof-read the forthcoming edition, the printers, speedy and dexterous, set hot type beside her, unneeded lead dropping to the floor at the end of a line.

Vietnam hadn't gone away. The US had been bombing Vietcong supply routes, crossing over the Cambodian border. Our anger escalated, day by day. I was exhausted and depressed, looking for any way to escape. I grasped at straws. Maybe I could go and study in England for a term?

*

Vicki had gone to the MIT Student Centre to join a sanctuary for Mike, a nineteen-year-old soldier and former draft resister, who was absent from the army without leave. Mike hailed from a small town in Maine. He went AWOL in mid-September from Fort Bragg, North Carolina and got in touch with the New England Resistance, the anti-war/anti-draft group, who in turn, put him in touch with the MIT Resistance who offered him safe haven. Unless the police came and they got busted, Vicki would be there for the rest of the night.

She listened to Mike take a long-distance call from someone who was also in sanctuary in New York: 'He was just a nineteen-year-old kid. The last thing they said to each other was "see you in the stockade".

'God,' Vicki said. 'To lay yourself on the line knowing that you're going to get put in prison?'

*

At 6pm on Monday 4 November Anne and I climbed into Volksie and drove to Yale. Escape! Escape!

We had volunteered to be guinea pigs in an experiment in five days of co-education. Yalies had vacated their rooms for us. They wanted to persuade alumni and supporters to donate the funds necessary to convert the 267-year-old bastion of male education to accommodate women. We arrived long after dark, four-and-a-half hours after registration closed.

Lights twinkled along the paths that ran through the quadrangles: massive stone and brick buildings that reminded me a little of Oxford, which I had visited the previous summer. There was a bit of confusion when I found the single room I had been allocated was occupied by two men. The scent of stale marijuana lingered in the hall. Doubtful that 'something would work out', I went with Anne to Jonathan Edwards College where our reception was considerably more welcoming. We were given a book of meal tickets, campus maps and a course timetable. And I was given a mattress for the floor in the room she had been given. It belonged to Jim, who was a bit of a square, insisting on being there all day. There were no concessions for women in the bathrooms which were down the hall.

We trawled through the mass of courses we could sit in on, trying to sort out a timetable and our way through a maze of buildings to lectures. We were advised that Reverend Coffin was speaking. That we mustn't miss Vincent Scully's art history lecture. It was packed out. Anne went to one on African music – it was way over her head. We felt just like freshmen again, strange and new, getting lost.

Yale didn't have the intensity and focus of Harvard. It was like their traditional colours, the heat of the crimson and the cool of the blue. The place seemed more laid back, less of a pressure cooker. Was it because during this experiment we girls were no longer quarry, but guinea pigs and potential competitors? Mealtimes were definitely better than any at Wellesley: an hour and a half and more, dense with conversation. There was lots more talk of Chicago. More advice on which lectures to go to, which concerts to hear. And masses and masses of politics. The next day, Tuesday, voters across America would go to the polls. The 1968 Presidential campaign had reached its climax.

That night we sat in front of the TV on tenterhooks, lapping up the coverage. Walter Cronkite's commentary was so level-headed, he was addictive. Our future seemed to stand or fall on its outcome. We didn't want Hubert Humphrey, who we saw as having compromised a once-sterling reputation as a liberal senator and foe of Jim Crow, by speaking up as Johnson's vice-president in favour of the war. But we REALLY didn't want Richard Nixon. 'Tricky Dickie' my dad had always called him. Just to look at him was enough to trigger loathing, to say nothing of his piggy-looking candidate for Vice President, Spiro Agnew.

The night went by. Anne and I moved from the International Student Centre to the Law School to the Yale Political Union, where there was a lot of beer and no one was interested in talking to us. Then squashed up against some boys we hadn't met before on big leather sofas in the common room back at Jonathan Edwards, where there was fresh coffee and a colour TV set. Slowly, slowly, the results came in. The contest was very close. We sat up until almost five waiting for the final outcome and finally went to bed and slept until twelve. We stumbled out into the morning, to learn that Nixon had won.

At Yale I dined with Linda's friend Bob, then saw him off and on over the next three days. We had fun. Given that Linda was also seeing him from time to time, I wondered, was this a *good* thing to do? Anne left in Volksie on Friday night to see Chi at Princeton. The next day Vicki and Linda picked me up to go to Diana's mother's Upper East Side apartment for the weekend in New York, where we entered a world of wealth and high society.

Diana in rose pink with a flowery silk scarf, Vicki slim in a navy shift, Linda in rust. Me in a brown velvet dress from London, pale tights, and those black patent shoes. We just had time to see a show of Italian frescoes at the Metropolitan Museum of Art, before heading to Madison Square Gardens and prime seats for the National Horse Show.

Like so much of what I did that autumn of my junior year, I hadn't intended to go on the annual Harvard–Toronto student exchange. 'But please, Stephanie, we're so short of girls,' the Harvard organiser pleaded when I got back from Yale and New York on Sunday night. 'We really need the ballast.'

At noon the following Thursday, I climbed into a bus for a fourteen-hour ride to Toronto for the weekend. We toured the university; I enjoyed looking at the city. There was a talk on the future of higher education. On Saturday night we dined at the President's house, warm and full of comfort, with rooms of paintings on walls of wood panelling, and big striking pieces of Inuit sculpture.

The sky was grey and heavy with snow as we climbed back into the bus for the long ride back to Harvard. I lay back in my seat listening to the swish of the wheels and stared out the window at walls of dark forest. Over the weekend in New York, I had turned twenty. Three days in Toronto made me realize how far I'd travelled from my old life in Canada, growing up on the move, at the convent and at the lake, wild toboggan runs down the heights from old Fort Henry. I thought of how lucky

I had been to be taken by Mike to some of those lectures with John Kenneth Galbraith and Henry Kissinger. Nothing I saw of the University of Toronto made me want to leave the urbanity of the Northeastern USA, or the rigour of the teaching I was getting at Wellesley. But I also realized: if I was serious about becoming a diplomat with Canada's department of External Affairs, I was not only going to need to be fluent in French, but to have some elements of Canadian Studies in my degree. For which, conveniently, I learnt on the exchange, Harvard had recently opened a department.

The day after I got back, I made an appointment to see Ramsay Cook, the new professor of Canadian Studies. Cook was a close friend of Canada's new prime minister, Pierre Trudeau. In his office off a corner of Harvard Yard, we talked things over. He was young and kind and liked the fact that I'd been to a French-Canadian convent. It was a no-brainer, it seemed, that he should admit me to his post-graduate seminar on French-Canadian Nationalism the following term.

*

I was reading Thomas More and Erasmus and Machiavelli; George Eliot; Rabelais, Montaigne, and della Mirandola. And I had 5,000 words to write on the methods of inquiry and trial of witches in seventeenth century France for Eleanor McLaughlin. And half as much on the 'Political and Moral Dilemmas of Sir Thomas More'. As ever, as pressure mounted, my brain seemed unable to engage. Late on the following Sunday evening, Vicki and Linda came into my room, full of accounts of their wonderful weekend before Thanksgiving: breakfast on Saturday with

Phil and Vicki cooking pancakes, Linda and the Ach arriving with a bottle of champagne. In the afternoon everyone went off to cheer Harvard/ Yale. And I felt heartsick – Mike had been there, and of course I was no longer invited.

★

In a letter home, I noted that in the newspapers a Boston research team had found the physical and psychological effects of smoking marijuana mild. I went to see *Marat/Sade* playing at the college. And radical feminists – a 'guerrilla theatre coven' of Women's Liberation, newly formed to disrupt the Miss America pageant in Atlantic City the previous summer – had taken two tables at the annual lunch and bridge party of the Wellesley Alumnae Club in Brooklyn.

Suddenly an alumna from the class of '67 stood up from the card-table: 'Oh, my God. I've spent years pounding my brains out and here I am playing *bridge?*'

With which the other table began a solemn incantation of a Jello ad: *What's the difference between a career girl and an old maid?*

Nothing.

And ran on through some choice selections of insulting adverts before ending with the Virginia Slim slogan for cigarettes: *You've come a long way, baby.*

Provocative – yes!

Hostile? No question.

A lady in Balenciaga rose: 'If you don't clear out of here, we'll call the cops!'

12

The pull of the future

I bussed into Cambridge for my first Canadian History seminar at Harvard. Tuesday 2pm, at Quincy House, a white room with windows overlooking some trees. In the centre was a white table, big enough for twelve. Only one other person was there. I took my time taking off my coat and hat, stuffed my gloves into my pockets and laid my green book bag on a square of table. Others drifted in, bringing the cold with them. Then Ramsay Cook came in, smiling. He nodded to the room and sat down at the head of the table: a small man in a tweed jacket and a tie, tortoise-shell spectacles, warm, interesting and, as they say now, 'inclusive'. He took his time introducing everyone. I was between a giant of a bearded, friendly Canadian called Bob Bothwell, who was doing his doctorate, and a diminutive Black guy called Howard, who I found out was big in Afro, the Black organisation on campus. Small and dapper, he was neatly dressed in button-down shirt and tie, and a good jacket. There was one other girl in the room; Howard, was the only other undergraduate.

Why was he joining us to learn about the nature of French-Canadian nationalism?

'I'm making a study of different forms of oppression.'

In the winter term of junior year, I also began commuting to Cambridge two or three times a week for a course at MIT. At the student union, there were silent, carpeted study centres and very comfortable chairs. Outside, the sidewalks were icy and treacherous, the narrowest of footpaths carved between shoulder-high frozen drifts. Early in February, three-and-a-half feet of snow fell in the space of twelve hours. I was sporting a moth-eaten black fur coat that reached my ankles, knee-high boots and a black beret I considered very dashing. At various events I ran into Mike. We chatted, kept our distance. I was still going about with my motorcycle riding friend, Steve, or a droopy, neurotic, desperately clever boy from Harvard called Van, who was writing a thesis on the Chinese invasion of Vietnam in 200 BC.

Meanwhile:

- It was official. Diana was in love with Douglas. She had more or less moved in with him at the Law School.
- No one could bear to read the newspapers. They were all about Nixon.
- From Vietnam, startling news. The North Vietnamese had fired rocket and mortar rounds into the southern capital of Saigon. US commanders warned this could be the start of a new general offensive.
- There was to be a panel discussion on campus with a female psychiatrist, Carola Eisenberg, from MIT to talk about marriage. Apparently the 'marriage lecture' was an annual event for seniors. But there was room for quite a few of us juniors too. The key issue of the night was — PREMARITAL SEX (!)

I sat at the front of the balcony, looking down on the floor below.

'If you're in the right place, at the right time, it can be a very beautiful experience,' Eisenberg declared, even as she went on to list all sorts of ghastly risks: unwanted babies, back-street abortions, STDs that would wreak untold long-term damage on your physical and mental health. 'But if you don't take risks, you don't really live,' she counselled. 'You merely survive.'

It wasn't long before the atmosphere in the hall took on the nature of a revival meeting. One after the other girls were standing up to account their experiences. The pressure to rid yourself of your tiresome virginity was plain to see.

'What's an orgasm?' somebody asked.

'How do you get one?' said another.

'These are medical questions and will not be answered here,' said the moderator. 'Go to the infirmary.'

- Two more feet of snow fell.
- Vicki's eyes were framed with huge dark circles. She was fragile, on the edge of tears, exhausted with the responsibility of being Vil Junior, overworked on her courses, and desperate to be with Phil. He was unreliable, didn't get in touch. When she was with him, he went about communication in a sparse New England way. She was paranoid about hemming him in, but found it hard to be in love with him without any strings attached. ('Not that I want them either!') Her father's heart condition, diagnosed the previous summer, was not getting better. She hated the college, the oppressive way it was so separate from the rest of real life.

- Anne and Chi decided they had better stop seeing each other because there was no future in their relationship. Although Anne would consider changing her religion ('I can believe in anything'), his family verged on Orthodox, totally family and synagogue oriented. And Anne just wasn't.
- Even Linda confessed to a certain curious mixture of alternating misery and cheer.

I was getting carried away with Canadian history: at last I was discovering what it was to be a scholar. There was so much raw material, so much research still to be done. After our seminar Howard and I would retreat to the library, and on the way he would tell me how much Harvard had to change to accommodate Black students. How he and friends had been working ever since Martin Luther King's assassination, trying to make it happen: basic stuff like what was happening at Wellesley, endowing a chair for a Black professor and establishing courses relevant to Black students. 'Can you believe it,' he told me, 'McGill and the University of Toronto are the best places for African Studies in North America?'

And it was not just me enjoying my work. In the evenings when we met, Linda and Diana were full of the wonders of Rembrandt's etchings and Ugo da Carpi's chiaroscuro woodcuts. One wonderful Sunday, Anne and I joined them for hours in the Boston Museum of Fine Arts, and then on to the Isabella Stuart Gardiner Museum.

★

The snows melted. On campuses across America the political temperature began to rise. In Chicago, eight men, among them Tom Hayden, Abbie Hoffman, Jerry Rubin and Bobby Seale, co-founder of the Black Panthers, who had been arrested in Chicago at the Democratic National Convention, were indicted on federal charges of conspiring to cross state lines with the intent to incite a riot. Their trial was set for the following September.

On 4 March, MIT shut down. Students, faculty and staff at MIT came out on strike. The physics faculty already had a long history of opposition to nuclear weapons. Recent research had revealed the institution to be the nation's largest academic defence contractor. Noam Chomsky and Harvard's George Wald, the 1967 Nobel laureate in biology, addressed huge crowds. I went with my camera to take pictures.

Wald said he had gone through a lot of history lately and found there was a trick to it. 'It isn't written out, but I think we established it by precedent. That gimmick is that if one can allege that one is repelling or retaliating for an aggression, after that everything goes.

'We are [now] living in a world in which all wars are wars of defence. All War Departments, Defense Departments ... The aggressor is always on the other side. How do you begin to define a war crime?

'After World War II everyone thought we would get back to normal American life one day. But what happened, under the plea of the Cold War, was not only that we built up the first big peacetime Army in our history, but that we institutionalized it. And built the biggest government building in American history – the Pentagon – to run it. Now more three and a half million

American men were under arms, in Vietnam, in 'support areas' in the Pacific; 250,000 in Germany.

'And there are a lot at home. Some months ago, we were told that three hundred thousand National Guardsmen and two hundred thousand reservists – so half a million men – had been specially trained for riot duty in the cities. As long as we keep that big an Army, it will always find things to do.' As for the draft: it was oppressive European countries and Russia where young men were forced into the army, not in a place like America.'

There was something even more important. 'Ex-President Eisenhower, in his farewell address, warned us of what he called the military-industrial complex.' But this, said Wald, was exactly what had happened. The country had been thoroughly militarised.[*]

*

Anne was focussed on collecting qualifications: applying for summer internships in Washington DC and becoming the news editor of the *Wellesley News*. She was unafraid of commissioning articles from anyone caught up in any fray. I rode in her slipstream, taking pictures, trying to keep up. Unlike her, I was baffled about what I could do in the future. Maybe, with my history, I could become an archaeologist? Choose academia? External affairs or the CBC? There seemed so much choice. Whatever it was it had to contain travel and feed my curiosity. I wanted to get out into the world. And NO MORE SCHOOL.

---

[*] https://elijahwald.com/generation.html

Over spring break, Anne flew to Washington for an internship interview with Edith Green, the Democratic Representative from Oregon, and chair of the House Representatives' Labor and Education Committee. She landed from Boston at around 2.30 pm for her meeting at 4.15. The day was heavy, with a sort of blue-greyness pressing down on the air. She strolled the streets to the Capitol steps and stood for a while on the esplanade, struck by its seeming Southern, butter-won't melt-in-the-mouth quality. Everything was so spread apart and white – or grassy – with a slow-moving, genteel appearance. She and I had spent the day before at an MIT Resistance meeting. Now she confronted the vast marble presence of the neoclassical Rayburn Building that housed the offices of the members of the US congress.

She wandered around, freaking out at the scale of the buildings. Everywhere there were flurries of American flags and gold stars, patriotism on every corner. She walked past the offices of a southern Dixiecrat, segregationist congressman, the kind of person she tried to pretend did not exist. She arrived at Edith Green's door.

'Well, I guess you think Washington will be a pretty sexy place to work,' kicked off Mr Feeney, Green's administrative assistant. Anne annoyed, tried to write this off as a poise-testing question.

Mrs Green was less combative. All the same, it was made clear half a dozen times over the next thirty minutes that any intern working for her would be responsible for their conduct outside the office: i.e. there was to be no war protesting or other 'wild-eyed radical activity'. Cited time and again, were the summer crew of '67, whose anti-Vietnam actions had nearly brought the House-financed summer internship programme to an end. The 'no funny business' warning was as clear as the point that she was being hired, not on her own merit, but as a favour to the professor who ran the internship programme on behalf of the Political Science department at Wellesley. To top it off, Anne was addressed as 'Diane' throughout.

While Anne was in Washington, I flew to Montreal to spend spring break with my aunt and to do some work on a paper for Ramsay Cook in the library at McGill. The day after I arrived, angry separatists took to the streets, planning to shut down the university. They were protesting the lack of university places for French Canadian students and demanding that McGill, founded by royal charter by King George IV in 1821, be made French. Huge spotlights were set up all over campus and armed policemen guarded the doors. At 4pm all the buildings were closed. By five the whole campus looked like an armed camp.

Six thousand demonstrators were on the move.

In Canada?

13

Living the contradictions

Nine weeks left of junior year. All the contradictions of our lives sprang into sharp relief. My room was decorated with pretty prints by Fragonard, intercut with strike posters I had picked up: 'Scientists for peace' at MIT, and solidarity with the Cuban revolution. Adverts for women's fashion still showed us as immaculate, in svelte shifts of silk or wool, hemlines sitting just above the knee. Manicured nails, pale lips, dark, brooding eyes. In fact, the nice all-American 'girl-next-door' looks of neat skirts and make-up that I and my friends had cultivated only a little more than a year before, had disappeared. The dominant look was serious and intense. I had grown my hair long, parted in the middle, severe, tied back low on the neck. Frequently I dispensed with a bra. I, who loved it so, no longer followed fashion, much less dressed as I once had in my big pink Biba hat to call attention to myself. No one flaunted sexuality. We didn't need men to hold our coats or open doors for us anymore. We swore like fishwives, talked of male chauvinism all the time.

No question: the women's movement was now a thing. I went to lots of meetings in small groups; there were debates at the dining table. Proselytes for women's liberation kept asking us just how free we thought we were. Wellesley was still such a terribly cautious place. Why, I fumed, did so many clever women still think the whole concept of sex equality ridiculous? So impossible to achieve?

That spring the traditional college Tree Day Pageant was replaced by a picnic and donations to support inner-city Black kids on Upward Bound. 'Liberation: A New Role for Women?' was a new course on campus. Run by students for students, it would examine 'The Position of Women in Contemporary American Society.' Why bother? Why not just get out and change things for the better? Meanwhile, Cell 16, Roxanne Dunbar's 'female liberation front', had started publishing a journal called *No More Fun and Games*. I added new terms to my lexicon of oppression: sexism and sexist.

At Easter Bob invited me to come to Yale for the weekend, in the blue *Bulldog* version of the romantic Ivy Dream. I was not sure what had happened between him and Linda over the autumn and made no effort to find out. I didn't want to hurt her. But I liked him. He was studying archaeology, a subject I could relate to. He had an open, fresh-faced look about him. He was funny and seemed keen to show me a good time. I said yes.

We took in *The Prime of Miss Jean Brodie* and *The Fantasticks* live on stage, then rode the train into New York. Stood in the subway below Grand Central, rusting pipes overhead, signs every which way, grime underfoot, the smell of steam in our nostrils. We went to the Frick (Ingres! Goya!) Ate the best hamburgers *ever*. Took the Staten Island Ferry in the rain. The Statue of Liberty up close, from low down in the water, a colossus. Back at

Yale on Sunday morning, Bill Coffin delivered the Easter sermon. I was amazed. The chapel was so crowded people sat in the aisles and on the chancel steps. During his sermon, people cheered and clapped. At the end, there were too many people trying to speak to him for me to get close to him.

Three days later, back in my room in Davis, Wednesday, 9 April dawned, a perfect spring day. I was tied to my desk cramming for a history exam, when the phone rang in the hall. Vicki was on the line. Students had invaded University Hall, Harvard's main administrative building, and bundled seven deans out of the door. They secured the building with chains bolted to the doors from inside and were reported to be rifling confidential files.

Harvard?

Oh, Harvard! To think that wholesale violence had arrived? I thought my heart would break. That beautiful tree-shaded yard, with the tall elms over the pink brick paths, the super-rational, civilised bastion of academic excellence – to me, the quintessence of a university. America's symbol of higher learning?

Things had been cooking for a while. Rallies protested the reduction in financial aid to students who had been placed on probation for attending a sit-in. A Student-Faculty Advisory Council meeting to discuss the status of the Reserve Officers Training Corps (ROTC) at the university had been invaded. What was happening now sounded like a copycat action of Columbia the year before.

The night before, Students for Democratic Society (SDS) had met to discuss tactics for getting the authorities to accept a series of demands, chief among them to get rid of ROTC, which was seen to subvert the spirit of liberal education from campus. By its very existence, let alone awarding academic credit to those who enlisted, Harvard was complicit in the military/political/intellectual machine engineering an immoral war. After hours of argument, the meeting voted not to occupy any buildings. They'd resume again in the morning. They had just come together to continue the debate, when a break-away group headed out to take over University Hall.

'*ROTC must go! ROTC must go!*'

Four hundred and fifty people piled through the doors.

'The fight is now inside!' shouted one SDS leader.

'Out! Out! OUT!' others bellowed back.

Linda, intent on buying wine and cheese for her twenty-first birthday party on Saturday night, wandered into the Yard with the Ach on their way to the Co-op. As they strolled through, there was almost a carnival atmosphere. Thousands of students and faculty had gathered and were milling about, waiting for what would happen next. People handed out leaflets. Groups hung around chatting.

Before long pictures were released of students carrying deans out of the building, draping themselves over statues and lounging in chairs.

The students who took the building set up a control point at an entrance closest to the Widener Library on Harvard Yard. Outside, television cameras gathered. In the Yard, crowds watched and waited. The choppity-chop of rising tension, miserably waiting to see what would happen. Four hours later, the Dean of the Faculty of Arts and Sciences, faced the building with a bull-horn. The students had fifteen minutes to clear the building, or be subject to arrest for criminal trespass.

The deadline came and went.

Shadows lengthened. Friends crept into the building with supplies of food and blankets. Darkness fell. The television lights blazed. Still nothing happened.

Just before dawn four hundred police converged on the Yard.

At 4.45 am the mayor of Cambridge told the occupiers to get out of the building. At 5 the police moved in: dark-blue shirts, the municipal police, messy and brutal, beating students off the steps with clubs. The light-blues, the state police, followed them inside and hauled the students out. It took just thirty minutes for one hundred and ninety-six bloodied kids to be loaded into police vans and taken to jail.

Witnesses wandered about the Yard in a daze. Many were crying, weeping about such tragedy. Groundsmen moved in to clear up the mess.

It didn't matter that Wellesley was fifteen miles away. This was our territory. These were our friends and people we knew, beaten up and arrested. There wasn't anything else any of us could talk about. Within an hour of the police raid, a meeting was called in the Memorial Church in the Yard. Two thousand students and professors crammed into the pews.

As soon as my exam was over, I bussed into Cambridge to

find strike posters with huge red fists pasted up on the walls. In odd corners, T-shirts were being silk-screened. Red armbands handed out. A three-day strike was declared from the next day, Friday.

On Sunday evening I dropped by Howard's room to see how he was taking things. I knocked and waited. No reply. I tried again. I was just turning to leave when the door opened a crack. Howard poked his nose out of it. He was wearing a black beret and a black shirt. *Howard is a Black Panther?*

'Steph, you can't come in right now.'

'Is something a problem?'

Howard said nothing.

'Hey – Howard, what's up?'

'Look – Steph, I'm sorry. This is no place for you right now.' And he shut the door in my face.

I walked back down the stairs, eyes smarting. Howard was my friend. As soon as I glimpsed his black beret, I knew as a white woman I couldn't come in. But still I kept feeling, how could things ever change, if he and the others couldn't trust people like me?

On Monday afternoon, 15 April, I inched my way along with a vast crowd through the gates of Harvard's football stadium at Soldiers Fields. So many mimeographed leaflets were shoved into my hands I could hold no more. Resolution for a referendum from the undergraduate council, more from a committee for Radical Structural Reform. A copy of *Old Mole*, the Harvard Socialist newspaper's 'Strike Special'. 'Housing in Cambridge — Some Facts' told how local people were being squeezed out of affordable housing by the university.

The sky was blue and the sun shone warm. We squeezed along the rows of hard concrete seats. Marshals in blue, red and yellow jerseys directed people, cleared the aisles and tested microphones. Paper airplanes zipped over the crowd. Cheering students swept a long red banner across the field and then climbed high into the bleachers, swirling it overhead. Bull horns honked.

The meeting had been called by an ad-hoc coalition of moderates to agree follow-up action to the strike. The idea that you could pull thousands of people together to discuss something and try and get a consensus for action had never happened before. A lot of work had gone into preparing for the meeting, and the drafting of proposals to be debated. How should it be run? Who would moderate discussion? What order would issues be discussed? More than that, how could you bring together the radical wing of the SDS and those who wanted no change, and persuade them to accept some kind of baseline to go forward? Said one professor: 'What we need is an escalation in co-operation.'

It all went on for *hours*. Run on the basis of British parliamentary procedure, moderated by a teaching assistant called Lance Buhl, all statements were strictly time limited. Marshals directed speakers to the nearest microphone. Representatives from Afro were soon on their feet. Voices condemned the anarchy of SDS. SDS called for an amnesty for those who had been arrested. Community leaders from the city of Cambridge called for local people to be given a say in the university's real estate plans. At last, all the resolutions had been put. Voting, section by section of the stadium, was tightly controlled.

It was weird. But all this stuff got pulled together: terminate the university's contract with the Department of Defense to get

rid of ROTC, build more housing in Cambridge, elect a committee of students and faculty to agree on how to discipline the students who occupied University Hall. A consensus had been reached. All of a sudden, there was a realisation of the tremendous power of all these people who had pulled together. Hope, optimism, and the power of collective action. We were euphoric. My friends and I gathered together later, so excited we couldn't talk of anything else.

At that moment, we really did believe we could change the world.

The next day, I saw Howard. He was jubilant. Afro had got what they wanted at Harvard, that is to form a fully-fledged department of African-American Studies, giving out degrees, and a chair in Black Studies. 'Within five years, we should be turning out the first experts in African and African-American history!' Howard was so neat and understated; I'd never imagined he could change things so profoundly. It was wonderful.

Five days later, Harvard was still riding high on the triumph of having settled their issues so peacefully, when the front page of the *New York Times* led with pictures of armed Black students at Cornell. Over the weekend, one hundred Black students raided the student union, and occupied the building. During the night, rifles and shotguns were smuggled into the building. Thirty-six hours later, after eleven hours of negotiation with the administration, they walked out brandishing bandoliers of bullets and their weapons. The report chilled my blood. Beside this story ran a column: 'Campus Unrest in Brief'. So much was going on: sit-ins and riots at the best universities all over the country. No question: something big was happening in America.

But if *students* were going to start carrying guns, what hope did we have?

*

There had been rumours for a while. Just before spring break it had been confirmed: for the first-time in Wellesley's history, a handful of unmarried seniors would be able to live off campus from the following September. Linda and Vicki immediately applied and began making plans to find an apartment in Cambridge that some or all of us could share. Anne didn't think it was worth it: she planned to leave Wellesley the minute she had collected all her requirements for her degree. 'My father won't dream of letting me do it,' said Diana. And I knew I had no chance of joining them; the terms of my scholarship required me to live in a dormitory. We three put in for rooms again in Davis for the fall.

The boys we knew were finalising plans for after graduation. The Ach had been accepted to go to Tunisia with the Peace Corps, but might want to teach in the inner city instead. My friend Van had enrolled in Divinity School (an occupation that was exempt from the draft). Mike had enrolled to study law at Columbia in September but was pretty sure he'd be drafted in December. Howard was going to do an MA in history at Cambridge, in England. Bob still had one more year to go at Yale. As for the girls: talk of doing PhDs seemed to be the only meaningful thing around. I'd been invited to two weddings in June and was predicting three more after graduation in a year's time, when Vicki, Linda and Diana would walk down the aisle.

I had been sounding out Ottawa on securing a job with External Affairs. My first step: an interview with M. Duclos, deputy Canadian Consul in Boston. It was a beautiful day in early May. I remember wearing my favourite pink two-toned slingback kitten-heels. The offices of the Canadian Consulate were in downtown Boston, an area I did not know well. I was excited and feeling slightly sick: this was my first interview, for a job I really wanted. I walked through the revolving door of an unremarkable building and was shown into a dull brown room.

Louis Duclos was not yet thirty, with a long face and head of thick dark hair. He rose from his desk, reached out his hand with a smile. Stacks of metal shelves bundled with untidy heaps of books and files filled the walls behind him. I could not help feeling, as M. Duclos unfolded himself from behind his desk, that these offices were hardly those of a great nation. As he gestured in an off-hand way to a chair, I found myself wondering what the Canadian Consulate had to do in a town like Boston all day long. (Perhaps Duclos thought the same thing too, as within five years he had left External Affairs to become the Liberal MP for Montmorency in Quebec under Pierre Trudeau.)

'So, you want to join External Affairs,' Duclos leant back in his chair and cast his eyes over his fingernails. 'What gave you that idea?'

I said something bright about having been brought up to a life of travel, father in army, wanting to work abroad, interest in foreign affairs.

'You think you'd be any good at it?'

Well, there were my languages: French and some Spanish; my history: I'd already lived in several countries – Germany, Britain and the US. I told him I was curious. I liked to find out about what made places tick. I liked to listen to people, to hear what they really have to say.

'Let me tell you something,' he said. 'The foreign service is no place for a woman. They don't make any allowances. Your first assignment – they'll send you off to some place like the capital of Bolivia, say, or Bogotá. And you'll be living in a one-bedroom apartment all on your own. And you won't be able to go out by yourself. You will always have to have a security officer with you.'

I told him that if a place was that dangerous for me as a single woman, then it must be pretty dangerous for men too and that maybe Ottawa might think twice about where they sent me on a first assignment. I was halfway through my argument when I could see he wasn't listening.

'They won't do a thing like that,' he said. 'Everyone is treated just the same. You have to put up with the assignment you're given.'

'I can do that.'

'This is no job for a woman,' he repeated. 'I'd advise you to think again.'

'Surely you want women in External Affairs?'

He made no answer.

'The letter I had from Ottawa said to come and see you, and then take the civil service exams. I can still go and do that.'

'Sure,' he said. 'You can still do that.' Duclos eased himself out of his chair and stood up from his desk. He held out a long hand.

'I wish you luck, Miss Williams. In some other career.'

Stupid man, I railed as I stomped back to the college. What does he know? How are women to get anywhere if they are never given a chance? I was due to write the Canadian civil-service exams, held once a year, in Washington DC in November. I would sit them, and I'd show them. And they would take me on.

*

Bob invited me to 'College Weekend' at Yale. This had been established to provide one last orgy before reading period and exams. It featured a Friday evening toga party at which there was to be dancing with a rock band and an exotic dancer (two shows and free lessons). This was to be followed at 11am Saturday with the 'Tang Cup' – a beer swigging contest. Moving on through the day, there would be an expedition to Holiday Hill, with two hundred acres of land, huts, grass, etc, for a barbecue, swimming, sports and rowing. In the evening there would be a beach bake, followed by another dance with a light show. All activities that by now were beginning to seem distinctly outmoded.

Especially given the opportunity that same weekend to attend the New England regional female liberation conference, which was to be held at nearby Emmanuel, a Catholic girls' college. Karate demonstrations, workshops of all sorts: sex, music, the workings of women's bodies (for our ignorance was still almost total) advertising and the media as oppressors of females, and the family as the basic unit of female oppression. There were nods to the concerns of Black women 'in a caste society', and interracial marriage. In short, it would be all about how to be liberated 'in an unliberated society'.

But true to form, I'd rather have fun instead.

While I spent my last weekend of the term partying at Yale, Anne went to see Chi at Princeton. 'REALLY GOOD – volleyball, Frisbee, running around, reading, TV, very relaxing.' She sounded so happy. Finally, it seemed, they'd got everything resolved. At the same time, she penned a short story: a sharp vignette of a woman who once talked revolution 'and things' with her professors, now trapped in a perfect suburban marriage with two darling children, aching for a meaning 'greater than frozen foods, possessing the latest consumer gadgets, and an identity not limited to 57 varieties'.

14

Summer of '69

Anne – I wrote, on Saturday, June 14 – *what did you mean by Hillary's 'coup' at graduation? I left the sacred U.S. of A. Sunday morning and saw no papers so heard no news. Is Wellesley famous?*

Well, yes.

Hillary had been nominated unopposed by her Class of '69 to be the first student in the history of the college to address commencement ceremonies, following the main speaker of the day, Massachusetts's Senator Edward Brooke. All the undergraduates had left for the summer vacation by this time, so neither I nor any of my friends was there. But you couldn't miss it.

In his speech, Brooke, America's first Black senator, suggested that students who protested about political issues were an elite set of ne'er-do-wells. Under a marquee on the spreading lawns in sight of the lake, Hillary abandoned her prepared script to take Brooke to task and defend the constitutional right to protest.

'Part of the problem with empathy … is that empathy doesn't do us anything,' she said. 'We've had lots of empathy, we've had lots of sympathy, but we feel that for too long our leaders have viewed politics as the art of the possible. The challenge now is to practice politics as the art of making what appears to be impossible, possible.'

Hillary's remarks did not just make the front page of the *Boston Globe,* but the *Chicago Daily News* and *Life* magazine, and have reverberated through her history ever since.

I'd heard Hillary speak many times. Often, I didn't agree with her. But, there was no question she was dynamic. 'We arrived not knowing what was possible, consequently, we expected a lot. We arrived and found there was a gap between expectation and reality. It inspired us to change.' She got things done, and for lots of us, she showed us how to do it. For the past three years we'd got into the habit of dreaming that things could get better, that by pointing out the errors of its ways, the world could change for the better, that life would improve.

And, thanks to our demands, the college curriculum and its domestic issues were being addressed. No doubt because the women in charge of the college, like the young women they presided over, were trying to do their best. They were uncomfortable hearing grievance and felt in fairness they should listen to both sides. The challenge was to chart some kind of middle way between the wealth and power of trustees and alumnae, whose donations were essential for the ongoing financial stability of the college and who wanted life for girls and women at the college to go as it always had done, and the demands of students for recognition of their right to take responsibility for themselves and drag the college into the late twentieth century.

But none of the men in charge of the nation, not one of those who oversaw the draft or the conduct of the Vietnam war, had shown an ounce of sympathy, much less a willingness to change the course on which they had embarked.

✱

All of us were scattered far and wide that summer. Linda was back in San Antonio, feeling 'nice and alienated'. She was to go to summer school at the University of Texas at Austin, where she would share an apartment with an old friend from school.

Diana's whereabouts are lost in time but would have involved the Upper East Side, Europe and as much time as possible with Douglas. Vicki and Phil had planned to work in New York, but out at Phil's parents' place in the countryside, they stood on the lawn gazing up at the stars overhead. How could they *even think* of spending the summer in New York?

Especially when it turned out that a guy called Dave was

advertising in the *Harvard Crimson* for passengers to share the driving across the country to San Francisco. Dave was going by way of Texas, and if Vicki and Phil could fly stand-by down to meet him in Dallas, they'd be all set.

In Washington DC, Anne started work as an intern in Edith's Green's office. She was 'largely surviving', trying to keep her mouth shut, finding it was impossible to be there '& not absorb & learn TONS.' It was such an exciting place to be. She had had little contact with Edith Green so far, but reported her Legislative Assistant was a fine man, 'very sensitive to the complexities of the campus scene, unlike most others on the Hill.'

'Congress,' she reported, 'was mad and is still mad at students.' Sixty-two bills had been introduced during the session to prevent riots on campus. These 'ranged from clear cut repression to moderate toothless proposals. The pleas of university presidents for the Federal govt to stay out of university affairs fell on many deaf ears, with the very existence of real aid to education at stake.'

At first Anne was asked to do nothing but type. One day she asked if there was anything else 'they needed help on'. She was lucky. Things rapidly improved. She was writing for Edith Green's newsletter – not about students, but about cigarettes, pay-TV and local issues. She started answering constituency mail, and doing more research.

In London, after a fruitless attempt at job-hunting elsewhere, I returned to working in my father's office for the Canadian Defence Staff in Grosvenor Square. I was doing lots of typing, drinking too much coffee and booking military families moving across Europe into hotel accommodation. At the end of June,

Bob arrived in England to do an archaeology course at Oxford for the summer, but before that we took ten days to go youth-hostelling in Scotland. All things considered – I struggled to maintain my temper when Bob's dry wit strayed into conde-scension – and hitchhiking in the drizzle in the empty Highlands proved a damp and tedious task, while climbing Ben Nevis in sneakers was perhaps not the best idea. But we were happy gorg-ing on Scottish history in Edinburgh and Stirling, and the Heb-rides were magical. I fell for Skye. Eerie, weird, and enchanting. The population was then about 2,000 and the whole place died on Sunday. We climbed cliffs and walked on the moors. It was so wild, its hills changing colour with the light, it made me feel like a Daphne de Maurier character. Bob and I parted in Glas-gow, slightly amazed that we had survived ten days together, while he went on to Carlisle to walk Hadrian's Wall.

*

Life in Austin was not turning out to be what Linda had hoped. The apartment was squalid. The drug scene was heavy. Not just pot and hash, but 'orange acid', mescaline, LSD, and something called PCP, an anaesthetic. Then she wrote, appalled. Her room-mate, an old friend from high school, had been raped four days before. She was walking home from her job as a waitress about 10pm, some guys came by in a car and offered her a lift. It was the kind of thing that happened all the time in a college town, where the boys looked like they were at college too and seemed safe enough. They were only five blocks from the apartment, on a relatively busy street. She climbed in. They dragged her off into bushes by the side of the road and, one after the other, raped her.

The weird thing was she didn't even think to get redress. After all, who would the men in the police force believe? *Three* boys versus *one* girl?

Linda couldn't get over it. She would never walk alone at night in peace again.

*

From me to Anne:

20 July 69

Now I am typing — guess what? Defence Research catalogues — top secret or highly confidential. Do you know what they mainly consist of? Descriptions & studies of such varied things as inflatable life rafts, various & sundry types of vacuum cleaners, tin openers, paper clips and gun carriage covers, not to mention the chemical formulas for making artificial tea. I figure I am totally sold out.

I felt like a curiosity, this strange Canadian girl in London, reputedly clever, reporting back from a foreign front in America to an uncomprehending nation. We agreed on Vietnam. We agreed on police brutality. And these particular military men in my father's office didn't like violence. They believed in war as a last resort – when all other means of reaching agreement had failed. There was little sympathy for the American conduct of the war, and none at all for the violence of their police. No one, not one of my English friends or their parents, could understand American student unrest, either.

'To people here it all seems so nonsensical,' I told Anne. In

Britain the idea of a military draft was nothing new. Memory of National Service, which ended in 1963, was still very much alive. Even if they regarded the war in Vietnam as a disaster, and felt that no person in their right mind would want to fight there, I was unable to convey to them what made us all so angry, in a way that they could understand. They were baffled by the obtuse, uncompromising attitude of both the government and the students.

'Well, of course,' they concluded, 'Americans have been brought up with violence. I guess they can see no other way of handling problems, of getting their own way. They're like spoilt children.'

Up in Scotland many who Bob and I met were shocked at the violence of the police. They wanted to know about the 'Black problem'.

'They sort of felt,' I wrote to Anne, 'the States is in a state of total anarchy, but they didn't really know why. Except that people "can all carry guns, can't they?"'

*

My English friends were heading off to the continent for a month or two in Berlin, Bologna, or Aix-en-Provence, using their university grants to live off. I spent a weekend visiting my grandparents in Oxford and seeing Bob. We went pub-crawling and punting on the Cherwell, and I wondered, dreamily, what going to Oxford, with all its green college quads would be like. All that summer, I felt myself becoming more in tune with Britain than ever before.

In London, I squashed up with my family to watch the live

coverage coming in from NASA. The coverage was all in black and white. Slow moving, grainy – it took hours. But we couldn't stop watching. We were amazed by what we were seeing: the inside of the NASA control room, the space suits, the rocket, the launch. Finally, the huge moment. I watched, my heart in my mouth, as the space capsule touched

down safely. Then waited and waited some more before Neil Armstrong at last climbed down from the space capsule to set foot on the stony surface of the moon – the first man ever to do so.

Bob wrote from Oxford, where he'd watched David Frost present the whole affair on ITV. His account of the British coverage was scathing. He conceded the British were generous with their praise, but Frost kept coming back to how much it had all cost. Then he made the mistake of referring to the poverty of America's inner cities. Now Bob went on to attack the dirt and poverty of much of Britain's old housing. 'I don't really feel the housing for the lower middle class here is that much better than the housing in our big city ghettoes.' I knew we were never going to see eye to eye.

In Texas, the Ach had been to visit. Linda wrote she was cooling on that front, moving into a Platonic mode. 'We get along well, and will see each other in the fall, ... but I guess I get classified as a free spirit.' More than once she had asked for Bob's address and wondered what he was up to. I knew she was keen to see him. I let her know that I thought he and I were in trouble. But I was sad that her relationship with Mike's old roommate was coming to an end.

'*Are you completely finished?*' I wrote back. '*I wish I didn't adore the Ach so. It's funny, but some days I just expect him to come towards me, waltzing down New Bond Street, dressed in frayed bell-bottomed trousers and sandals, and navy turtleneck jersey, and hair standing out all over his head in the bright sunshine at noon.*' I went on tell her, in slightly lunatic phrases, how my feelings for Bob '*descend & descend... The climax may never come — next Saturday may kill us.*'

For me, it was a summer of mindless inertia, feeling suspended between the realities of past and the future. My father was retiring in the autumn. He and Mother had decided to stay in England and were house hunting in the English countryside. I could see that Mother was living a much richer life in London than she had in so many places where we had lived in Canada, meeting women of her generation who had held serious roles during the war, or were designers and writers. She was doing things she really enjoyed: the theatre, the opera and the ballet. Even so, I wasn't sure I liked the idea. I couldn't understand why they didn't regard Canada as home, why they couldn't go and settle somewhere beautiful, like ...Victoria or Calgary or the Maritimes or ... ? But after a lifetime of moving around the world, where, exactly, could they be happy?

At the end of August Bob came up to London for our last date of the summer. We went to see *Hair*, the hit show described by the papers as the 'American love-rock musical'. Lots of naked bodies, bed, sex (all sorts) and – long beautiful hair. 'Shining, gleaming, streaming, flaxen, waxen ... shoulder length or longer.' Make love, not war: a celebration of freedom and the hippy life in general. The problem was, here was this guy offering up his girlfriend for the night to someone who was just off to Vietnam, while she stood demurely by, happy to do her boyfriend's will. The tone was horribly reminiscent of running the gauntlet of baying males at a mixer at Dartmouth. I emerged with Bob onto Soho's crowded pavements, baking in late night diesel fumes with an unpleasant taste in my mouth.

And I wondered: do the women on the stage feel exploited as tools and playthings? Probably not.

✷

Early in September I flew back to Canada. I'd promised to see Rob, an old friend who had kept up with me in the time I'd been away. Rob had always been quiet: tall and gentle, unadventurous. His university career at Western, in London, Ontario had been a disaster. He'd spent most of his time selling dope and failed his degree. 'I tried hard in the last month to get things together, but it was too late for assignments,' he told me. Now he had to be in summer school at Queen's and was living back home in Kingston with his parents.

I climbed down from the bus in Kingston: full of curiosity to be back in the town I'd known so well. It was late afternoon, warm, the maples across the street, still in leaf. The vacant parking lot in front of the bus station looked just the same, the depot was still not much more than a shed. It was quiet, no one much about. Nothing looked any different. It felt slightly surreal, as if a lifetime had passed since I last stood on this spot on the day I climbed up into a Greyhound to go away to Wellesley and waved good-bye to my family.

Disappointingly, but not surprising, Rob was late to pick me up. Standing by the curb with my bags, I noticed a slight, pretty girl with long dark hair and freckles. I knew her, I knew she had been one of the most popular girls in my high-school class, the year I before I was sent away to the convent.

'Hi, Stephanie.' Her greeting was mild, uncurious, as if she'd only seen me that morning. 'How are you?'

I looked at the thick fringe of her eyelashes, into her warm, brown eyes. Of course – 'Suzanne!'

'You getting the number 69?' The bus that used to serve my route from town, out to old Fort Henry.

'Not today. Waiting for Rob to come and get me.'

'Oh.'

She nodded at my bags. 'You been away?'

'Yeah.'

'Toronto?'

'No, the States.'

'Oh. Was it nice there?'

'It's okay. What are you doing these days, Suzanne?'

'Nursing.'

'You training?'

'No, got my RN last year. I'm working at the hospital.'

Rob had finished summer school. He'd got a job with a construction company managing three buildings going up in town and was living with his parents until he went back to Western in a year's time to finish his degree. His father, retired from the army, was working for the vice principal at Queen's University. Their house was in a new sub-division surrounded by big trees that backed onto Lake Ontario. His father played golf at week-ends; there were neighbourhood barbecues. It struck me that the place had become a retired army officer's paradise. So many of them now worked at Queen's. And I knew it would not suit my father.

Rob drove me out to see the house where I used to live – the standard military issue three-bedroom at Fort Henry Heights, the army base on the outskirts of town. It sat high above the St Law-rence River, commanding the point where it flowed out from Lake Ontario. Over the road was old Fort Henry, Kingston's major tourist attraction, begun during the War of 1812. We went to take a tour and say 'hi' to several friends from high school. They had been working there as guides all summer, and were dressed up as British Red Coats. Now they were about to enter their final year at Queen's. That evening we went out for a beer, sat around in a bar with pine-panelled walls and a big pool table.

It was all so familiar. It was all so strange. No one asked me where I had been or what I had been doing. My old high school had a new storey on top of it. Kingston had expanded beyond the city limits. Everyone assumed that now I was back with them, our lives would go on as they always had. Their future – managing the local sports shops, teaching in the high-school, running a car dealership, getting married to someone from their class, living in the suburbs – was all laid out as I had imagined it would be when I decided I must leave. I felt as if I had stepped back in time, as if I had never been away. Or maybe, all this time at Wellesley, I had been enchanted, in a deep, at times, disturbing sleep?

15

Widening horizons

Linda and Vicki picked me up among the lines of taxis waiting at Logan on a hot day of blue skies and blazing sun at the end of summer.

'Look who's here!' Vicki reached out and hugged me close. She looked in good shape, her dark hair long and heavy, her brown eyes with their thick lashes clear and bright. We piled my cases into Linda's car – a 'new' second-hand Opel – and I climbed into the back seat.

'Just gotta tell you – I've been on the most amazing diet,' Linda turned to look at me, her eyes crinkled with mirth. 'You have to eat lean meat, fish, eggs, cottage cheese – that is, solid protein – and drink eight glasses of water a day, plus tea, coffee, diet drinks, etc – and you're supposed to lose 5% of your weight the first week.'

'And did you?'

She drew herself up tall. 'Can't you tell?' We collapsed into laughter.

There was too much to say. The Ach had gone part-way to the Woodstock Festival but gave up when the traffic just became too much. 'Half a million people turned up for a festival billed for 100,000. It was insane.'

'How is he?'

'We're easy,' said Linda. 'We're both going to see other people.'

'And you're going to see Bob.'

'That's right.' She eyed me in the mirror.

I smiled back. 'I wrote him on the plane. It's over.'

'And how was your summer?' I said to Vicki. 'Can't say I heard too much from you.'

'Aw, you know I'm no good at writing.' Vicki threw her head back and laughed. 'But it was great. Things went really well with Phil.' Like Linda she was excited about the fall. She had designed an autumn with courses at MIT, centred on one on landscape architecture, and planned to go out to Wellesley as little as possible – for a seminar in sociology and, possibly, a course to meet the science requirements for her degree.

We were driving the scenic route from the airport to Cambridge, along Storrow Drive by the banks of the Charles River. The sun shone and the water gleamed blue. I could see the brick and domes of Harvard's buildings in the distance. My throat tightened. Mike. Again. I am walking with him through the Yard, wrapped in his Harvard scarf, his arm around my shoulders.

'What about you, Steph?'

I thought about how I was going to be living in Davis out at the college, working nights in the language lab. Putting in the hours in the library, carrying on as if nothing had changed, while Vicki and Linda would be free to live as they chose in Cambridge. 'I just can't wait to get finished. All I want is to be free. Free to go anywhere, do anything. No time limits. No ties.'

'Uh huh,' said Vicki.

Their new apartment was on the second floor of a rambling timber block on Chatham Street, ten minutes' walk from Harvard Yard. The hall ran from the front to the back of the house, bedrooms on the right, living room near the back. It wasn't large, furnished with one or two forgettable chairs and a shabby velvet sofa of indeterminate hue. Linda had hung some coconut prints made by her mother on the walls. The sofa had a great high back and sagged in the middle. Vicki had already permitted a mean black cat to stray into the apartment: 'one of those cats that if you pick him up and he doesn't want to be picked up, scratches the hell out of you,' she warned. 'He takes shelter down between the cushions of the sofa. And if you made the mistake of sitting on him – he'll go batshit.'

At the end of the hall, overlooking a back porch of sorts with a fire escape going down to a yard, was the kitchen – the centre of life in the house.

For the next couple of days, I wandered about in shorts and sandals, helping them scrub and paint. Such a lot of Dylan on the record player while Phil wandered in and out, handsome and languid in bare feet, his fair hair now down to his shoulders. He never said much to me. Then Anne's good friend Charlie, who had moved in around the corner, dropped by. Over the summer his fuzzy hair had grown into a wild Jimi Hendrix halo. Charlie always made me crease up with laughter. Like Puck, he would perch on the edge of the kitchen table, swinging his legs and scoffing bananas. 'Woe is me,' he would wail before launching into a crazy account of his latest disaster.

Late the second morning, Mike walked in. He had come to bequeath Vicki and Linda his whisky glasses before driving down to New York to start law school at Columbia. He'd spent part of the summer in Canada. He loved it, he told me.

He knew how much I had longed to show it to him.

That so? I said.

*

I arrived out at the college as Anne came in from putting *News* to bed. She and I had succeeded Hillary in the best suite at Davis: two rooms and a bathroom *all to ourselves*. The main room was enormous, lined with bookshelves that ran under the eaves, and a window overlooking the lake. She set up her bed near the window and put a stack of Aretha and James Brown on the record player. I opted for the smaller bedroom, away from the action. We piled our books for the new term onto the shelves. For me, volumes on early Italian humanism, the education of Tudor women and books for a course on the Modern Novel: Austen, James, Conrad, Norman Mailer and *Women in Love*. For Anne, Black history: WEB Dubois, Floyd Barbour's *The Black Power Revolt*, the *Autobiography of Malcolm X* , and *The Making of Black America*, only just published.

At the end of the summer, Anne had said good-bye to Chi. It was one of those quirks of the way our social lives worked, that I had never met him. I told her I had put an end to things with Bob. We agreed we were no longer interested in playing the dating game. New conquests, if required, would be made off the pitch.

We had nine months before we graduated. Then it would be all over.

*

Across the hall Diana's new room had a range of Gothic windows overlooking the front drive. The floor was the usual chaos of clothes and bags, books and an open suitcase. She cleared a heap from an armchair.

'Sit,' she said, and passed me a cigarette. Kool, a green pack, menthol flavour.

'These are new.'

'Uh, huh.' She took her time taking her own from the pack. Her fingers on the cigarette were shaky, the skin on the back of her hand with its light freckles almost transparent. She lit it, inhaled deeply. After a moment the smoke that curled from her mouth was blue in the light. She followed the cloud with her eyes, then looked away into space.

'What's up?' I said.

She looked unnervingly pale for someone who had just returned from a summer vacation.

'Oh, the usual.'

'You mean Douglas?'

She nodded. 'What can I do? I am in *agony*.'

It was my turn to inhale. I'd heard this sort of thing so many times before. Diana, the mistress of neurosis. It was like a disease that was catching. She encouraged detailed dissection of every feeling. But I hadn't realized that after the summer she would still be so fragile. As she had been all the previous year. The depression – and her recurring bouts with blood clots in her legs. She knew she shouldn't take the pill. But still she insisted on doing so. I settled back in my chair. 'What's happened?'

'Oh, you know. It's his mother! Didn't you realize – she won't let up on him for a moment. She's always getting at him. Douglas this, and Douglas, that. He's always having to do what she wants. And he does it!' Diana paused to take another drag. 'The other day she called him up and told him he just had to go over right away and take her out to lunch, just when we were going to go out to Marble Head.'

'Oh, poor Douglas.'

'I know. He hates it. It's her way of getting at me. You know she doesn't like me. It's even worse because he's Jewish. His parents are doing everything to stop us getting married.'

'They can't. Not in this day and age.'

'Oh, but they can.' She inhaled. 'Anyway. You know what happened last night? Simon called.'

Simon was not a good thing. He dominated her time in high school. Haunted her even now. Every time Diana seemed to reach some level of equilibrium he turned up and took her out. Whatever happened when they were together, she was in a state of nerves for days.

'He's coming out later to see me.'

'Diana—'

'I don't know what I feel.'

'Diana, you do. You *know* you love Douglas. You know he loves you.'

'I just wish it was that simple.'

✳

The first edition of *News* was out. Lead story: 57 Black girls were among Wellesley's incoming freshman class, thanks to the recruiting efforts of dozens of students. This was for its time, a respectable percentage. Plus, Tom Atkins, Boston's first Black City Councillor, was to join the political science faculty. The Boston Draft Resistance Group was now entering its third year of operations. It had a new coffeehouse and a counselling centre and expected to advise as many as 50 men a week. Hillary's speech from Commencement was printed in full, plus a piece by Anne on what eighteen interns had learnt over the summer on Capitol Hill: in short, why things happen in Washington as they do, and why other things never get done.

It wasn't long before I realized I was living with a minor celebrity. *Newsweek*, newspapers and television companies, people on the Hill, contacts at Harvard and MIT – the phone rang constantly for Anne. People dropped by all the time. Everyone wanted to know what women on campus were thinking.

I would come back from a seminar to find our rooms full of people. Girls in jeans and sweatshirts curled up on our baggy armchairs or lounged on the floor, drinking tea and talking issues. The college had set up a commission on its future.

Like, what I mean is, how can the college survive if it doesn't go co-ed?

Yeah. Now that Yale and Princeton and Harvard have started taking all the good women, how can this place hope to maintain its academic standards?

You're right. As it is, all anyone cares about is their Saturday night date and getting a new dress.

You really think what we need here are a few men to keep things cooking?

Actually, I do.

So how would you do it?

More or less immediately. Announce that we will accept five hundred men including freshmen and transfers from September 1970.

You think men will want to come?

Just took at Vassar.

That's what I mean. They'll all be second-rate.

We decided to form a committee to make the college go co-ed immediately – to accept 500 men, freshmen and transfers, in the following September. The first step was to survey opinion at the college to find out what everyone really thought.

And then there was Women's Lib.

At the end of September, fifty women announced the setting up of Bread and Roses, a revolutionary socialist women's group. The name came from a song taken up by striking women from a textile factory in Lawrence, Massachusetts in 1912. It was to meet on Monday evenings in Cambridge.

White, middle-class, college-educated – they were older than us, in their twenties. Some had kids. Its roots were in SDS and the radical political movement against the war. All that sign painting and silk-screening of posters calling for strikes, making phone calls, and typing lists to aid the Resist movement by women; all the big calls on organisation and strategy decided by men. All the polite expectations of how girls and women should behave pertained: be too ambitious and it looked like ball-busting. Shouty speaking sounded bitchy. Put down or ignored, girls turned to flirtation, and thus into girlfriends – who took the minutes and did the typing. Now they were refusing to be treated as objects to be possessed.

Bread and Roses didn't just want equal rights. They wanted *liberation*. Freedom from all forms of male oppression. Besides the Black Panthers at home, they supported liberation struggles around the world.

All that door-knocking and leafletting on the campaign trail for Eugene McCarthy: I had been too much of a novice in American politics to do other than trail in Mike's slipstream. It had never occurred to me to resent merely being handed a piece to write up for a circular. I was just too glad to help.

I thought Bread and Roses sounded too radical for me. But Anne was keen to go. She set off in Volksie, crammed with four more women. The sun was still high, the evening light and warm, when somewhere on Route 128 she felt the steering wheel begin to pull.

'Ladies, we have a problem.' She changed lanes, slowed to the edge of the highway, stopped and got out to see what was going on. One of the back tyres was flat.

'Just our luck,' Anne fumed.

The girls piled out and stared at the wheel. No one had a clue how to change it. So, it was indeed fortunate that before long, a young man saw their plight, stopped and, in less than ten minutes, had changed the tyre.

Anne drove on to the meeting in silence.

A week or two later, the first meeting of Women's Liberation was held on the campus. Bread and Roses came out to talk. I wondered what I'd make of it, and if the college, so full of women, was ready for this. I noted the atmosphere: hesitant, locked up. Fearful? People were smart and they knew it. The questions came.

What's the problem?

Do we need this?

Look, we're free. We have the vote. We can work.

Yes, came the reply. As receptionists, secretaries, schoolteachers. And we work for a lot less than men. We don't get lots of jobs because we're not men. Look: we're half the population but hold less than 1% of elected offices.

Of course, men earn more, came back the reply. They have to, in order to support you and your family. And why do you say men *ought* to change diapers?

Have you ever heard of a husband putting his wife through grad school?'

Surely that's asking too much.

There were calls for the college to set up a day-care centre for children and provide birth control information and contraceptives to any girl who asked for them. That's good, I thought. But this idea was in turn disputed. The possibility of setting up a study group about woman's place in society was mooted.

It was all so earnest. So tentative. As if everything had to be analysed, disputed, bureaucratised, when all I wanted to do was to seize the reins of power and take them into our own hands.

But maybe they were right.

What I didn't realize then was how new Bread and Roses was – with no hierarchy, no group image, it was nothing more than a group of 'collectives' each with about ten members. On that evening a small group of 'silent radicals' formed at the college: they would meet again in one week's time.

＊

For me, above all else, there was the fight to end the war in Vietnam. Every morning the headlines delivered more bad news. The men I knew drew closer to being drafted to join the crazed and hopeless nightmare. I could no longer bear to watch the television news. The crump of bombs, the walls of flame cascading over grassy villages. Swathes of jungle charred and blackened into stumps and heaps of pale ash. Wailing half-clothed children fled barefoot. Crouching mothers shielded their babies. Clattering choppers hoisted stretcher-loads of bloodied soldiers.

The pain and horror just kept on coming. I felt like a patient being tortured by a dentist with his drill. This was no way to wage any kind of war, let alone on peasants subsisting on rice paddies, of whom America knew nothing. It was morally indefensible, and I felt culpable.

By now, too many 'victories' in Vietnam had turned out to be empty. Too many American boys had been killed or wounded. Public opinion was swinging against it. Rumour had it that Nixon had started to think up feasible ways to withdraw the troops. A glimmer of hope that peace might be on the way? Tricky Dicky might end the war? No one trusted him.

Over the summer in Washington, Anne had met some 'movement' people – activists who had worked on the Eugene McCarthy campaign and who wanted to give the movement to stop the war a respectable face. Using their contacts at colleges and universities, civil rights organisations and churches, they were planning a series of strikes and demonstrations that would bring the country to a standstill. The first 'Vietnam Moratorium' would be a vast co-ordinated nation-wide demonstration on 15th October.

'Look,' she said. 'We do an icebreaker for one day on 15th October. Then two days in November, three days in December and so on. If we can just get enough people onto the streets to protest, we're going to convince the President the war *just has to stop.*'

Watch out for news of Chicago Oct 8 – 11, I wrote home. My family were in the throes of moving out of London to an ancient timber-beamed house in the Surrey countryside. *The place is going to blow sky high when the 'Chicago Eight' have hearings then. They were members of the New Left (McCarthy people etc) and Black Panthers who were arrested at the Democratic Convention last year. SDS, that is the more radical wing of it, has decided that the time for the revolution, full scale, blood and gore et al. And I am afraid they mean business —*

It was clear by now that the 'movement' was out of control. As if seeking revenge for the violence of 1968's Democratic Convention, the Weatherman faction of SDS – very pure, utopian, apocalyptic, and totally reckless – launched its National Actions, the 'Days of Rage'. Wielding clubs and pipes they raced through Chicago's wealthy near North Side, smashing into police cordons, windows, cars and windows. The National Guard arrived. Six people were shot and wounded, dozens of police and demonstrators injured, and two hundred and fifty arrested.

I wept for the bloodshed and the violence. The Weathermen were thrilled with their audacity. The student movement, they said, was too small to remake America root and branch, to fight for the Blacks, the working class and the Vietnamese people.

They put out a call for an 'anti-pig self-defence units' modelled on the way Chinese revolutionaries mobilised the peasantry and set to work. 'Long live the people's war!'

Fear heightened the atmosphere as I gathered with friends to march for the first Moratorium on 15 October.

Could our plans for peaceful protest hold?

*

It was a perfect autumn morning. Dew on the grass, sun glittering on the lawns, the lake pure ultramarine blue. The leaves on the trees were turning scarlet and gold. From the newspaper we learnt that all over the country huge rallies and marches were to be held: Washington, New York, Chicago, Los Angeles, and on campuses across the country: Oklahoma, Virginia, Arizona State.

I joined the march from Harvard Square to Boston Common, big Peace button on my lapel. Around me were medics in white coats, high school students with Peace signs, and men carrying the Stars and Stripes. Others raised Vietcong flags. By the time we got to the Common it was massed with thousands of people. There were all sorts: businessmen in suits, ladies in hats, toddlers in strollers and thousands of students. People laughed and smiled, savouring the camaraderie and the sense that everyone knew why they were there. Measured chants of 'PEACE NOW' chimed with church bells tolling for the war dead. 'Woodstock was Beautiful But Only Temporary,' read one banner.

At Copley Square in front of the Boston Public Library, Linda handed out leaflets. She got called 'sweetie' by all the truck drivers going by, who took a leaflet if they were stopped by the light.

She 'ma'am'-ed and 'sir'-ed like mad, so the middle-aged and little old ladies didn't have much choice but to take her hand-outs.

'Stay out of American politics,' my parents wrote.

'Face it, the war must be ended, and if I can help in any way I will,' I told them. I was vaguely aware that if I was arrested it might be embarrassing for my father, still on the Canadian Defence Staff in London. 'I am only marching in the streets, not really involved.'

American politics might not be my business, but how a nation conducted a war on the international stage was.

*

The pull of the future intensified. The time was coming when we had to grow up, to enter the world. Anne handed me a piece from the *New York Times* on salaries. They didn't break the numbers down by male and female. We didn't know yet how far women were discriminated against. What she learnt was that there weren't many history professors, and they didn't get paid much. Lawyers did. She was going to have to support herself. Law school it was.

Scholarships for women to go to graduate school were vir-tually unheard of and I didn't have the money to go on with studies in history. To pursue my goal of getting into External Affairs I registered for Canada's Civil Service exam which I learned I must sit at the Canadian embassy in Washington DC. The job market was tight in Canada, and there was a freeze on hiring in the government. I decided not to think about the fact that the exam was scheduled for 15th November, the same day as the next march for the Vietnam Moratorium.

To be honest, I was petrified of leaving the Boston area. With all that was going on, it felt like the centre of the universe. And I didn't want to go and live in England. I really didn't want to live the working girl's life I'd seen in London – basically, typing, maybe, if you were lucky, in publishing; sharing a flat with other girls for the week, and weekends in the country. Lots of fashion, art and theatre might be great – but for LIFE? The careers office pointed out a teaching post at Chung Chi College at the Chinese University in Hong Kong. The idea of China where my mother first grew up intrigued me. The job sounded possible but scary. I decided to apply.

Now that Vicki and Linda were living off campus in Chatham Street, our social circle expanded. Vicki had policy of inviting anyone at a loose end for dinner. A new guy called Foss, a deeply committed conscientious objector, had taken to hanging around the apartment. In place of serving in the army, he was required to teach school. At the same time, he was trying to keep up with his third year of a PhD in physics. Foss had intense blue eyes, a thick shock of fair hair, a pale beard and a habit of studiously analysing everything and everyone with punishing intensity, from *Steppenwolf* to ee cummings, or whatever his current enthusiasm. He latched first onto me, and a couple of months later, Anne. His rigorous examination of *every detail* proved increasingly exhausting the more you knew him.

Meanwhile, Anne introduced, Joseph, who she'd met in DC through the League of Women Voters. He had just arrived at Harvard as a Junior Fellow. He was Black, good-looking, pipe-smoking, and full of charismatic talk about the power of students to make change. Anne thought he was close to being a genius.

Vicki prepped at the kitchen table. Her trademark dishes stretched to feed indeterminate numbers: spaghetti, lasagne, zucchini, tomatoes and brown rice. One night she was cooking Chinese, hot and sour soup and a huge stir-fry. I sat by the table and watched pans steaming as she gave the kitchen floor a quick clean, walking around on damp towels and shoving them in various directions.

Also present was someone called Stanislas, another apparent genius with a challenging personality. Stanislas was not tall, a little plump, with brown eyes so dark they were almost black. He had charm, was obviously clever, and rather too eager to reveal that his uncle was Vladimir Horowitz, the world-famous pianist. Stanislas talked and talked. Before long, he had drawn me into conversation about Russia and our families.

Like my mother's mother, Stanislas's family had fled Russia – from Leningrad as the Germans set up a blockade to besiege the city in 1941. His father, a Russian Jew, had been involved in the revolution with Trotsky. From Finland they travelled through war-torn Europe to Paris, finally landing in the US in 1948.

'Stash', as he liked to be known, did not hold back on the marvels of his history. Educated by his mother and father, he went to Columbia at 14, graduated in music at 18. Then to Belgium for a couple of years, back to the US to Harvard in medicine for three years, then to Mexico for a couple of years to help run a cattle ranch, time in the Yucatan, living with Mayan Indians. Who knew if any of it were true? He had spent last year doing cancer research, pioneering a breakthrough in leukaemia.

Every claim was more and more wonderful. Now he told me he was starting a PhD in Biology at MIT and writing poetry and articles for the *Partisan Review*. Stanislas wrote out his address and shoved it into my hand. He insisted I come to visit him the next day.

'I have so much to show you.'

Sure.

But anything that might shed light on the mystery of my grandmother's life in Russia held me in thrall. Mid-afternoon on a sunny autumn day I walked over to his place, Simon and Garfunkel's *Bridge over Troubled Water* sounding in my head: up the timber steps of a blue shingled house not far from Harvard Yard, into a tiny space with a sofa and a couple of chairs. Stanislas cupped my face in his hands and kissed me three times on the cheeks ('let me show you the Russian fashion'), poured me smoky Russian tea and showed me round, talking all the time.

We were in a library. It was extraordinary. Every wall was lined floor to ceiling with books: books in Russian, French, books in Spanish; art, literature, medical textbooks, and music. Down the centre of the long main room ran a floor to ceiling metal bookcase packed with LPs on both sides. I had never seen anything like it outside of Wellesley's music library.

I tried to persuade Stanislas to tell me more about Russia. His father had known Trotsky? I told him my grandmother had run guns during the Revolution. He brushed this aside and pulled out another volume.

'Next week, I will call you,' said Stanislas.

★

We had to get on with our studies. I was deep in Dante and Petrarch, engaging with heresy and testimony from the Spanish Inquisition, and studying early Christianity – reading church fathers in the original (or as 'original' as you could get). Anne was studying urban history and preparing work for her thesis with her advisor, a Marxist historian called Paul Worthman. Vicki was doing a project on Boston's Storrow Drive for a course at MIT on urban design. Linda, too, was doing urban planning. She and Bob interviewed Marcel Breuer about an engineering lab he had designed at Yale and wrote it up for a magazine.

*

Stanislas called. He demanded – not asked – to see me. He did not offer (as polite convention of the time still suggested) to pick me up, but told me to come to him. I can't remember what we did – went to the movies? A concert? He talked non-stop, about extraordinary things: Stravinsky, the Russian poet Yevtushenko, the engineering of a molecule. He was obsessive, neurotic, insecure, completely unreliable. I found him Tolstoyan, mesmeric, and fascinating.

My little group of friends and I were making our separate ways. Not much time now for long heart-to-hearts. Linda was having a good time visiting Bob at Yale, cautiously optimistic as to how things were going. Diana, of whom I had seen little this autumn, had more or less de-camped to Douglas's apartment. Their friends at the graduate schools were older, seemed more worldly and sophisticated than I was. In spite of her constant tales of his parents' opposition to their relationship, we were sure her brains and beauty would persuade them to relent.

We expected her to appear with a diamond any day. Vicki spent every spare moment with Phil at Harvard.

✱

A late night gathering in our rooms at Davis. Anne was sitting crossed legged on her bed, sipping tea, a box of cookies from her mother open beside her. Who else was there, sitting on the rug on the floor or in my comfy red corduroy chair? The talk was of marriage. For all of us, what we understood of it in its traditional sense, had become unreal as a future possibility.

'I don't think I can accept its limitations,' said Anne.

Neither could I.

The issue of children did not come into our discussion. None of us could conceive of motherhood, a concept so alien it did not even cross our minds.

We were on the cusp of change. Caught between so-called 'normal' men and traditional, 'bourgeois' dating patterns – the football weekend, the movies and candlelit dinner à deux, for which you dressed up and did your hair. He collected you, opened doors and helped you into your coat, and paid for everything. You pleased the man, otherwise you didn't get the husband.

Promoting the new role for women were the 'weird and wonderful', deeply intellectual types who declared themselves all for 'women's liberation'. What they wanted were independent, freedom-loving women as partners. To be one you scraped your hair back, wore the same jeans you'd been in for the past six weeks, packed spare underwear in your bag, rustled up the cash to go Dutch, and trailed them down the pavement.

'Normality' was being expected to sit back and bask in the reflection of some wonderful male, who you must please or else abandon the relationship. 'Hip' was intense and stimulating conversation combined with complete lack of consideration of the need to balance the dependence/ independence unavoidable in any relationship – described by him as a hang-up.

It was clear that Stanislas, Foss and Joseph fell into the latter camp. They declared they were searching for strong women who would not be dependent, who would maintain their own lives and identities, separately – albeit in conjunction with them – and who wouldn't mind too much if they invited you to a poetry reading and, on the way back to their apartment, picked up the girl with whom they had arranged to spend the night.

Intellectually, this was 'freedom'.

Emotionally, it made you a mess. And it displayed a contempt even more malign than the traditional 'double-standard'. It was as if being 'liberated' meant you were expected to have no feelings, to play your part in a free-for-all, having sex with no matter who, whether you cared for them or not. Men still called the shots, started up or called off a relationship. However well you debated, however good you were in bed, you would never be their equals. Meanwhile, it was up to you to take care of birth control.

Such were the headlines of discussions among us in the dorm. They were accompanied by a sub-text on free love, otherwise described as 'sleeping around', and uttered sotto voce: anyone know how you got rid of herpes? Thrush or cystitis? There were whispers of syphilis. Someone else had the clap. No one knew anything much at all about the hazards of sex beyond getting pregnant. Our ignorance was so vast. We still knew next to nothing about the way the female body worked. Men's were a mystery too. There was debate on the life of a foetus and abortion: who would have one, who would not. We operated on speculation and rumour, and above all, fear of what our parents might find out.

*

As long as there is private property and while money is the standard of all things, I do not think that a nation can be governed either justly or happily ... Social evils may be allayed or mitigated, but ... there is no hope at all that they may be cured.

I was steeped in the philosophy of Thomas More who was martyred for his refusal to endorse King Henry VIII's decision to overthrow the Catholic religion of his country so that he could marry Anne Boleyn.

'Government should be about life,' George Wald had said last spring.

We were threading our way through a maze of ideas and arguments. Marxism, Castro's Communism, Mao's Cultural Revolution. Heroes like Che Guevara, Stokely Carmichael, Malcolm X. We disdained wealth. We hated privilege. We sympathised with the oppressed. We had seen gross injustice meted out to the Black Panther, Bobby Seale, who, shockingly, was bound and gagged in a courtroom when he begged for the right to legal defence. We longed for the common good. We despised

* Thomas More, *Utopia*.

the rat-race, the Establishment job, and the home in the suburbs. Among the Weathermen, we heard, monogamy was outlawed. 'People who live together and fight together fuck together.'[*] Everyone slept with everyone else – male/ female/ whatever.

Our education had taught us to think. Now we had the tools to research, summarise and conclude. Better minds than ours had been investigating the conduct of the Vietnam war for years. In the process they had uncovered all kinds of unsavoury ways in which America operated: through insider deals and the ruthless quest for profit, companies habitually trampled over communities and pristine places, heedless of the welfare of ordinary people. The ideal of 'individual opportunity' – the one, above all others, that defined America – had been corrupted. A new meaning had been applied to the word 'opportunity': the chance to put your own interests before the welfare of others.

What now the price of liberty?

The license to do as you will?

By now we had some idea of how far servicing the requirements of the largest military state in the world had infiltrated American life. Our immediate example lay at MIT, where contracts for the Department of Defense not only provided more than half its operating budget, but funded research into missiles, radar systems, helicopter stability, and psychological warfare. The most top-secret war research went on in the I-labs, in a building that was federal property: no one was allowed there who wasn't authorised; the guards were armed.

A large sit-in in MIT's administrative building and a march

* Todd Gitlin, *The Sixties. Years of Hope, Days of Rage. 1993*

on the I-Labs was planned for 4th November. Besides representatives from around twenty colleges in the Boston area, another
ten organisations ranging from Bread and Roses to the Black
Panthers and the Weathermen were going.

In other words, a highly volatile cocktail of various philoso-
phies, pacifist and anarchist, Socialist and Communist; everyone
anti-war, anti-racist, anti-male chauvinist. And a whole lot of
others prepared to take things into their own hands.

Everyone was edgy.

Perhaps just as well, it rained.

*

For my 21st birthday party in early November, a friend loaned
me his apartment. The whole thing was created in a huge rush
on the day – buying and cooking the food and also – tying up
the results of our student poll on co-education at Wellesley and
racing out to the college to present the numbers to the commission on the future of the college. (This proved an important learning exercise in how NOT to design a survey: don't ask
too many questions. In brief, 86% wanted change, almost 29%
wanted immediate full co-education, and 14% to remain an all-
girls school.) Anne and Vicki and I drove back down the turnpike in time to go to the Harvard/ Princeton football game in
the afternoon.

But in the evening, everyone was there: Vicki and Phil, Diana
and Douglas, Anne and all my closest friends. In an unconven-
tional step, modelled on 21st birthday parties I had heard of
in the English style, I invited grown-ups as well, two or three
of my favourite professors, including Eleanor McLaughlin and

her husband. The wine punch tasted so awful, the men bought in some Scotch. The spaghetti ran out too soon. But there was loads of cake and ice cream, and the conversation was good. People sat around on the floor, talking and talking and *talking*.

To her mother, Linda pronounced it a great success.

I was 21, and ALIVE.

★

All of us were going to DC for the next Moratorium march on 15th November, a Saturday. Vicki and Phil were billeted with the Dean of Washington Cathedral, along with thirty or forty other people, laid out in sleeping bags. Even Linda, famously non-political, had known that here lay a divide. You were either for the Vietnam War or against it. It took her ten hours driving with a friend in an ancient Carmen Ghia to get there.

Two days before the march, Anne and I drove south. On the way, I wondered what I should do. My Canadian government exam was scheduled at the Embassy at 10 am on the day of the march.

'You can always come and find us when you're done,' Anne said helpfully.

By the time we got to DC it was close to midnight. The white dome of the Capitol shone brilliant against the black night sky, baroque, snowy white and glittery. We headed to the Asbury Methodist Church, headquarters of the New Mobilisation Committee, to offer help. The place was crowded with people from all over the country. I spotted two or three Canadians from my Harvard/Toronto exchange. One of them asked me to write an article on what was happening for a magazine called *Peace*. Anne was at the desk for the March against Death.

The march had already begun at the Arlington National Cemetery six hours before. Each marcher was to carry a placard with the name of an American serviceman killed in Vietnam, or a Vietnamese village said to have been destroyed by American action, and walk in single file from the cemetery past the White House to the Capitol. Anne was assigned a name and picked up her placard: Christopher Schroeder, from New York – a name which she hunted for thirty years later and could not find on the Memorial Wall, built later to commemorate those fallen in the war.

We were staying in an apartment just off Constitution Avenue behind the police department. Picking up food for my friends on the way, I passed the White House. A neon blast of search lights swallowed up the building. Silent files of marchers bearing candles wound slowly along the sidewalk in the direction of the Capitol where eight representative coffins lay in state at the base of the Capitol steps. With woolly hats and scarves, they looked to me like Christmas carollers – except their scarves were black, and they had white placards and mourning bands.

On Friday morning, Anne led the way to Edith Green's office where she had worked last summer. On the way she gave us a short tour of the Capitol. The vast marbled halls, the efficient-looking men, short-back-and-sides, suits and ties, moved purposely along. Everywhere long-haired and bearded students were jamming the elevators and crowding the subways between the buildings. Everyone was on their way to see their representatives, to make their views on the war known. I felt strange, here in the heart of America's political establishment, in my black stockings and scuffed shoes, black beret and scruffy clothes. Office workers stared at me as if I were a creature from another planet. They in turn looked impossibly remote, detached from the heat of the reality we inhabited.

Waking early on Saturday, I found the floor of the apartment covered with bodies in sleeping bags. I rose and went to the window. Dawn was breaking, crisp and clear. It looked very cold. Across the street was the long rear facade of the police department. The road below was silent and deserted. Except for a line of armoured cars and a couple of tanks.

Tanks?

The US government was prepared to use *tanks* against its own people?

There was no question of writing a Canadian civil service exam that day.

I dressed for the march in my light brown coat, thick black tights and my black wool beret. My hair was tied back in pigtails. On my arm was a black armband, on my lapel, my big red and white 'PEACE' badge. Down on the street, the chill in the wind took our breath away. We shivered as we walked along, the streets eerily empty and clean. No people, no traffic.

Before long we found ourselves walking along a row of National Guardsmen, boys in blue holding guns, looking resolutely straight ahead, as if unaware of anyone passing. Anne and I tried to engage. Clean shaven, pink cheeks, blue eyes staring straight ahead they seemed, as we looked them in the eye and said hello, even more frightened of us than we were of them.

Everyone was determined the march should be peaceful. All along the route, student marshals from MOB (pronounced with a long O – the Mobilization Committee) stood in line, arms locked, to prevent any breakthrough of Yippies, Weathermen or other troublemakers. Instructions were to keep us moving. We were in a fine humour, laughing at clever banners 'Make Pizza not War' and the 'Active-duty GIs Against the War' who marched in step shouting: 'Your left. Your left. Your military left.'

Then I caught sight of a Canadian flag, flaring down the street. It was huge enough to top a building. I said good-bye to Anne and leapt over to join three students who, it turned out, came from Ontario's University of Waterloo. I was so proud to find fellow Canadians marching in this cause. It wasn't long before more and more came to join us. We soared along, fifty of us at least, striding out in the sun on that crisp November day, waving the flag over our heads, people cheering as we passed.

'What are you doing here?' people shouted.

'Canadians care about Vietnam?'

'Right on!'

We felt like celebrities. 'Peace Now! Peace Now!' All along the route, people paused to cheer our flag, until finally, we stepped free of the marshals and strode out across the grass of the Mall to the base of the Washington Monument.

There we took a stand and mounted the flag on the base of the hill. In the distance, towards the Lincoln Memorial, we could see a platform. Someone was speaking. Shaky phrases reached us from a microphone, blown away by the wind. Coretta Scott King? Eugene McCarthy? For as far as the eye could see were bodies of people, young and old, Black and white, packed so closely you could barely move between them. Never had we seen so many people gathered together.

It was not long before a CBC television crew and the rest of the Canadian press, reached us.

'What are you doing here?'

'We've come to tell the President to stop the war and get out of Vietnam.'

'What right have you got to be here?'

'This is not a case of nationality,' I told the CBC, 'This war concerns everyone in America – and in the world.'

Distant cheers were greeting the speaker at the microphone. The wind was growing colder and splashes of rain were in the air. Anne and others arrived to find me. Shivering with cold, sorely in need of bathrooms and cups of hot coffee, we left the Hill and walked into town. Store keepers were lowering their shutters. 'Closin' up.' Cafes and small restaurant owners frowned at us. 'We want no trouble here,' and locked their doors. Privileged Wellesley women that we were, we made straight for Garfinkel's, Washington's smartest department store.

Inside we found crowds from the march lining up to use the bathrooms and taking seats in the restaurant. Parents with children and middle-aged couples who looked like picnickers were coming in for a drink or holding forth beside the perfume counter and among the ladies' evening bags.

By now it was nearly dark. The crowds were dispersing. Police were everywhere. The White House was sealed on every side by bumper-to-bumper lines of buses and police officers. We headed home, footsore and hungry, perishing with cold. We knew there was a line of cops behind us. I don't remember the noise or the sound of their feet. The wind whistled. Behind us, sounds of crashing. Swarms of Weathermen were smashing cars and hurling rocks into the Justice Department.

Pop, pop, pop.

Anne shouted 'run'.

And the gas came down, blinding, choking.

We crammed a lot into that weekend in DC. Sunday was spent in the National Gallery, soaking up pictures: Botticelli, Leonardo, Durer, Titian, Raphael, Rembrandt. In the late afternoon we drove to Philadelphia to stay with Lenny, now at the Law School, and where Anne had an interview first thing Monday morning.

I returned to Wellesley, unaware that my statements had fronted the CBC's Saturday evening news, that in England my father had been fielding outraged calls from the family across

Canada about my behaviour. I knew Dad supported me. I was high on adrenaline from the march and steeped in the art of the Renaissance. I must go to Florence or go mad.

The future. Oh, the future!

Anne steeled her nerves as she handed me the keys to Volksie. She was teaching me to drive. Together we drove off into the dark on the roads around Wellesley, my foot careful on the clutch. As Christmas approached, I had got to the point of driving halfway to Cambridge on Route 9, the four-lane turnpike. We both knew we were running around too fast to know who we were or what we were doing.

Then Anne realized that she had fulfilled all the requirements for her degree except her thesis. She decided to move off campus into an MIT fraternity house in Cambridge after Christmas. I wanted to join her but I knew I would have an uphill battle trying to persuade the scholarship office to commute the award I had for room and board at the college into cash for rent on an apartment. I could only imagine how much I would miss her.

On 1st December, President Nixon announced that selection for the draft was to be turned into a lottery. Random dates of birth for all men born between 1944 and 1950 were to be drawn to establish priority for those who are to be called up. Anyone with a high number no longer had to worry about being sent to join the army.

Linda's Bob was 130. He would need the fact he had been hospitalised for asthma after the age of 12 to clear him.

Phil was in the 200s. He would apply to become a conscientious objector.

I heard that Mike would come to take his physical exam in

Cambridge at the beginning of March. He expected to be in Vietnam by September.

Early in December I decided to forgo the possibility of an honours degree and drop my thesis. I had spent so little time on it, it was going nowhere. I wanted to spend my final term working on my courses. I renewed my attack on the scholarship office to try to commute my dormitory allowance to live off-campus next term.

If I couldn't find any other solution, Foss told me I could live free in his basement. I thought of Foss's bearded face, his punishing intensity.

'Exactly what did he say?' said Vicki.

'Well – I hang loose…'

'You mean you don't mind the stereo going full blast 24 hours a day?'

Linda: 'Or filth, a lot of mess and pie fights?'

'Yeh. And I'm hip…'

'You can carry on an intellectual conversation?' Anne.

'And I'm radical… !'

Dissolve into laughter all round.

Two days later, I had an interview to teach history at Chung Chi College at the Chinese University in Hong Kong.

16

Separating out

My Christmas vacation was spent at my family's new home in Surrey, a brick-and-timber house dating from the fifteenth century, with a sloping red-tile roof. Inside the floors were uneven: stone flags and brick passageways, and wide oak boards, blackened by time. It was called Stonelands. My bedroom was a white-plastered, black-beamed cupboard at the top of the stairs, the door so low I had to stoop to enter. There was no central heating. Layered in sweaters and shawls, I set up a card table in front of the fire in the sitting room. All day long I researched and wrote, researched and wrote: Mary Tudor. Machiavelli. Constantine's Christianity. I had four papers to deliver by the end of January.

Outside, cawing rooks roosted in great nests of sticks in the tops of trees gaunt and black against the winter sky. They leapt up, angry and protesting, whenever I came near. Daylight came late in the morning; it was dark not long after 3. I existed in chill and deep damp, walking the dog with my mother on sodden paths beneath dripping trees in the nearby arboretum on breaks from my labour. It was very quiet. With my father I practised driving on narrow lanes edged with steep banks and bare, dark trees. From time to time I took the commuter train to London, full of men in suits and bowler hats, briefcases and neatly furled umbrellas under their arms, to go to the dentist or meet one of the girls who I worked with last summer for lunch. The air was dank with mist and the smell of coal.

From the US, everyone was reporting a calm and unflustered reading period – writing papers, heads in books. Milk and graham crackers. I was still in England, only because I had no exams to write.

A scrawl from Anne:

Stephanie
URGENT!
The housemother says our suite is needed ... I said that was OK because I knew you wouldn't be able to keep it alone. Now, the problem comes with where you want to live. I told them you definitely wanted a single room. I'll try and fend them off from moving your junk, but that may not be possible.
(When are you coming back?)
Stanislas called.

Anne met me at the airport on 2 February. She was wearing a new 'Loretta Young' style muskrat coat with a high collar, that she had bought for a song at Goodwill. It flattered her, as snow fell, flakes glittered on it. We went off to Elsie's for crab sandwiches and hamburgers. She was her usual understated self, cracking jokes and telling me she'd found a place to live in a large attic room with a couple of freshmen ('yes, male') at the top of an MIT fraternity house just across the Charles River on Commonwealth Avenue in Boston.

'It's right at the top. Fourth floor. Long walk up. I've got a bed and desk and a chair – and it's cheap. $50 a month. It's saving Mama some money, which is good. Thesis materials are all piled in boxes, which is not ideal. The main hazard though is getting dressed and undressed without the guys seeing me.' I wondered where she would work.

She dropped me out at Davis. I lugged my stuff to the top floor to find my new room a shambles. The girls who had moved into our suite had piled all my stuff, and a lot of Anne's, on the floor.

'Welcome back,' I thought. It took me a couple of hours to clear the bed to get some sleep.

All the work that I had done in England had paid off: for each of my papers – just a straight plain A. And it felt good. I prepared to get down to work: a course at MIT on history and psychoanalysis, McLaughlin again for medieval heresies, more on the education of Tudor women, and a glorious treat of a course on the history of print making. I was told there was only one other girl in close contention for the job at the Chinese University in Hong Kong. She was a friend, who had majored in Chinese.

Hong Kong. I'd seen snapshots in my grandparents' albums, taken on voyages they'd taken for home leave. The idea of living somewhere so far away and foreign was a challenge I felt I could face. Hong Kong was a favoured destination for R&R for GIs from Vietnam, as well as foreign correspondents and military observers. Close to the action, but not in it. A British colony, where English, not just Cantonese, was spoken, set in a beautiful harbour, exotic with banyan and palm trees, hot and steamy. 'Of course, it's not really China,' my grandfather had said.

In London, I'd picked up a trendy new maxi coat with military buttons from Biba. To maintain my smart new Mary Quant bob, I resorted to setting my hair with rollers. This prompted astonished remarks – 'What did you to do to your hair?' said Foss in surprise. 'It certainly looks nice.'

At the apartment in Chatham Street, Vicki was not herself. Phil had spent Christmas down in Mexico with his parents. All autumn, he'd been distant and unreliable – although sufficiently devoted to exhibit unpleasant signs of jealousy when a friend she had dated before she met him came to stay for Thanksgiving.

So, when he rang from Mexico and asked her to type a paper for him – typing papers for boyfriends was one of the things we all did – of course, she couldn't find it in her heart to say 'no'. And so he proceeded to dictate a twenty-page paper to her over a dodgy long-distance line. She took it down, typed it up and dutifully handed it in for him on time, raging all the while. Knowing it was over.

Now she was miserable, nervy and skittish, needing to be so busy she would have no time to think, asking all of us to do things with her. She had enrolled on a new course organized by Harvard graduate students. Run out of Harvard's Design School, the focus of 'Change' was on how to implement the new ideas attacking the status quo: from education, the position of Blacks, and women, to the decline of America's cities, the desecration of forests and polluting the environment. It was a hardly a step from there to protesting the war, or – and this was what they were doing: using that activism to infuse other issues.

The five of us were running in different directions. Anne was working part-time for Joseph. Before getting his fellowship, Joseph had been student president at the California Institute of Technology – Caltech – where he'd led changes that gave students more say in the institute's decision-making bodies. He'd set up a research centre directed by students. On top of his academic work in history at Harvard, he had a grant from the Ford Foundation to chart student activism at colleges and universities around the country. Anne was helping collate the research. They were tracking down little-known disturbances.

'Did you ever hear about the Orangeburg Massacre?'

'Massacre?'

'Unbelievable. Two whole years ago – back in Feb '68 – three Black students were killed and *no one even reported it!*'

In between she was commuting to Haverhill, a former shoe factory town north of Boston, to collect information on the social mobility of immigrants from 1870–1910 for her thesis. Everything had to be recorded and tabulated by hand.

Linda had the overwhelming feeling of being a squirrel in a cage, running on about five treadmills: work, friends, running the apartment, and commuting to see Bob in Yale.

I went in search of Vicki. I knew she was hanging out with a group of architects and urban studies people who were living in a commune. She was picking up a new life, pouring herself into becoming an activist. Friends had started a crazy macrobiotic restaurant, called 'Corners of the Mouth', a long way east of Harvard, in Inman Square. She went down there to shop for brown rice and fresh vegetables in a Portuguese fish market.

I found her in the Great Space inside the Design School, a vast room equipped with silk screens and printers. She was bent over a silk screen, too thin, in her navy sailor's pants and dark sweater. I watched her work, back and forth with the squeegee, printing a poster. I looked around. I knew no one else in the room. She paused, wiped her hands, and smiled. She told me everyone was focussed on some kind of artistic project connected to themes of saving the earth, the brainchild of a junior senator from Wisconsin. Gaylord Nelson had long been campaigning on the deteriorating condition of air and water in America. Following a massive oil spill off the California coast near Santa Barbara in January, he announced plans for nation-wide teach-ins to be held on 22nd April, to be christened 'Earth Day'.

I was going around with Charlie with his big head of brown Afro hair, off to the movies, getting some dinner. He never seemed to be serious; all we did was laugh. From time to time, Foss and I had supper. I didn't need to meet anybody new – Stanislas was still making demands – and I especially did not need to meet John, another implausible character who told me he hailed from Seattle. John towered over me, with his huge head of dark, curly hair and a beard; warm eyes and a big, wide smile. He wore a lumberjack shirt, sagging jeans and work boots. He told me he was a teacher, but just then he was driving a taxi. Uncle Sam was due to take him in a month. He was applying to become a conscientious objector. Meanwhile, he seemed to know his way around. He was jokey and charming and kind, and unnervingly keen to take up as much of my time as he could. I found myself powerless to keep finding excuses as to why we could not meet when we both finished work at 10.

Mike appeared from New York. He was staying with one of his old roommates. They came over to Chatham Street to spend the evening with us before their physicals for the draft the next morning. It was a night of high good humour, terrible jokes, much food and drink, all taken in the spirit of eat, drink and be merry for tomorrow we die. Two days later these super-fit young men learned they had failed their physicals. One of them, a 240lb shot-putter, had been eating so many hamburgers, he'd almost become obese. As for Mike: it was something to do with his heel.

John wanted to be a writer. On the first Monday in March, he took me to hear W H Auden read. Auden was now 63, but, stooped, he looked older. I listened to his gentle English voice, not realizing he would sound so northern, and let my mind drift.

Our earth in 1969
*is not the planet I call mine...**

I was not sure who John really was, but I could not help liking him. He told me he'd once started training as a minister. That he had nearly finished his degree. He was writing a screen play. He was living in a commune of MIT folk, but when we went to pick something up from his room it was in a shabby walk-up in a queasy part of South Boston. He was living out of a sleeping bag and a rucksack, with a Nikon camera and a note-book in which he wrote interminable streams of consciousness that included a lot about nature that I did not understand.

The snows melted. Blades of new grass spread a green haze on muddy yards. There was no question that Nixon's tactic of introducing the lottery had taken the heat out of the issue of

---

* W H Auden, *Doggerel by a Senior Citizen*, 1969

the draft. He had been pulling troops out of Vietnam. Even though rumour had it that an air war had begun over Laos, things seemed to be settling down. But the sense of living in an exploitative and unjust society rankled. Poverty and racism in the cities only seemed to be getting worse. The nation fouled its rivers and polluted its air.

Early in March reports came in of a massive fire on West 11th Street near Fifth Avenue in New York. It took days for forensic officers to discover that what happened was not merely a gas explosion. A group of Weathermen were building nail and pipe bombs when someone connected the wrong wires. The explosion ignited the gas main. Three were killed. The undetonated dynamite could have blown up a city block. The news unnerved me. They were all so young, just like us. How much more would it take before one of us decided to throw in our lot with the radicals?

At last, the news Anne and I had been waiting for arrived. Not only had Anne received offers to do graduate studies in history at the University of Chicago and for Law School at UC Berkeley, I had been offered a two-year contract for the job in Hong Kong, generous expenses and the tutoring to become fluent in Chinese. I put my reservations about a requirement not to return to the West for two years aside. It was thrilling and exciting and I couldn't wait to go.

★

I went home with Vicki for spring break, company to soothe her heartbreak. We left at noon on a Thursday and drove all night to Cincinnati. For me, it was a bit of an eye-opener to discover that Albany didn't look so different from Syracuse, which wasn't much different from Buffalo or Cleveland or Columbus. While Vicki slept, I took the midnight shift to 4.30 am. The two-lane black-top was dark and empty, with only giant trucks for company. I learnt the trick of coming up behind them, flashing my lights to overtake. They winked me forward when the road ahead was clear.

I liked Cincinnati, its parks, trees and nice neighbourhoods. It was clean, quiet, conservative and stable, with much less long hair in evidence. Vicki's parents made me so welcome, I realized how much I missed my own in England.

But I was disappointed at how much of America seemed to look the same – the freeways and the strip malls, and the tacky urban dross. In England I had noticed how much the construction of older houses changed – from flint to brick to stone – even within a short distance. I supposed there was a certain security in knowing that doing all kinds of basic things, like eating hot dogs or peanut butter sandwiches or hamburgers and drinking Coca Cola across so vast a distance, were essentially the same. That you would find the same stainless steel bathroom cubicles with toilet flushes, big sinks and wide mirrors everywhere, from museums, to bus stations and airports, to say nothing of our own dorms.

I sensed the same conforming spirit everywhere I went and felt maybe I was getting ready to leave America.

Both Vicki and I, in different ways, were in thrall to our men. Cross with ourselves that we were spending so much energy on them. Struggling to break free of the emotional hold they had over us. John did not want me to accept the job in Hong Kong.

He told me he was getting serious. For all his hints I knew he didn't need a wife right now and while traipsing off on a hippy-like existence for six months or a year with him might *really* be fun (I could scoop ice cream and he could be a janitor and we could live on peanuts and raisins and California wine), I wasn't ready for any of this. I knew we wouldn't last.

'Dear Vicki, here is the CO stuff.' Phil wanted her to write him a reference to support his application to become a conscientious objector, on the toughest of grounds: of conscience, as an atheist. 'I don't have to have it until after the vacation.' He told her where to send it. 'It doesn't have to be more than a page long, and it shouldn't be more than two, if you can help it.' There was no word of thanks.

As we set off to drive back to college, we were feeling devil-may-care. The spring weather was beautiful. Before long, we picked up a hitch-hiker, some guy with a rucksack wanting a lift to Philadelphia. We cruised along in the sunshine, the air crystal clear, the scent of fresh greenery sharp on the wind. I was the one who was driving as we came down a long slope on the Pennsylvania Turnpike, knowing I was going too fast. I pulled back from a curve and headed into an uphill straight. Behind me, I noted flashing lights. A siren sounded, a little blip and then full-on. A state trooper pulled up alongside, waved me over. He parked up in front, got out and came to my window.

'Licence?'

What I had was a little red book, a learner's 'provisional' licence from England with a gold crown on the front. The policeman stared at it, turned over the pages, and said 'what's this?'

I put on my best English accent and explained.

'We'll see what the judge has to say about that.' He shrugged. 'Come on. Out you get. There's no point arguing. The radar caught you ten miles back and you've been going over 70 ever since. I'm taking you back up the pike to the courthouse.'

All three of us stumbled out of the car and we set off back up the pike in the police car, maybe 15 miles, to the little town of Somerset, 'the Rooftop of the State'. We parked outside a small stone-built County Court. The policeman set us down on a bench at the back of the entrance hall.

'Don't try anything silly,' he said to me. 'Just plead guilty.'

The judge did not look up. He heard the charge, stamped a form, said that will be $15.00. There was a scramble among us for so much cash. The policeman drove us back down the pike to Vicki's car.

That night we stayed with Lenny in Philadelphia. The next, with friends in New York.

On Monday morning, 'eyes closed, and fingers crossed,' I signed my contract with the Foundation to go to Chung Chi in Hong Kong.

17

Things fall apart

Two months to graduation.

Vicki could not bear the idea of leaving the Northeastern United States. She was planning to join a commune with some of her new friends next year. Anne had accepted the offer from UC Berkeley and would go to law school in California in September. This was brave. At this point in time, no more than 3% of lawyers in the US were women. Linda felt as if she was in suspended animation, with no idea what the future might hold. And Diana and Douglas would *finally* get married on July 11th.

The tutor who was in the post I was to take up in Hong Kong wrote me a long letter. 'Don't believe everything they tell you in New York,' she said. Chung Chi College was deep in the countryside in Hong Kong's New Territories, just outside a new town under construction near a Chinese village called Shatin. Accommodation was in tiny rooms in student dormitories, and in such short supply that I might have to share with a Chinese undergraduate. Transport to Hong Kong Island was slow and unreliable. As for the students, they relied on rote learning. She said she would be the only other unmarried Westerner teaching on campus.

A great weight came down on my head. What I dreamt about most upon taking my degree was independence, an interesting job and somewhere to live that I could call my own. The thought of life confined to a student dormitory in what I imagined as a quasi-monastic institution in rural Southeast Asia sounded too remote and too much like a conservative women's college for me. Under my contract, I was to travel to places like Taiwan in vacations and otherwise further my knowledge of China. It was six thousand miles away. No return to the West for two years.

I was thrown into a maelstrom of uncertainty. John had never been able to see the point of my going so far away. (I subsequently learnt that he would not obtain a passport until the age of 59.) He was funny, confident, persistent, so present in the here and now, his jeans strung together with a piece of string at the waist. He kept tempting me to come away with him, to go picking apples for his uncle in his orchard outside Yakima or make ice-cream somewhere in the Pacific Northwest. Everything would work out fine. A life of freedom. No responsibility. We could get married in a year.

None of it felt right.

*

My exhaustion and confusion were mirrored by fury on the political front. Now things were all coming together. Everything that had been building up over the past four years. The long trains of civil rights marches, the humiliations and the griefs. The burning of Detroit. The viciousness of race riots in Los Angeles. The bitter loss of Martin Luther King. The murder of Bobby Kennedy. The ferocity of the police at the National

Democratic Party Convention in Chicago. The brutal injustice meted out on Bobby Seale. The arrogance, injustice and deceits. The never-ending war in Vietnam, the horrors and the slaughter. Fighting the draft. The fruitless, endless, calling, and calling and calling for peace. Lately the newspapers had exposed the massacred women and children of My Lai.

Over and over and over again.

The same phrases, getting tired. *The war must stop! The troops must leave.*

Now I had been schooled: all the things that we had been raised to believe in, all the systems we had taken for granted, all the big corporations, like Proctor and Gamble, Ford and General Motors, the people who brought us our household names; the Congress and the Senate and the President himself, the very structures of government, not perfect, but relatively benign. This was the system, that for whatever its faults, had kept us secure growing up.

All of it now, we knew, corrupted and degraded. Two-thirds of government resources devoted to war and outer space. Basic human dignity, to say nothing of basic rights – food, housing, education, employment, justice and peace under the Constitution – denied to Black citizens. Our own role as women of no consequence, so often menial, so open to exploitation. The planet threatened, not just from pollution and overpopulation, but nuclear annihilation.

Who could you trust in authority anymore?

The answer was: no one.

We had seen the shattering of principles. Principles of kindness, decency, and goodness, and starting with the Golden Rule: do unto others as you would have them do unto you. Once we had believed them sacred. Now they were shown to be worse than hypocrisy, sacrificed to greed.

We had been such innocents.

Now that innocence was gone. For me, my loss was no worse than untold others have had to endure, but still, it was hard.

*

Wednesday 15th April. The April Moratorium. The date was significant: it was the final day to file Federal income tax returns. The rally wanted to protest the use of tax money to fuel the war. It was also the day to protest the injustice of the trial of the Black Panther leader, Bobby Seale.

The mood of the crowd in Boston was different this time. The atmosphere was no longer sweetness and light. There was no overwhelming sense of camaraderie. This wasn't just about the war in Vietnam any more. It was about racism, poverty, the state of the Earth and the kind of society in America that seemed to require ten kinds of insurance policies just to live.

All kinds of factions and splinter groups were calling for attention. Women's liberation, gay power, Bobby Seale, the Black Panthers. The Suffragette's Brigade was drowned out by a woman from the Progressive Labor faction of SDS. The Black Panther speaker, Douglas Miranda – 'My message to the youth of America is to pick up guns. Pick up guns! It's not 'off the pigs' anymore. It's 'kill the pigs'* – is drowned out by peace chants. If a lot of people weren't that keen on killing the pigs, a whole lot of others were fed up with just about everything.

---

* *Boston Globe*, 16 April 1970

One, two, three four we don't want your fucking war.

As the cast from *Hair* – banned by Massachusetts obscenity laws from appearing on stage in Boston – sang *Let the Sun Shine In*, groups got to work and cleaned up the garbage. Thousands more set off to march across the Charles to Cambridge.

Power.
All power to the people.
Red, red power
For the red, red people.
Black, black power
For the black, black people.
Power.
All power to the people.

The huge crowd turned onto the Harvard Bridge to cross the Charles River from Boston. A sound truck plastered with peace posters nursed them along.

'Right on to Harvard Square. Come on now, brothers and sisters. Keep it together. Let's close the line up. There's a lot of brothers and sisters behind us. An awful lot.'

Then.

'Listen up. There's a lot of pigs in Cambridge. They don't want us to get to the Square. But that's home turf. That's safe ground. Just keep cool, keep calm and just keep marching. We'll all get to the square. Safe turf. Right on.'[*]

In Massachusetts Avenue, just off Harvard Square, a phalanx of police stood waiting in neat rows, two deep, armed with long

---

[*] *Boston After Dark*, week of Apr 22, 1970

nightsticks, wearing blue and white helmets. Not much later Vicki exited the Great Space at the Design School on her way home. She stepped out of the shelter of Harvard Yard and into a riot. She pulled her navy cape over her head and ran. A policeman caught her.

'I'm a law-abiding citizen!' She fought off blows to her head and squirmed out of his grasp. She ducked into the doorway of Elsie's. A waitress pulled her inside.

Anne was in the thick of it. As she put it, she joined 'the troops' on Mount Auburn Street, on the pavement in front of the Harvard Lampoon Building. Protestors were prying bricks out of the sidewalks to hurl at the police. Running through the streets brought back memories of childhood games, only this was deadly serious.

John and I came out of the movies, smelled the tear gas and saw the streets crawling with armed police. There was a lot of broken glass and mess underfoot. He took my arm and steered me rapidly towards Chatham Street. We had hardly got in through the door before Vicki burst in, white faced, a bloody towel over her head.

'There's a *huge* riot in Harvard Square.'

We comforted her and calmed her down.

'There was blood in my eyes. I looked into the face of that policeman and realized he was just as scared as I was,' she said. 'They're scared. We're scared.' Her face contorted. Tears filled her eyes. 'What would I tell my parents if I ended up in jail?'

The next morning, I crawled over the news. Over 200 had been hurt in the riot. Fires, looting, rocks hurled. From all accounts, it sounded like a planned confrontation of students and police

– *by* the police – waiting in Harvard Square for the return of students from the rally on the Common.

And that night was the unforgettable night when Anne and Charlie, John and I, sat high in the box at the Boston Music Hall to hear Jefferson Airplane.

We were high on excitement. But beneath it we were bruised and raw. Anne told me she hadn't been scared – she figured she'd exhausted her terror at the Chicago Convention. But I noticed a new set to her mouth. She was hardened, more resolute; there was a fierceness in her eyes. Recently she had been off with others, allied to a more radical group who I didn't know. She said they gave courage to each other. They were preparing to fight back. This was no longer a question of emotion. This was duty.

The concert didn't offer catharsis. It only stirred up more rage. I was fired by the music, wound up with fury at the senselessness of authorities who would set violence on students. Revolution! To hell with it all, I thought. If they think I'm an outlaw, so be it. I'll go to California and join the Weathermen!

Anne was cooler. Grace Slick's attempt to inflame emotions with thundering, pulsating music, scared her. 'It was almost like a ritual,' she said. Slick had stood, army-jacketed, and brought down what she called a political rap. Visions of Nazi theatre flashed through Anne's mind.

Anne announced she would go to New Haven on May 1st to protest the treatment of Bobby Seale.

*

The day after the concert, two days after the riot, bomb threats closed the main libraries at Harvard. On the next day, Saturday, in Mount Auburn cemetery: Stanislas's 'conjugal ceremony'. Was he serious? A few days before, his invitation – I certainly didn't know he had a serious girlfriend – arrived out of the blue.

It was an early spring day, chilly, a mixture of blue sky and white cloud, the smell of new grass sharp on the air. A collection of people, few of whom I'd ever seen before. John and I and Anne milled around for the longest time, until at last, the bride arrived. Was her name Alexandra Maria Ulanova? She was tall, with long, dark hair, in a slim-cut white lacy dress. She had the kind of grace and sophistication that spoke of the Upper East side, frankly at odds with Stanislas's eclectic, boisterous style. But that day Stanislas himself looked quite unlike himself too, in a well-cut dark suit. He called us all to order and announced the beginning of proceedings.

He climbed a tree above his brother. The director, Fellini, might have been directing. A hush fell. We waited for words of conventional introduction. Instead, his brother turned to the bride.

'Will you, Alexandra Maria, support Stan?'

'No.' She was clear. 'I love him, but I will not support him.'

'Wise girl,' Anne whispered to me. 'The man's a parasite.'

Upon which Stanislas climbed down from the tree, kissed Alexandra on the cheek and moved off into the crowd, broad, unfazed, and took up the arm of another girl.

'The party goes on,' he declared expansively, and led the way back to his apartment for 'feasting and music'.

The next day was Sunday, 19th April. Swarms of police manned the gates to Harvard's Athletic fields. Here at *Welcome to the land,* the mood was mellow and the sun was warm. People lay about on the grass, smoking dope, listening to music, playing frisbee and picking up free asparagus and melon. 'Earth people' had travelled from all over New England to be here.

Vicki had been working for weeks to bring the Earth Week festival to life: silk screening posters and T-shirts, writing leaflets, tie-dying purloined sheets from Harvard dormitories, and helping organize food. Because of the riot in Harvard Square, the festival had been cut down from two days to one. I wandered about. Lots of music, tepees, and air bubbles – the Design School had built a plastic air-house. There was face painting, and homemade kites, and bags for collecting garbage.

'Share your car or don't use it!' 'GREEN ENERGY!' Between music sets, various speakers made various pleas for people to do various things to save the environment.

The mood ran on. The following Wednesday was the world's first Earth Day. All over the country hundreds of thousands took to parks and streets to protest air and river pollution, and rallied support for the idea of keeping  the earth liveable. New Yorkers jammed 5th Avenue, gas masks sold out in Omaha, and a 'dead orange' parade took place in Miami.

Out at the college I listened, alarmed, to a talk on how the 'ecosphere' – the fragile cycle connecting all living things on the planet – was breaking down.[*]

---

[*] Barry Commoner, *Wellesley News*, 30 Apr 1970

*

It was one week later, on Thursday, 30th April, that the big move came. At 9pm President Nixon went on television to tell the nation he had ordered the invasion of Cambodia. The day before, three divisions of American troops had crossed the border from Vietnam to destroy enemy camps and supplies. These movements were preceded by attacks by B52 bombers to clear the ground. I felt our world implode.

Even as we had gathered for Earth Day, students at Ohio State University had begun clashing with police and National Guards in an action that would ultimately end with 13 students shot and wounded, dozens more injured and 100 arrested. Anne was among thousands on their way to New Haven, to gather on the green in front of the courthouse for a weekend rally in support of Bobby Seale and the nine other Black Panthers who were facing charges of murder there. First aid stations had been set up around the Yale campus, and special facilities at the hospital. US troops as well as the National Guard and state police were on stand-by in New Haven in case of trouble.

That was before news of the invasion. In Washington DC, the Vietnam Moratorium committee called for immediate, massive protests. Plans for demonstrations around the country were announced. Already at the University of Maryland, the National Guard was on the alert. At Princeton, students and faculty voted to strike. At Stanford, a demonstration developed into a rock-throwing melee. There was a sit-in in downtown Cincinnati, more action in Philadelphia, and in Appleton, Wisconsin, high school students walked out of their classrooms. The call went out for a nationwide student strike.

By Monday, 4th May more than thirty universities had joined the strike. At Wellesley, an all-college meeting was called for 4.15pm in the Chapel.

Even before we got there, more news was coming in, so shocking we could hardly take it in. Around lunchtime, four students were shot dead at Kent State University in Ohio. Others were wounded. At Wellesley 970 students and faculty voted to shut down the college.

'But four are DEAD,' Anne kept saying to me. 'It's happened. I can see more fervently than ever that there is no turning back, no piece-meal solution. For the first time I'm beginning to glimpse an inkling of the long term nature of this ordeal. It all feels immense.'

All over the country, people came out onto the streets.

'Do you sense, in my attitude, a sort of "up against the wall" unwillingness to compromise?' I wrote home the next day. 'You may be right. Today I feel as hard as nails and absolutely livid with this country. Wellesley, Harvard, MIT, Yale – the list goes on and on – are all on strike – to protest the re-escalation of the war, and President Nixon, and just about everything else. – Bobby Seale's trial, etc, etc.

'What is bothering most people here is that Nixon refuses to formally say that we are at war, although now committing more troops and weapons without the consent of Congress.

'I cannot sit still when four students are killed by the National Guard in Ohio. You simply cannot remain unmoved by the dreadful spirit of repression here ... you can feel a civil war is really coming. People are talking about the revolution – I doubt there will be a real revolution here – but there sure is going to be a hell of a mess. That riot in Harvard Square, and yesterday's

incidents at the University of Maryland and Kent State in Ohio, I think are mere warnings of what is going to happen.'

I was at supper with my favourite history professor, Mrs McLaughlin, comfortable round the table in her kitchen. All the talk was what would happen now the college was on strike. Would there be examinations? Would there be graduation? Nobody knew. All we could talk about was the illegality of Nixon's actions, the disgrace of pitting the armed National Guard against students. Meanwhile, Boston University had closed, and its students given twelve hours to be out of their dormitories.

Writing home again: *'Princeton (!) has closed until next November so that students can work for peace candidates for Congress. The Senate is talking about rescinding the Gulf of Tonkin resolution; people are talking about impeaching Nixon. All I am afraid of is violence. 4000 auto workers have gone on strike here to support the students. It looks like France, again, my dears. I feel this country is in a state of emergency.'*

Linda got into her car and drove to New Haven to seek refuge with Bob at Yale. I took over her bedroom at Chatham Street. The apartment was grungy. The refrigerator a disaster area. But when Vicky and I went to the market to buy fresh food, the weather was gorgeous, just like summer. We were in strappy Marimekko sundresses and white sandals. We went wild over the fresh vegetables and fruit: zucchini, pineapple, three kinds of lettuce, eggplant, crabs, cheese. Back in the kitchen, Vicki set to slicing and chopping for ratatouille and brown rice – she had been living as a vegetarian for the past month – and making oatmeal bread, her routine twice a week. Then the Grateful Dead set up on the steps of the MIT student centre and the music played on and on for hours – and we just wanted to dance and play.

But we didn't. We got down to work for the strike. We went down to the Great Space, now a clearing house for printing strike posters, great red fists raised, leaflets and badges. I helped stack leaflets and draft letters for people to send to their congressmen.

*

15th May: Two more students were killed and twelve injured when city police and highway patrolmen fired on a dormitory building at Jackson State College in Mississippi.

*

There was not a lot of room now for reasoned debate.

Nixon: 'You see these bums, you know, blowing up the campuses. Listen, the boys that are on the college campuses today are the luckiest people in the world, going to the greatest universities, and here they are burning up the books, storming around about this issue. You name it. Get rid of the war there will be another one.'*

In Ohio, no inquiry into how students were shot to death during a fusillade which violated both federal and state laws had been announced. There would never be one. So, it seemed,

---

* *New York Times*, 2 May 1970

the National Guard could fire guns without any order to shoot. The Chicago trial of the Black Panthers had just been shown to have had no grounds. More than ever Linda and Vicki were aware of the huge chasm that yawned between their lives at Chatham Street and at home in San Antonio and Cincinnati. Vicki's father, in a rare display of temper was heard to say, 'I wish I'd never sent her to that damn Eastern school.'

★

John had gone home to Yakima in Washington. He had won his case. In my fury with the world, I could no longer see the path ahead. Taking up the job at Chung Chi was proving complicated – where, exactly was I resident for visa purposes? Somehow, I had to find somewhere to learn Cantonese in London over the summer. More and more I felt trapped by the uncertainty of where and how I would live, but most of all, unable to declare I would not come back to the West for two years. I pulled out of my contract. John would meet me in Vancouver later in June so I could meet his parents and twin brothers and see how we got on. Then I would go to England and figure things out from there.

I went back to my room at Davis to pack. I had five suitcases, my dad's old tin trunk and a crate of approximately six cubic feet that Vicki and I planned to drive to Montreal for safe-keeping with my aunt, on a super-quick 14-hour return trip. I sent my books off to England by surface mail in a 65lb sack.

Diana was in her room. She made me tea. I handed her a cigarette. Only two weeks ago, we had celebrated with her and Douglas, high on their plans for their wedding, scheduled for 28th June. Everything was to be staged at the Ritz in Boston. It was to be very small. When Douglas wasn't listening, she whispered to me that she had bought the most beautiful dress you could imagine – $500 in New York.

Now she was on the verge of tears.

'*I am really going to need you there.*'

I took a breath. 'What's up?'

'Douglas's parents have just told him they will not help pay for a thing – ring, reception, champagne – *nothing*. Furthermore, they've just told him they won't be coming to the wedding.'

'What?'

'It's because I won't convert to Judaism.'

'Oh, Diana – why not?' We had been over this a hundred times.

'I just can't do it. And I don't see why I have to. It's just not in me.'

★

Anne had begun to talk about dying young. Dying for ideas and hopes. A sense of apocalypse loomed over us. We realized we could have children and never see them grow up.

'It's what people have been predicting. That killings would go from Southeast Asia to the streets. Now it's happening: Kent State, Augusta, Mississippi – Jackson College – the next is only a matter of time and an unsubtle state government. Death soon is a real possibility.'

I listened to her and my blood chilled. One of her friends from home had already committed suicide in the week after the invasion of Cambodia.

But I knew exactly what she meant.

'You remember how I hesitated to go to the Vietnam March on the Pentagon in sophomore year?' she said. 'The fall of '67? I was afraid that, if I got arrested, I wouldn't be able to get a good job later. So I didn't go.'

'Yeah.'

'That's inconceivable to me now,' Anne said. 'There is no question of the rightness of what we feel and think about now and about the future. And the rightness wouldn't be *right* if it weren't worth dying for.'

From England, my parents wrote that they were nervous. They were sickened by the shootings. Incredibly shocked that the National Guard should be ordered anywhere near students. 'It's just asking for trouble,' Dad said. In a few days they were flying to Canada – on the verge of retirement, Dad was needed at meetings in Ottawa. Mother planned to travel to see me graduate – it was a big, expensive deal. Should she come? In the meantime, my father sent me 'bug-out' cash so I could get out of town fast.

In the end, Mother came and stayed in an empty room next door to me at Davis.

∗

I do not know what a proper Commencement is like at Wellesley, for we did not have one. I can imagine it. Cups of tea in china cups on the green lawns, the sweet scent of new mown grass, white marquees, polite conversation between parents who have never met before, proud hands on daughters' shoulders. Congratulations and smiles all round. That didn't happen this time. Or, to be precise, maybe it just didn't happen to us.

I took Mother to hear the Yale Chaplain, Bill Coffin, deliver the Baccalaureate address. The long talk I had with him after midnight on my first trip to Yale in freshman year about civil rights and opposition to the draft still rang in my years. I wanted Mother to appreciate him. I was also curious to hear what parting words he might have for us as a graduating class.

But Coffin was disappointing. Falling back on erudition, his speech was dense and convoluted, saying a lot about Jonah but making no mention of the whale. Or maybe I just wasn't listening. It was basically about the evil of holding grudges and the need to love good more. 'The skies are eclipsed by evil,' he said. 'We've got to learn to endure the darkness while we continue to struggle, and in a dark and wintry world, we've got to learn live as the first swallows of a new summer.'

Graduation Day dawned, a day of sheeting rain. I was required to remove all my things from my college room by 3pm. I dressed in my black academic gown, tied on a white armband symbolising peace and a red one in protest at injustice to Black Panthers.

I sat through the ceremony in a packed Alumnae Hall in a kind of daze. Linda and others raised banners in protest as the class sang *America the Beautiful*. Claire Parkinson (later of NASA), winner of the senior prize for maths, was not there: rather than pay a $20 fine she was in jail serving a 20-day sentence for her part in a protest against the draft at the Boston Army Base. Anne graduated with double honours and took the Bollard American History prize. Who knew she was doing so well? Vicki too had done brilliantly.

Somewhere in the distance I caught sight of Diana, surrounded by parents. Douglas was with them too. Linda waved. Outside in the rain there was a chance for just one snap.

It was too late to say good-bye. Waving farewell to whoever I could see, I walked back with my mother in the soaking rain to collect my luggage from Davis. The taxi to take us to the airport arrived on time. We stepped into it, and an instant later we swung out of the gates of the college.

A couple of hours later, I sat in silence on the plane to Montreal and wondered: was that it?

It was all over.

18

Pray, silence

And that was it.

Not for a moment were any of us aware how far and fast we would be thrown apart.

We were never to live together again – not even on the same continents. We kept in touch, of course. Letters flew back and forth at first. Then they dwindled, rescued in the early 90s with the advent of e-mail and cheaper air travel.

But: back to our abrupt departure from college. We'd done this before. The summer was the summer, when each of us went our different way. From Boston, I flew to Montreal with my mother to stay with my aunt, and then travelled west to Alberta to stay with more family in Calgary. From there I flew to Vancouver, dropping down on what was a virtually empty plane into Kamloops in the middle of British Columbia, to pick up a gaggle of housewives, kids and businessmen – plus two Mounties with a boy hand-cuffed between them. John met me in Vancouver and we drove south over the border through a place called Nighthawk, straight out of a Western: dry, rugged country with no one anywhere around. In Yakima, I met his twin brothers and his parents: warm, close and comfortable. From there we left on a road trip through Mount Rainier National Park and on to Seattle, from where we drifted down Route 1 to California, pitching our sleeping bags under the stars wherever it took our fancy, and spent a couple of days in San Francisco. After two weeks I flew to England and my family in the Surrey countryside – a future with John still a question mark, the hunt for a job before me.

By then Vicki was living in Cambridge with Phil again – it was all getting hazy for those of us who were bystanders. Anne was on a graduation trip to Europe: Copenhagen, north Germany, Geneva and Paris, from where she sent me a letter. 'Lots of greasy grimies who proposition you at every step. ... Women's Lib has a lot of fresh ground awaiting it over here.' She was heading on to Avignon and Spain, before coming to England to stay with me for a couple of days.

Linda was home in San Antonio, 'pretty consistently in a blue funk' after stringing out her farewells with Bob for as long as she could after graduation. Her father seemed 'oblivious to the possibility that I might not want to stay in San Antonio for a year as a deb,' as opposed to going to Philadelphia to be with Bob where he was starting law school. She missed him badly. Meanwhile, the wedding season was upon her. 'And everyone keeps coming up to me at parties and asking if I'm going to make my debut in the fall.'

Diana was travelling in Italy and Yugoslavia with Douglas. 'I drove this gear shift Fiat and could do everything except put it in reverse and take off the brake.' In the middle of July, she arrived at our house in Surrey. 'It is so old and fairytale-ish – I think you'd be crazy about it,' she told Linda. With help from associates of her father, she hoped to find a job in London. Three young accountants in a house in the shadow of Chelsea Football ground were looking for a pair of tenants. 'We can share a room,' she said.

I got a job working at Britain's Royal Town Planning Institute. Vicki's work in urban design had persuaded me that thoughtful design and architecture could improve the lives of ordinary people: a belief echoed in those I met in London. The job was fast paced and hectic, my boss hesitant and neurotic. It wasn't easy to come home after working eight hours and find Diana unable to get out of bed from depression. She had never shared a room with another female before. She couldn't get the kind of job she wanted in a gallery; now had one in computer programming. She brooded over Douglas, showing off the gorgeous diamond ring he had given her and going into paroxysms of delight when an exquisite lace mantilla Linda's mother had made her arrived in anticipation of her wedding. She told me his parents no longer seemed to oppose their marriage so much now. I couldn't understand how she could declare herself so much in love with him, and endure this trans-Atlantic separation.

Before long before we discovered that the accountants from whom we rented our room, were living there for free, while we paid their mortgage. We said farewell to Fulham and moved to a pretty flat in Notting Hill – trees, spacious white Kensington houses. But – no surprise – by October, Diana had had enough of London and left to find Douglas in California.

Anne started Law School at Berkeley. 'They tell you what to take, when to take it, etc, and I'm not in much of a mood to be told what to do. How does 'Property (real estate marketing, and conveyancing, etc) three times a week strike you? Somehow, I just can't believe I'm doing this.' She had a seat assigned where she was to sit in a lecture hall, and tons of work. She was diligently going to classes at 9am every day, spending from 3–6pm in the library, having something to eat, then back to the library from 7–11pm. Out of three hundred and twenty people in her class, only fifty were women, many of them from Wellesley – 'twice as many as in the third year'.

It was hard. In huge rooms full of men, male assumptions everywhere, she felt on edge the whole time. One day, as she stood at a photocopier waiting for her work, one of her professors came up. 'Can you do ten copies for me?'

'It's like living with the enemy.'

As quickly as they had started, politics in America seemed to die down. Students returning that autumn pronounced things dull. Anne had joined a radical study group of other law students, to go over cases they had to discuss in class, looking for points they could challenge. 'The atmosphere is definitely that of easy living.' She could not believe how staid Berkeley – once in the vanguard of radical politics – had become. All the fire seemed to have gone out of protests.

We burrowed away at our new occupations, not quite believing we had left all the intensity of what had gone before. We heard rumours of friends, hitchhiking across Canada or dropping out to live in a commune and grow their own food. People who weren't committed to graduate school were looking for work in alternatives, futures that would keep them away from the capitalist rat-race, in ecology groups, street theatre; or where they could do good, like teaching. Those at law school, like Anne, were trying to see how they could use their new knowledge to help others.

John wrote, putting off the question of when he would come to see me in England, to tell me that he had locked himself away in a cabin at Indianola on Puget Sound. He was reading Thomas Wolfe and writing short stories, and I could feel the distance between us growing wider and wider.

It wasn't until late October, on the eve of her 22nd birthday, that I heard from Vicki. She had been offered a great job not far from Boston – working for an alternative education project in Worcester, Massachusetts. She was to have her own apartment and be sent on an Outward-Bound course to get fit before she could start work. Only later was she told by her boss that one of the reasons she was hired was because she had great legs.

'Jeepers! And now I'm supposed to know something. Probably the only thing that I do know is that I don't know anything at all – which is of course, false modesty, because when you realize you don't know anything you are actually being very wise.' She was feeling low. 'Part of the trouble is that I haven't quite realized that this is not just summer vacation and we won't be seeing each other in another month.' The situation with Phil was at an end. 'I loved him – I think. He didn't love me.'

She hadn't seen him since the end of August when she had been despatched on the Outward Bound course in Minnesota to prepare for her job: 'beyond description. There were times when I thought I would never get through it. Imagine me running eight miles one week after arrival. Portaging an 85-pound pack through one and half miles of swamp. *Oooah.*' Now she was settling in for the winter: 'this is a fantastic job, if I don't end up burning myself out before it is over.'

But even by spring, she could not accept that we would not all be coming together again soon.

We were lonely, overworked, tired and uncertain. Male criticism was coming down fast and hard on Anne and me. Our judgement was questioned, our egos shattered, again and again. In this new world, men were carrying on as they always had, taking command. In London I was reading Doris Lessing, deep in Germaine Greer's *The Female Eunuch* and making friends with like-minded women who had been to university in Britain. We compared notes on fielding male banter, removing hands from hips, diving out of 'awkward' situations into the Ladies. Everyday harassment was just 'men being men'. One look at the government's Civil Service pay-scales – and in my job, I had them right there in front of me – and there could be no doubt: women were graded lower and earned less, for the same job.

That dark winter in London, I suffered serious depression. No one around me had any idea why I grew so angry whenever the ongoing Vietnam war was mentioned. Being an educated girl, especially from North America, meant you were distinctively odd-ball. The boss who had hired me because he wanted to have a graduate to be his PA could not adjust to the facts that I could not take shorthand, that my typing was terrible but that I often dealt more efficiently on the telephone or with issues of administration than he did.

At Berkeley, professors thought Anne must be a secretary. She found herself unable to speak up in rooms full of men – unable to face the possibility of being put down – and often discovering that men who she at first thought sympathetic to women, were as ever, still only interested in getting them into bed.

Diana, after doing 'menial things' in an art gallery in San Francisco, 'trying to work out the morals of whether or not I can pass this stuff on to customers in good faith', had tried to get a new job that didn't involve typing. In the meantime, she was working for the local historical society.

I divide my time between Hazel in book-keeping and a very particular lady who is so anal that she makes my drawers look thrown together. This woman is, truly, a Champion of Compartments, a Queen of Trivia! She makes it her business to govern you down to the way you take your finished paper out of the typewriter, the way in which you erase your mistakes, the method by which you find the exact center of the paper.

Down in Texas, Linda was in thrall to her father. He still wanted her to be a debutante in San Antonio, to 'coronate' at Fiesta. She was finding it impossible to resist him – or her feelings for Bob. She could not face making a debut, the whole purpose of which was to meet the person you would marry, and be integrated into the social structure of your parents' world. But, dazzled by the 'Coronation' from the age of 12, when her mother had been Mistress of the Robes, she had agreed to do the 'whole damn thing' and was to become a Duchess during Fiesta Week the following April. Meanwhile, she was learning to type at business school ('unfortunate but necessary'), and applying to graduate school at Bryn Mawr, near Bob. By Christmas, she had agreed to marry him.

✳

Linda and Bob's engagement was officially announced immediately after her appearance as the Duchess of the Underwater Gardens of Atlantis during Fiesta Week in April 1971. Her dress, in turquoise velvet and silver lame, cost over $3,000 – as much as her Wellesley tuition during senior year (a fact that was not revealed to us until the writing of this book) – and required a serious fitness regime to prepare her to manage the train and support its weight of over 100lbs. She and Bob were married in August, a little more than a year after our graduation. They moved into a 'functional' apartment in Philadelphia. Linda settled down, happily, to become a proper wife. She worked two days a week as an assistant librarian and attended seminars at Bryn Mawr, joined the Junior League, and cooked and cleaned.

By the end of her first year at law school, Anne had decided to take a year out. She was deeply disillusioned: *In so many ways I feel this year's been such a waste. My level of concentration is about negative 45; the distinctions judges use in cases strike me as so arbitrary & meaningless. And the cases we read, all appellate decisions, are so far removed from the actuality of most courts' processes. I still have only the vaguest notion of what a lawyer really does, day to day.*

She got a job typing, but with time enough to begin working with others to develop brochures to encourage more women into the law. After a couple of months, she set off to travel east through the Rockies and Arizona, to her home to Illinois. Then on, to her old haunts, in Washington DC, Philadelphia, Princeton and Boston. Her idea was to collect source material on women in labour history.

Vicki wrote. She had spent the summer travelling on her own in Mexico – a revelation. Once again, she was hopelessly entangled with Phil, but still enjoying her work and a new spacious apartment. But Worcester was lonely. Work was consuming, and exhausting. 'The rest of life slowly crumbles around my ears ... the old green Chevy is lurching to a slow and painful death,' and she faced dental bills amounting to several hundred dollars.

By November, Linda was planning a small cous-cous dinner party for Bob's birthday. Diana was back in Boston with a $130 apartment, bad plumbing, a cat and no job – 'that's all I know,' wrote Vicki. Over Thanksgiving ('we had a feast here'), she saw her. 'And she seems quite good – maybe a little lonely. Things with her and Douglas were good last time she saw him, but she isn't doing any planning or defining. Things will go the way they will go and she'll see...' Anne stopped in last week – 'she's like a breath of fresh air.'

I envied them their reunion. But for me in England, life was improving. My boss had dumped a load of interesting administration into my hands, including setting up a new Commonwealth organisation for town planners. I had just returned from ten days in Ghana for my job. I had always intended to go back to Canada to get a 'proper' job, (it was not too late to apply to the CBC) but after a year in London I was broke. I had also begun to realize that I was meeting a range of people I would meet nowhere else: architects who had worked with Le Corbusier, actors from the West End stage, lawyers, journalists and people making their way in national politics.

By early 1972, Vicki had decided she would not continue in her job another year – Worcester made her miserable. She was setting the next week aside for the beginning of the new job hunt: 'mostly so that I feel I am doing something concrete about my life for next year ... I really have no idea where to head next.' Meanwhile: 'I have decided that all men should be summarily eliminated – they seem to cause us so much trouble. Of course, getting attached or married doesn't seem to be quite the answer either.' She'd seen Bob and Linda over Christmas, and while they were doing well, 'I'm not sure it's the sort of life I would want. Linda seems so dependent upon him I'm having a bit of trouble defining her as a person any longer.'

Neither she, nor Anne, nor I, could see ourselves settling into conventional marriage. We wanted our own roles in life, in some way to make a difference.

By February, Anne was back in the Bay area and had landed two jobs: one, with a Prison Law project, a 'movement group of attorneys who only have prisoners for clients', challenging abuses in prisons on a class action basis, as well as helping out some individual prisoners '(tho' there's not the staff for helping all)', where she would work for virtually nothing, and as a law clerk with a small general practice firm, for proper money.

'I'm going back to school next fall, not too enthusiastically. However, I do think I'll be a lawyer (what else? I can't do tricks well enough to join the circus) and that's the easiest way, at this point.'

*

The telegram arrived in London on a glorious July day in 1972. I tore open the envelope, hoping, half expecting, a jokey love token from my newly acquired (English) boyfriend. Instead, from Vicki:

DIANA DIED YESTERDAY BOSTON GENERAL HOSPITAL.

I waited to put in the call until she would be awake on the other side of the Atlantic. Beneath her calm hello, her voice shook. 'Oh, my God...'

She paused and got a grip.

'I don't know exactly. We still don't know. All I know is that she wasn't feeling good. She was in a lot of pain. She went and checked herself into the hospital about twelve. It turns out she was having a massive haemorrhage, but no one seemed to know what was wrong with her.

They couldn't get it stopped. You remember she had to take that medicine to stop the blood clots in her leg when she was taking the pill? Well, they couldn't get the bleeding stopped. She died an hour and a half later.'

How could it be possible to be well enough to walk into hospital and be dead an hour and half later? 'Was anyone with her?'

'They couldn't get hold of anybody in the time. Her mother's just come up from New York. Her father is flying in from somewhere or other. I've told Andrew, the guy she was dating. But Douglas is the one who's really cut up.'

Oh, Douglas. The love of her life.

For the longest time I could not get the image of Diana alone on a death bed out of my mind. Frail body tucked into starched white sheets, face as pale as ashes, hair splayed auburn across the pillow. I realized then how fragile had been her hold on life, how close to the edge she'd been at times. For all her contradictions, I loved her. Golden, gifted, exquisite – and crazy with insecurity. She rose like Icarus towards the sun.

After a while it was as if she wasn't gone at all. 'I suppose it will never seem real to any of us,' Vicki wrote. For me she was just very far away, living across the Atlantic. The tragedy of Diana's death is that had birth control been legal, had she not been prescribed anticoagulants, had the medicines been less crude, had we women known more about how our bodies worked, had we only known that you could be pregnant while on the pill, had we even heard of the existence of ectopic pregnancies, Diana need not have died.

✳

For Vicki, Diana's death marked the beginning of a string of tragedies. Little more than two months later in September 1972 her father died. By then, she had begun work for the Appalachian Mountain Club, hiking and maintaining trails in New Hampshire, and falling in love with a handsome climber called Mark. By the following summer they had begun making plans to marry. Towards the end of July, Phil, who had spent most of the year in California, departed for Upper Volta (now Burkina Faso) with the Peace Corps, thanks, in part, to Anne, who provided a reference saying how good he was at showing people how to do things without making them feel hopelessly stupid. But little more than one week later, on 12th August 1973, Mark, died in a rock climbing accident. Nine years later, Phil too was dead from virulent pneumonia, caught on an engineering assignment in Cape Verde.

For Vicki, an awful lot of death so early in her adult life.

✳

Five years after graduation, Linda, Vicki, Anne and I still had little time and not much money. We had seen each other two or three times, on holidays that one or other made to England or I to the United States, though never as a four. We battled on in our various careers, fighting back when men put us down at work, trying to get ourselves into positions where to be a smart girl was no longer a negative. In 1975, Britain passed the Sex Discrimination Act. By then, I was happier, working as a journalist – a tough field with just a handful of women – and, having thrown in my lot with a disconcertingly clever and funny British lawyer who saw me as a partner, had been married for two years. Linda and Bob were in Washington DC, where he was now a qualified lawyer, and she continued to eschew the career path. Anne had emerged from law school, and was working in the legal department of the United Automobile Workers Union in Detroit, juggling a marriage at long distance that would soon be on the rocks.

'I remain opposed to the institution of marriage as it oppresses women,' she wrote in reply to 'a very sexist questionnaire' sent by our class for our fifth Wellesley reunion.

We seldom heard from Vicki, who was now the staff coordinator of the New England office of the Sierra Club, hiking and developing environmental education. She had always known she'd never be a real hippie. 'I couldn't drop out of society. I hadn't been raised like that.' Still, she could not bring herself to work for the 'Establishment'.

And so it goes on, and so we grow older.

By 1980, things were beginning to change. More than half who replied to questions for our Wellesley reunion questionnaire were describing themselves as full-time professionals. Many had been to graduate school. About two-thirds were married. Three quarters of those who were wives had taken their husbands' surnames – but 25% hadn't. Nearly half the class had children. Of these, one quarter described themselves as full-time mothers. Others had found ways of balancing the demands of children and work: sharing jobs, sharing child-care, living in communes. It was clear men were taking more of a share in childcare and household tasks, some couples going so far as to split the role of child caring completely between them. Replies showed that the conflict between career and motherhood was really kicking in.

- 'As I sit here surveying the rubble of toys all over our living room. I've been in search of The Perfect Career to augment my sagging self-esteem.'
- 'My "career" so far has consisted of supporting (with my mind, heart and feet) my husband, and recently, my little guy.'
- 'For the last ten years I've been leading with my uterus. But I have my track shoes waiting at the front door. When my youngest, now three, arrives in first grade, I'm heading back to work.'

Women had seen themselves side-lined, unable to compete. Many had discovered how tough it was to hold a job and bring up children – let alone to win a promotion as a woman. A number were re-evaluating their lives.

I was an outlier, living in Hong Kong where my husband's job had taken us, with two young children and full-time help which enabled me to work as a journalist. Vicki, on the hunt for fresh pastures, was doing a post-graduate degree at Yale. Linda and Bob had moved south to Baton Rouge, where they now had two young daughters.

Anne was divorced. She had given up working as a staff attorney at the International Union of the UAW and followed her heart to marry a German architect/ civil engineer co-ordinating the German government's Volunteer Services projects in Peruvian schools. Her letters now came from her home in Peru, by the headwaters of the Amazon, from where she wrote, 'I see boats, logs, turtles and occasionally jumping dolphins, on their way to Brazil.'

*

In England, where my college experience in America was completely alien, my time at Wellesley was sealed in a box and put away. This was true for Linda, too, most of whose friends back home in Texas had simply partied through the sixties. For Anne and Vicki, it was more like a dirty secret, to be stuffed away in a bottom drawer. If you dared to pull it out, your heart beat fast, your stomach tightened. A wave of depression and anxiety rose up. Self-doubt and misery, unrest and confusion melded with memories of that final spring before we graduated, when day after day shocking things kept happening and you kept asking yourself, will this never end?

It was not until 1997, more than twenty-five years after graduation, that the four of us came together for a reunion in the south of France. We were almost fifty. By that time, Vicki too was married. All of us were mothers, and except for Linda, had significant careers in the world. Vicki was chair of a department at a business school in Boston; Anne, who had emerged after two years in Peru, a senior lawyer with the International Labour Organisation in Geneva. I was writing, working on my third book.

We realized as we sat down to talk, how few others shared our past. When we went to college, less than 10 percent of people in the United States – 7.4% of all women – went to university. Neither our situation, more or less sealed in an all-female bubble, nor the times, had been normal. Major convulsions exploded ideas. We had been clever, but oh, so young, so innocent! Like the scant knowledge we had of our bodies, issues of sex, gynaecology and birth control, we had not known what we did not know. We had no idea how shackled we were by what was expected of us: to be seen and not heard; that parents – especially fathers – knew best; that marriage was inevitable. About this, there had been a conspiracy of silence, until, in the end, the phase of women's liberation we embraced at college began to break it down.

At Wellesley, the education had been superb. In the classroom, you didn't need to worry about being clever, or challenging a point of view as a girl. Professors pushed us to ask questions. The downside was an almost crazed level of intensity about almost any issue, and an angst about how we should comport ourselves. You had no way to make friends of boys, no way to interact that was not automatically overlaid with sexual overtones. We were tight-buttoned, trying to figure it out. There was no one we knew to offer guidance. As for the men, whose isolation from women was equally extreme the same anxiety manifested itself by getting drunk and by boorish and overt sexist behaviour.

Question sources, question assumptions, question a whole bunch of stuff. Once you start asking and investigating, you discover things are not as they seem. That all sorts of things you thought were part of an upright, stable world were simply facades for nefarious dealings. We started college with one set of dreams, a certain set of values, and an expectation of a certain way of life – perhaps not unlike our parents, in future. During our four years, we underwent a critical transformation of values and loyalties. Never again would we trust authority, never again, trust a government. We didn't trust the police. Nor men – much.

As in convents, there is a chemistry that develops between women when they live in close quarters. Everyone has a good idea of what others are thinking, when things are not going right. We all knew, more or less, when everyone was having their period, or having a fight with their boyfriend. We knew when someone had something awful going on at home. As women we had learned to trust one another. It was no accident that Betty Friedan, educated at Smith, found it natural to send a questionnaire to her classmates to find out how they were doing in life after graduation. And it is no accident, that the Boston area, with so many women's colleges, became a place in the second half of the 1960s where adverts appeared on dormitory bulletin boards, on flyers and in local newspapers calling for women to come together to discuss the situation of male dominance. Talk that rapidly developed into a demand for wholesale change in the power structure between men and women.

Dealing with change is messy and painful. Stress leads to a particular anguish. We didn't know what we were doing, breaking with authority, gaining the courage to challenge taboos, groping towards 'liberation'. For a long time it seemed that nothing had changed. But – slowly – our dreams for a better, more equal way of living took root. Our marriages have been different from our mother's marriages. Our sons and daughters' relationships are different again. Some things will always be the same. But no question: there has been a change in the culture.

And it is not finished yet.

Acknowledgements

After I left Wellesley in 1970, my experiences were so unlike those of any of my new friends in England that I locked them away. Yet they haunted me. Twenty years ago, I started work on this story designing it as fiction, but it ran out of steam. During the pandemic I turned to it again, this time corralling my dear friends Anne Trebilcock, Linda Helland Bowsher and Vicki Van Steenberg Lafarge on Zoom calls to try and pull our memories together. We dug into boxes of old letters, bits of diary, clippings, and other snapshots. Without their trust, belief and help, this book would never have been possible. The mistakes here are mine. To them, I am more grateful than I can say.

Thanks to the staff of the archives at Wellesley College and Yale University.

This book would not have seen the light of day without the encouragement of Audrey Mandela, who invited me to deliver the Barbara Ilias Memorial Lecture in September 2024 in London, which gave me the impetus to put this book out into the world. Or the hard work and sage advice of Gillian Stern, Ag MacKeith, Joe Ewart and Iram Allam. Thank you to Jane Bellhouse, Sybil del Strother, Sarah Ross Goobey, Angela

Neustatter, Sam Knight and my sister Sue Williams, for reading, wise counsel and fine friendship. To Priscilla Mensah for talks about race. To Janet Reibstein who lived through the period at Sarah Lawrence and Columbia, for great discussions, and close reading. To Gill Coleridge, Theresa Marteau, and Victoria Flexuer for belief and enthusiasm. Finally, to those without whose love and support little in my life is possible, my beloved Sarah and Ian, Sam and Polly; Will, Freddie, Aggie, Tess, John and Arthur. And to the rock of my life, William – THANK YOU.

Illustrations

Every effort has been made to trace copyright holders. Unless otherwise noted, all illustrations are the property of the author.

Printed in Dunstable, United Kingdom